Dedicated to my late brother, Teddy, the inspiration for Alex Nicholas, and who kept a copy of my books on his bed stand to the very end. I will miss you.

CHAPTER 1

Now he remembered everything. It began with the murder—
his murder. Who remembers such a thing?

He was at his old restaurant, Grimaldi's in Whitestone,
Queens, sitting across from Maria, the woman he sold it to
years ago. Veal parmigiana, bubbling tomato sauce, and mozzarella still sizzling on his plate. Alex was feeling his age, his
knees ached, his shoulder sore under his custom-tailored blue
sport jacket, the second Chivas just beginning to dull the pain.
Too many years playing ball, too many late nights at the bar.

He felt the bitter winter breeze as the door from the street
opened. Looking up he watched the kid with the Mets cap
enter and walk up to the bar, brushing off the snow from his
oddly light jacket. He looked out of place among the bar's
typical late-night clientele of tough guys in leather coats.

He turned his attention back to Maria, a beautiful woman,
long dark hair, and a perpetual tan, in her late forties, who

had accidentally become too close a friend for him to pursue romantically. He wished he'd caught it in time.

There was sudden movement, heads turned toward the kid in the Mets cap, who was approaching him—too quickly in a place where sudden movements weren't welcomed. Alex knew right away he should have paid more attention, and that whatever was going to happen would be too late to stop. He tried to quickly get up from the table. Maria, her back to the action, looked at him, clearly puzzled. He saw the silver gun barrel pointed at him and then a flash, the sound of thunder, the smoke from the gun, a sharp burn tearing through his chest, and then, as the kid put the gun's barrel to his head and fired, a sense of imploding inside his head.

And then, again, just to be sure, more shots. Each a lightning strike inside his brain.

Yet his eyes still worked. He saw his plate of half-eaten veal parm, now a darker shade of red than the tomato sauce that had been there. It was blood, his blood, blending with the molten mozzarella. He wouldn't touch it now, not that he'd get the chance. Funny the things that run through your brain just before the power goes out.

━━━

Alex had slept well. At least that was what he thought. He felt renewed. Or was it…refreshed? Maybe like his old computer after he turned it off and then back on. Suddenly, he found himself recalling new things, scenes he thought he missed but had heard about from others. They had now entered his mind. He could see them, vividly.

There was more gunfire as his cop friends bolted up from their drinks and dinners and shot the kid who murdered him. *Good*, he thought. Whoever the hell he was, he got what he deserved. Then the conversations they thought he couldn't hear as everyone knelt over him, cushioning his bloody head. His friends didn't care if they got blood on their clothes.

"He's gone," someone said. "It's over."

He could hear sirens in the background, cops on walkie-talkies, women, screaming. Maria, the beautiful bar owner he had been having dinner with, "Oh my God, Alex, oh my God."

You can tell who you friends are when you're shot dead in front of them.

Then there was the hearse…he loved black Cadillacs; the funeral, and the casket he had always thought he would want closed but now was happy it was open. Not that it mattered—from his viewpoint he could see everything; he was just glad they could see him.

Michael was giving the eulogy.

"I'm Alex's brother. We were ten years apart in age…

"Alex's loves were his friends and family—his son, George, all three of his wives, Pam, Greta, and Donna—he was the first one to admit he wasn't a good husband—baseball, the Yankees, music—Sinatra, Johnny Cash—women, particularly younger ones. Oh, and he loved his dinners.

"He was a great athlete and would have signed with the Pittsburgh Pirates out of high school if our parents hadn't forced him to go to college.

"As popular as he was, he took a neighbor to her high school prom, a dwarf. He knew no one else was going ask her...

"He'd fight—often picking on the bullies, never the weak...

"He was tough, stubborn, and he had a temper, but underneath, he was vulnerable and he had a huge heart that he hid beneath the tough-guy persona we all saw...

"Alex wasn't built for old age. Perhaps he was fortunate to be spared those years.

"We will miss him. If there's a God, Alex is in heaven—and God will have his hands full."

From inside, he looked up at the white silky, cheap polyester ridges of cloth liner; the casket's fabric acting like a frame around each mourner as they filed by: his son George had finally put a tie on, not bad for forty; his brother Michael; his old friends; and a few enemies.

He watched as his wives, the three of them in succession, each younger than the last, passed, in the chronological order of their marriage, by the coffin. They all had at least two things in common: perfectly proportioned size 34D breasts, compliments of Alex's good friend, Dr. Armand Simonetti, the famous Park Avenue plastic surgeon, and they all wore Chanel No. 9 perfume. He loved the scent. Even now, he could smell them through the funeral lilies. He gave the same perfume to all his wives—and lovers. It came in handy on those nights when he cheated on them; they'd never catch a different scent from another woman.

First came Pam, the original love of his life, the blond, perpetually tanned cheerleader from high school. They married young, too young, yet had a great relationship both before they married and after they were divorced. Not so much in between. He would continue to see Pam after their divorce and throughout his next two marriages.

Then Greta Garbone, the horrific mistake anyone who is married three or more times must make, although she did give Alex his only child. Greta had married him because she thought he'd make her a movie star. Right after they were married, she changed her name from Rosemary to Greta, figuring it would look better on the movie credits. She wanted Alex to move to LA. "Yeah, we'll move to LA," he told her one night when they were both drunk, "when you look like Angelina Jolie." It all really soured when he tried to get her to star in a porn film. She finally ran off with a magician who she thought had an upcoming act in Vegas, but it turned out to be Asbury Park, New Jersey, instead.

As it turned out, it was Greta, bitter over her divorce and blaming Alex even for her split with the magician, who put him here in this casket. She and some much older, washed-up Mafia guy, Joseph Sharkey, fell in love—and Sharkey hired the kid to shoot Alex. She got revenge and Sharkey got in her good graces. It didn't end well for Greta, though, but that was another long story.

Finally, Donna Finkelstein, his widow and possibly the happiest person in the church. She would be rich now. That said it all.

His brother Michael, dressed in his stylish navy suit. They'd never been quite as close as he'd hoped. Michael was so different. More into books instead of bookies, so straight, hard to get close to. His wife, Samantha, a good-looking blond but not Alex's type, too smart, pushy. Their daughter, Sophia. Tall, good-looking, too. Another smart one. Nice. All of them, including Michael, who was a little snobby for Alex's taste, but who didn't act that way toward him?

Then his friends—all of them for most of his life—Russell Munson, Fat and Skinny Lester, Shugo the bartender, Joe Sal, "the surgeon," who owned the biggest auto body shop in Queens, Jerry, Freddie the barber, the other Jerry, Raven, John, and so many more.

He heard the music as they were carrying him out of the church, felt the casket being tilted—they must have been going down the front steps of the church—followed by the ride in the back of the hearse. The drivers didn't give a shit, they were talking about getting home for dinner. One of them stole the ring off his finger before they locked the casket.

He could smell the grass as they opened the rear gate of the hearse and carried him out to the—his—gravesite. It was almost over, like the last moments of a killer's trial; soon it would just be him, trapped alone in the cell, the jury, judge, family all gone home from the courthouse.

The Greek priest Father Papadopoulos gave his sermon. What was he *thinking*? Did he really believe all this stuff he was saying? Alex would be the only person there who would know the truth.

People were probably thinking: *It's almost over.* Saying to each other, *You wanna meet for a drink?* The sound of the dirt falling on his coffin as he was dropped lower and lower, being let down into the earth. How long would it take before the seal of the casket gave out and he was …exposed to…whatever else the dirt held? He wanted to open the lid, hoping against all hope that Fat Lester would reach down with his meaty hand and pull him up from the dirt before it was too late, before everyone threw their roses and walked away to go home or out for dinner, leaving him, alone, buried under the earth, at the mercy of the gangs who came at night, drank vodka, smoked weed, and pissed on the headstones.

But he was still there.

CHAPTER 2

Washington, DC

Inside the Oval Office, surrounded by history, President Harry O'Brien sat in his upholstered wooden rocker, a coffee table separating him from his French counterpart, Francois Payard. Grateful for the time alone with the Frenchman, the President looked over at the antique clock above the fireplace; only fifteen minutes left before the door to the outer offices would open, bringing in their respective aides and selected members of the press. Until then, he could speak from his heart.

"The Greeks may have mishandled their economy but the Germans are destroying any chance of restoring it—or, getting their money back. Even the IMF agrees with the assessment."

"You and I are in complete agreement," Payard said, "but Madame Merkel has much pressure on her, the politics, you understand."

"I know, I know. It's the same here."

The President was enjoying the easy exchange. For once, he was meeting a foreign leader who had no contentious issues with him.

"So, will Mister Sarkozy run again…against you?"

"Surely, as long as he thinks he has a chance. He will run. If nothing else, he must please his wife, yes?"

"I understand," the President said, smiling. "It's the same here."

Payard checked his watch, his expression turned serious, he suddenly appeared tight. "Mr. President, I have a serious issue to bring to your attention…It concerns the missing airliner."

CHAPTER 3

Normandy, France

Before he buckled himself in, Captain Ernst Kruger double-checked to be sure he'd securely locked the cabin door. Tonight, he would be alone in the cockpit, flying the jetliner by himself. Given what lay ahead, there'd be no question about him staying awake.

While doing his final pre-check, reading the instruments, his eyes couldn't help moving around the cockpit. He looked closely at the windshield and controls around the co-pilot's seat. The cleaning crew had evidently meticulously removed all traces of the Richard Le Clerque's brains and blood.

The rest of his copilot was buried in the woods outside the old hangar.

Two days ago, as Kruger was implementing his planned hijacking, LeClerque, not part of the plot, had ingested a poison Kruger had dropped into his coffee. Prematurely realizing what was happening, he unlocked the cabin door, calling out for help. Suddenly a burly Russian passenger in first class rushed in to assist him. As a weakening Le Clerque tried to override Kruger at the controls, Kruger reached into his black pilot's case, pulled out a Walther P5 9mm semiautomatic pistol, turned and fired two bullets into the Russian's heart and then one into Le Clerque's face, sending their blood flying through the cabin over the maze of dials and controls, splattering on the windshield and turning the scene into a blur of red as though someone had thrown in a bucket of red paint.

He would inform the passengers and the uninvolved flight attendants that his copilot had attempted to hijack the plane, that it was unfortunate that the passenger, in the rush of events, had misread the situation and had to be shot, too. He reassured them he had it all under control, but they had to now make an emergency landing on the northern French coast.

All communications from the plane had already been blocked and the transponder disconnected to prevent tracking. Next, Kruger lowered the oxygen level in the first and main cabins down to a level that gently incapacitated the passengers, keeping them, for the most part, quiet until they landed in Normandy where the aircraft was towed directly into an old, refitted Luftwaffe hangar, where the passengers and crew were held captive and under constant watch.

Inside the hangar, they were all confused, with no idea what was happening or for what reason or cause. Despite the terror they'd witnessed on the plane and then being held captive against their will, they were perhaps convinced they had been chosen to survive the remaining ordeal.

=====

He switched on the PA system. "This is your Captain, Ernst Kruger. I know we are all happy and relieved to be back on board and getting airborne. We have been instructed to proceed directly to the US. I'm sure at some point we will be receiving a military escort so in case you see jet fighters around us, be assured it's for our safety. Our flight time to Washington will be seven hours and ten minutes so sit back and let our terrific flight attendants serve you. Since I'm alone here in the cockpit, you won't be hearing much from me from here on in. I hope you'll enjoy your dinner and get some well-deserved rest before we land."

Although his address was carried throughout the cabin on the PA system, he was talking to himself.

He wasn't sure they'd ever make it to their destination but, getting close enough to be shot down by US fighter jets over Washington with a Russian dissident, his entourage and members of the Russian press, totaling more than a hundred Russian citizens onboard was enough to accomplish his goal. Both Moscow and Washington would be enraged, its leaders hungry for retaliation, its military and air defenses whipped into a jittery, paranoid frenzy.

The stage would be set for the rest of Dietrich's grand plan.

"Flight attendants, prepare for takeoff."

Tonight, Kruger would see to it that Herr Dietrich's plan succeeded. In executing the great man's vision, he would happily give his life for what would follow.

He entered the GPS coordinates into the flight management system's GPS: 38°53'51.61" N -77°02'11.58" W:

The White House.

This time they wouldn't miss.

CHAPTER 4

Michael Nicholas had a secret, one he feared was about to be discovered. This secret had already changed his life.

It had been nearly three years since his older brother, Alex, was murdered at a restaurant in Queens. At his funeral, the Greek Orthodox priest had pronounced that Alex was on his way to heaven. Michael remembered hearing a low murmur of light-hearted dissent coming from the pews behind him.

Standing beside Alex's casket, he remembered telling everyone in the church that he couldn't believe that he—and everyone else listening to his eulogy—would never see Alex again.

Several days later, though, Michael realized he would.

In fact, he saw more of his brother now, post-death, than he had before the murder.

It was the secret he feared would be revealed. A revelation, he knew, would change—everything.

Samantha was sound asleep. Michael quietly got up out of bed, walked out of the bedroom, down two flights to their basement, and entered his wine cellar, closing the heavy door behind him.

Surrounded by a thousand bottles of wine, beautifully displayed in symmetrically stacked custom wooden shelves, Michael sat down at the heavy antique oak dining table, pressed the switch underneath, and watched as a large screen silently rolled down from its recessed compartment in the ceiling.

Staring ahead at the screen, touching the wireless mouse on the table, Michael moved the computer cursor on the screen to the ancient gold Greek cross icon, tapped twice, and typed in his password: *mickeymantle7*.

There, on the giant screen, the image of his brother instantly appeared.

From the monitor, Alex seemed to take in the room, his head moving from side to side. "You can't possibly ever drink all this," he said.

Michael, accustomed to his brother's cynicism about his supposedly snobby tastes, laughed. "I guess your computer geeks never programmed in cocktails for you."

"They hadn't gotten around to it, but I didn't expect to get shot, either. But artificial intelligence is getting more advanced every day—and I've been able to tap into the new systems, everything on the Internet and now, even the Cloud. Not drinking doesn't hurt, either. My mind's pretty sharp, sharper than…before."

"Healthier maybe," Michael said.

Although the voice sounded the same, this wasn't Alex's typical brand of conversation. Terms like AI and the Cloud weren't part of the old Alex's vocabulary. This was Alex 2.0. Or was it?

Alex continued, "But, I do miss the food, the dinners, roast beef, spaghetti and meatballs, the things you take for granted." He sounded like his old self again.

"I know. Growing up, our dinners around the dining room table, they were important, more than I could have imagined at the time," Michael said, remembering years of suppers with their parents in the comfortable Queens home they'd grown up in. It was part of life he'd never forgotten as he and Samantha continued the tradition with their daughter, Sophia.

"Yeah, I remember," Alex said, then stopped.

Michael knew when something was bothering his brother. He'd get that pained expression, wiping away his grin in an instant.

"What's wrong?" he asked.

"People are hacking into my software," Alex said. "Something's going on. It's bigger than when the so-called priest Schlegelberger hacked into your computer and found my site. Much bigger."

"Well, at least he's dead. But what do you mean, *much bigger*?"

"These are sophisticated hacks—or attacks—I'm not sure how to describe them. They're not coming from some com-

puter whiz but from…someone—no, not a solitary person…
maybe an agency, a country."

"A country?"

"Yeah, these are powerful probes, trying to break through—
and they just keep coming, almost faster now than I can block
them."

"What does this mean?"

"It means it's just a matter of time until they're going to
find our secret. They're going to find…me, copy my software,
and…from what I've intercepted…there's more."

"More?"

"Me, they'll just *delete*, but they'll *kill* you."

CHAPTER 5

40,000 feet above western France

"Ladies and gentlemen, we've just hit our cruising altitude of 40,000 feet. I've turned off the seatbelt light, which means you are now free to move about the cabin. However, for your own safety, please fasten it when you are seated in case we encounter any unexpected turbulence."

Alone in the cockpit, Captain Kruger looked out the windshield into the dark, ignoring the tray with his pre-prepared meal. He was relieved he wouldn't need to go to the bathroom again. He didn't fear death but he feared the dead, and so he double-checked the locks on the fortified cabin door.

He thought about how his family, which consisted only of his elderly parents in Munich, would view him once this was over. He felt a twinge of pain, no, guilt, in the pit of his stomach. They would never understand, and the note he left for them would do little to assuage the shame that would be coming their way soon, if it hadn't already.

Although any word or news from the outside world had been blocked from entering the hangar, he knew that, as the pilot of the missing airliner, his past and every miscue or flaw in his life had likely already been dissected by the authorities and revealed in the press and on television. They would have seen his confidential medical records and know about the diagnosis he had concealed from the airline: a slow but sure death sentence, twenty years of American Marlboros having taken their toll. Depression, no longer held in check by the medication he dreaded, made his decision…easier. Or so he thought.

At least he would die for a cause, for something that mattered, yet, even as he listened to them in his head, the words sounded hollow. And what about the terrified humans, passengers and crew, in the back? Were they casualties of war, of a revolution long overdue? They had looked to him as their protector, not suspecting he was the chief instrument of the hijacking and their kidnapping. Earlier, he had seen the hope in their eyes, their trust in *him*, as they passed the open cabin door, filing into their seats, the same ones and in same class as they had reserved on the initial flight. Everything was in order and now their captain would bring them to their destination safely.

As he stared ahead into the blackness, he could see his face looking back, gaunt and hollow, a newspaper or CNN image, etched in contemporary history like the 9/11 hijackers. But the next generation would hail him as a hero…Wouldn't they?

And would God see him the same way?

His thoughts returned to his parents...the innocent passengers and crew...the children in the rear. Things were no longer clear, except for his image, staring back at him from the dark.

CHAPTER 6

"It's astonishing to me," the President said, pulling his iPhone out of his suit coat pocket, "we can pinpoint a missing iPhone within ten feet or so from anywhere in the world, yet we can still find no trace of a missing airliner with hundreds of souls on board."

It had been two days since the French airliner had mysteriously gone off course over the Mediterranean Sea and disappeared from sight, defying the world's exhaustive search efforts.

"It is a mystery to me, too, Mr. President. Both our countries have citizens aboard that plane."

"Yes, and at least one hundred Russians, including a fierce critic of our good friend, Mr. Putin." The President's expression gave away his suspicion, well known among allied leaders, that the Russians were always at work advancing their expansionist agenda and eliminating their leader's adversaries.

"I agree, foul play is at work here," Payard said, "but I must confess this incident may be more complicated than most. I fear dark forces, of a unique nature, are at work here and that we have not heard the last of this."

"*Dark forces?* Which ones, exactly? We have so many now."

Payard appeared hesitant, suddenly uneasy. "We have detected unusual messages across the Internet. Thus far, we have not discussed these discoveries with anyone outside our own security agencies. We came upon highly unusual…conversations…from our monitoring of the Vatican."

"The Vatican?" The President laughed, then caught himself. "You've been eavesdropping on the Pope?"

"I must admit, I was somewhat surprised myself when I received an internal briefing from my security advisers. It is one of the reasons we have not disclosed this intelligence outside of France; we would prefer not to have to reveal our monitoring, so to speak, of the Holy Father. My director of security will be briefing your CIA director later today on this matter. So you know, Mr. President, this only came to my attention four months ago, after the Pope passed away…if that is the correct description."

"Do you suspect he didn't die of natural causes? We had no reason to doubt the Vatican intelligence reports of food poisoning, complicated by his advanced age."

Payard grimaced, "The Pope was *murdered*. Indeed, it was food poisoning in the strictest sense of the phrase. But the poison was *administered to him*."

"My God, by whom?"

"We believe," Payard continued, somberly, "by his close aide, the man in charge of overseeing his personal security, a Monsignor Kurt Schlegelberger, supposedly referred to inside the Vatican as *Monsignor 007.*"

"And where is this guy Schlegelberger now?"

Payard paused, seeming to collect his thoughts or measure his words. "He is dead, also murdered. Just a few days after the Pope's death, Schlegelberger was found in the basement storeroom of one of our hotels in Paris. His neck had been broken."

"And, what does this—the murder of the Pope by this man—have to do with the missing airliner?"

"We believe Schlegelberger was part of a secret neo-Nazi group called The Free Forces Party. You know, Mr. President, all these neo-Nazi movements are now referred to as *alt-right.* And although this particular party appears to be quite small, they have people in powerful positions around the world. They are also well funded, by Nazi gold hidden after the Second World War, we believe."

"But what about the missing airliner? How does that fit in?"

"We are not sure yet, except that we uncovered Internet communications—hacking perhaps—with the airliner just before it disappeared from the radar screens. We have traced those communications back to…Schlegelberger."

President O'Brien's head jerked back. "Schlegelberger? But you said Schlegelberger died right after the Pope was poisoned, four months ago. The airliner disappeared two *days* ago. So how could he have been communicating with the airliner…months after he supposedly was dead?

"We don't have the answer to that yet."

"So, is he really dead?"

"We believe he is. But that's only one of the mysteries, Mr. President."

O'Brien's face conveyed something between confusion and skepticism. "Okay…so what's their goal, this Free Forces Party?" he asked, wondering how all of this could be news to him and, he assumed, the CIA.

"Their objective, Mr. President, is to finish what Adolf Hitler began. It is to disrupt the world order and security and, in the resulting chaos, to…rule the world."

"And—besides the usual terrorist plots—how do they plan on doing that?"

"We believe they will use some sort of proprietary, or as you say, breakthrough technology to initiate conflict between Russia and the West, particularly America."

"What do you mean, 'proprietary technology'?"

"This is another great mystery. And it involves one—two, actually—of your citizens. They are brothers, a Michael Nicholas who is the CEO of a financial services company, Gibraltar Financial, and his brother, Alex Nicholas."

"I have never heard of either of them but I'm sure our intelligence services will find them."

Payard hesitated again, he looked at the President, as though embarrassed. "You will have no trouble finding Michael Nicholas. He appears to lead a double life, running Gibraltar Financial—"

"Yes, I'm vaguely familiar with the company," O'Brien said.

"He also secretly heads up an illegal, global loan-sharking and sports-betting operation called Tartarus. It is active not only in New York but also in Paris."

"Interesting," the President said, slightly confused.

"Yes, indeed. It gets much more interesting, Mr. President. You see, Tartarus was his brother's business."

"Alex Nicholas?"

"Yes."

"And Michael took over Alex's illegal business?"

"Precisely."

"So, what is Alex doing now?"

"This is where the story takes on another very mysterious turn. We are not sure. Our security services have intercepted another series of emails—and a FaceTime type of communications—over the last several months between Alex, Michael and, even more curiously, *before* his murder, Monsignor Schlegelberger."

"This is fascinating. And where, pray tell, is *Alex* Nicholas now?

"Alex Nicholas, Mr. President, has been dead for two years."

CHAPTER 7

The pilot picked up the microphone. "This is Captain Kruger. We're approaching the east coast of the United States. I hope your flight has been a comfortable one so far. We expect to be landing at Washington's Reagan Airport shortly."

Why did he make the announcement, or even the other ones for that matter? Was he losing his mind? Was it habit, or did it help him preserve his own sense of some normalcy despite all facts to the contrary?

This time he didn't mention the fighter escorts that were sure to accompany them once he turned the transponder on, allowing the aircraft's detection.

There had been no attempts to contact him from the ground and no sign of any aircraft around him. So far, it appeared he'd been successful in evading detection. He checked the cockpit indicators for the aircraft's precise location.

He had deviated from commercial airliners' usual path, instead staying away from the coast and flying farther out, over the Atlantic.

He looked at his watch. It was not yet time to move into the traditional airline traffic path and to engage air traffic control, alerting them that an airliner, missing for days, was suddenly coming in out of the sky, only minutes from Washington yet hitherto undetected. He would respond to their queries—but he would not deviate from his course. Perhaps indecision or a delay in the approval to shoot him down would allow him to reach the White House. More likely, they would shoot his plane out of the sky, its steel and human pieces scattering on the ground to be picked over by the men in yellow jackets...unless...

Unless he...followed their instructions, proceeding to a safe landing field, most likely an isolated, military base, away from populated areas. Then, he would be safe. He would live, at least as long as his disease allowed. He would have a wife and children of his own. Maybe he would be a hero. Or...he would be the only one they'd have to blame. Things seemed less certain now. Kruger felt...confused.

In the coming days, weeks, and years, he knew the world would replay his conversations with the control tower—and the fighter jets that would soon approach them—over and over, his photo simultaneously appearing on television screens around the world.

The plan was for him to continue undetected before turning the transponder on as he approached the restricted air space around Washington. That was the plan. Reality, though, began to feel different.

He reached over and switched on the transponder.

His headset came alive with static and voices, at first undecipherable.

"This is Reagan Tower air traffic control, unidentified aircraft you are entering a controlled airspace. Identify yourself and state your intentions."

Then he listened as the tower contacted another, evidently nearby, aircraft: "United 128, this Reagan tower air traffic control. We have an unidentified aircraft on our radar close to your position. Do you have a visual of the aircraft?"

"This is United 128, I have a visual of the aircraft at my eleven o'clock, fifteen nautical miles in front of me at 40,000 feet, heading west."

"United 128 what type of aircraft is it?"

"It's white, looks like an airliner, I can't make out the markings but I believe it's an Airbus 340 or 350."

"United 128, we will make contact and advise." A pause. "This is Reagan tower, please identify yourself. I repeat, please identify yourself. And your intentions."

He thought again about his family, and then the passengers and crew in the back. He had made a terrible mistake.

It was time for him to speak. "France Global 509. This is Captain Ernst Kruger, requesting vectors for direct approach to Reagan."

Other than static and the air-traffic controller and at least one other pilot talking over each other, there was silence for several seconds, then: "France Global 509, please confirm… Where the hell have you been?"

But the connection went silent and another voice came through, as distinct and clear as if it came from inside the cabin.

"Captain Kruger, *Ernst*, what are you doing? This is not the plan. You have engaged prematurely."

He recognized the voice with the German accent immediately but…it couldn't be. He switched on his microphone.

"Herr Schlegelberger?"

CHAPTER 8

Washington, DC

Dick Dolins had rehearsed this day a thousand times but he never thought he'd see it, and especially not from the White House roof.

As he looked out through his binoculars at the clear Washington sky, he pressed his earpiece firmly into his right ear. He'd been patched in to the JOC, the White House Joint Operations Center, listening as they tried to communicate with the incoming aircraft.

"This is White House security. You are approaching a restricted air space. I repeat, this is the Joint Operations Center. You are entering prohibited air space. You must alter your flight plan now. Make an immediate 180. Do you read me?"

"It's not responding, sir," another voice said.

Others joined in, their voices a jumble on the staticky line.

"The aircraft is now inside the prohibited air space."

"We've just lost radar contact, no visual either. It doesn't make any sense. My screen's clear."

"Keep trying, it's out there."

Turning quickly with his binoculars, Dolins scanned the skies until…"It's not small, it's a large plane, an airliner," he called out into his microphone. "I have a visual now. It's flying low, very low…maybe ten miles out, closing in."

"Confirmed, it's an airliner, sir," another voice said. "Looks like an Airbus from our radar. It just showed up again."

"Where the hell are our F-16s?"

"They've been scrambled and are in the air, sir."

"How'd this aircraft get this far? What's going on?"

There was no response from anyone to the question. Dolins looked through his binoculars. The aircraft was still in the distance but getting closer. He could see no other aircraft in the sky, so the airliner had an open path and was heading straight for the White House—and him. Despite the rush of adrenaline his mind wandered, would he be able to get a last message to his wife and daughters? No, there was no time. Where were the Air Force interceptors?

He heard the JOC voice again, "I repeat. This is FAA security. You have entered prohibited air space. Identify yourself and alter your flight plan now. Do you read me?"

Dolins heard another voice cutting in, "France Global 509, this is tower, on Guard frequency. Please confirm…Where the hell have you been?…How many persons do you have on board?"

"Jesus, it's the missing airliner," Dolins whispered. Clearly, this was no accident.

"Intercepts are on the way, estimated time to contact, three minutes."

"It'll be too late. We'll need to use the Stingers."

The JOC voice spoke, "Is anyone getting a response from the aircraft?"

"Negative."

"Where's the President?" Dolins said, speaking into the microphone on his lapel.

A new voice answered, "In the Oval Office, sir."

This time Dolins shouted into his microphone, "Get the President down to the secure bunker, *now*."

Without warning, the door to the Oval Office swung open, startling the President. This was no time to be interrupted; no one should have come in for at least half an hour.

But O'Brien instantly read the distressed look on the face of the head of White House security, Johnny Bennett, who'd burst through, followed closely by Jim Goodrich, the director of the CIA.

"We're under attack," Bennett said. "We need to get downstairs—both of you—*now*."

The President's mind flashed back to the images of a frozen George Bush at the moment an aide whispered into his ear about the second 9/11 airliner crashing into the World Trade Center. He rose up, quickly gestured with his arm to President Payard, and they both moved through the door and to the waiting entourage of nervous Secret Service agents.

"Run—we need to run, sir, quickly," the agent said. Another agent gestured to Payard, signaling him to come.

"Where's the attack, *exactly*?" the President said, grabbing President Payard's arm as they both hurried to follow.

"It's right here, sir. It's an aircraft heading directly for the White House. It will hit us in two minutes."

"An aircraft?" he echoed.

The agent looked back at him, his eyes betraying his fear, "An airliner, sir."

Jim Goodrich, too, was trying to stay calm as he raced behind Bennett and ushered the President and Payard into the elevator.

It was a thirty-second ride to the underground bunker and operations center. "What the hell's going on?" President O'Brien said. "What happened exactly?"

"The missing France Global airliner just appeared over the Atlantic, out of nowhere, and it's asking for clearance to Reagan but we think it's headed for us. Air traffic control is telling us it suddenly showed up on ATC radar after the pilot—who has identified himself as the same one who was in charge of the original flight—apparently switched on the transponder."

O'Brien tried to process Goodrich's news. "Where have they been? The airliner, I mean. It's been, what, two days? What about the passengers? Are they on board?"

"We're still trying to get answers, sir. In the meantime, the Air Force has dispatched F-16s. They'll have a visual on the aircraft any second now. These are all questions we'll be asking as our jets intercept."

As the steel elevator doors opened, the president leaned closer to Goodrich and whispered, "What the hell else is on that plane?" An airliner was bad enough; a bomb on board an airliner would be even worse. The doors to the operations center conference room opened. By O'Brien's watch, it had taken ninety seconds to get there.

As they entered, Goodrich glanced down at his secure cell phone. "The pilot just confirmed there are two hundred and forty people on board."

CHAPTER 9

Uzes, France

Traveling through the south of France, Michael and Samantha had just arrived at their hotel, L'Artemise, in the ancient town of Uzes. Samantha was fluent in French, which was fortunate since Michael had buried several French instructors at home in the States. Despite years of lessons, he had only a rough comprehension and a basic ability to speak the language. But combined with Samantha's fluency, his effort, regardless of how butchered, to speak and understand the language gained him a relatively positive reception in most of his French encounters.

Samantha was already at the pool, leaving Michael alone in their room overlooking the plush gardens of the seventeenth-century inn, once the grand home of an archbishop, now redesigned as a stylish luxury chateau with six guest rooms, each featuring exposed beams, stone walls, and contemporary art.

Sitting on the comfortable white linen upholstered chair, a glass of local chilled rosé by his side, he opened his laptop and clicked on Alex's icon.

"Schlegelberger's back," Alex said.

"He's dead. I know that better than anyone. There's no way he ever walked out of that hotel in Paris; he had to have gone straight to the morgue."

Alex laughed. "Yeah, just like I never walked out of the restaurant in Queens. I went straight to the morgue, too."

"What are you saying? That he's in the cloud like you?"

"Exactly, Sherlock. He got his hands on my software before he died. I think when he hacked into my account, he found out the identity of the AI geeks I'd hired."

"I'm trying to understand all this…Does it mean, since he's got the software, that he can somehow destroy you?"

"I don't know what he can do. I know it's not good. Like me, he's probably trying to figure out how much power he has. I don't care about all this power shit for myself—but he does."

"Could he be the one you said was hacking you? The one you thought was an organization or government?"

"It's possible, but it still looks more like it's bigger than one person…even a dead one like Schlegelberger. Could be someone else discovered one or both of us and is trying to figure out what we're all about, what's going on. Eventually the NSA or the Russian or Chinese equivalents of it has got to stumble onto of us. That's when the fun will really begin."

Michael paused to let it register. "So, that means—"

"What it means," Alex looked straight back at Michael, wide-eyed, "is there's *two* of us."

Just as it was beginning to sink in, Michael noticed a flickering on the screen.

"I think I'm losing you," Michael said. "Sometimes the Wi-Fi's weak here in this part of France."

He heard Alex's voice but couldn't make out what he was saying, and then it sounded like a jumble of static and then… another voice, throaty and guttural, someone who'd smoked for too long.

"Alex, are you there?" Michael said. "Is someone else…?"

And then he heard the voice again. He recognized the German accent. It was Schlegelberger.

"Well, what have we here?" Schlegelberger said. "You don't mind if I join your little chat, do you?"

Michael's computer screen was restored, the images and sound as clear as ever. The screen split into two images: on the left was Alex, exactly like before. On the right, was Monsignor Schlegelberger, dressed in his black clerical top and white collar. He looked as Michael remembered him: a wiry older man with white hair and dark circles under his eyes.

"There's nothing more pathetic than a dead priest," Alex said.

Schlegelberger shrugged. "My neck appears to have healed well enough."

It was Michael who had broken Schlegelberger's neck in the basement of the Hotel Lutetia that night in Paris. Schlegelberger had been desperate to get his hands on Michael's computer, but Michael, with the unexpected but welcome appearance of Sindy Steele, was able to overpower the priest while Steele put her stiletto into the hit man who had been about to murder him. What neither Michael nor Schlegelberger knew at the time, however, was that Schlegelberger had already been duplicated onto AI software after he found—and murdered—the computer duo Alex had employed to make the AI breakthrough.

Now, Schlegelberger was back.

"It's a shame you won't join me in my endeavor. We could be powerful together."

Alex's eyes narrowed, his forehead furrowed. "Are you fuckin' nuts? All I want is to figure out how to get a good meal again and maybe who's going to win the Super Bowl. I have no idea what the hell you want out of life, or death, or whatever the hell this is."

"What do you want?" Michael asked the priest. "And what do you want with *us*?"

"It's simple, Michael. I want you both to cease to exist, to disappear, forever."

"What difference does it make to you, especially now?"

"*Now*? You don't understand, do you? My life hasn't ended, as you can plainly see. In fact, it's only beginning. Soon you will see what I am capable of." He moved as if to check his watch. "Very soon, in fact."

"Well, I hate to tie you up with so much going on," Alex said.

"Unlike you, I am using my powers to achieve something worthwhile, not to try to fill my stomach or anticipate a soccer match."

"It's football, not soccer. Google it," Alex said.

"You are a fool, Alex. Before the day is over, you will see how small you are and how easily expendable you and your brother are. Today is simply the appetizer. Unfortunately, you will miss the main course."

CHAPTER 10

40,000 feet above the Atlan-
tic off the Virginia coast

The voice echoed through Captain Kruger's earphones.

"Herr Schlegelberger? I...thought you were...dead?"

"Evidently not, my friend. You are deviating from our plan. Reset your autopilot back to the coordinates for the White House, immediately."

Kruger was confused. Schlegelberger had been found dead in that Paris hotel. Dietrich was the new leader.

"What about Herr Dietrich? Where is he?"

"Dietrich is awaiting word from me of your mission. Let's not disappoint him. Cut off your transponder, stop all communications with the ground, and resume your course toward the target."

Kruger was paralyzed. His fingers reached for the autopilot control, which he'd changed to the airport coordinates.

Voices were coming through his earphones again, "France Global 509, this is on GUARD frequency, we have you on radar, please respond…"

Then Schlegelberger's voice again, "Ernst, plug back in the coordinates of the White House."

He ignored him, pulling his hand back from the autopilot control.

"Tower, this is France Global 509, we need your assistance—" But as he spoke into the microphone he no longer heard the unmistakable static that accompanied his back and forth with the US authorities, only a hollow echo. He'd been cut off. He tried again, "This is France Global 509, I repeat, this is France Global 509, come in Tower…Request coordinates to land directly at any secure airfield."

But it was no use, his mike and earphones were dead. He looked at the display: the destination coordinates were changing in front of his eyes. He recognized the new one, it was the same one he'd just replaced with Reagan Airport. He was heading once again for the White House.

He pulled up slightly on the plane's sidestick control, expecting the plane to pitch up, but nothing happened. He tried other controls, and then attempted to manually turn off the autopilot, but, once again, the plane didn't respond. Instead, it appeared the aircraft was being controlled from somewhere else, by someone else. He flicked one switch after another, but the aircraft carried on its way, banking slightly left, in defiance of Kruger's efforts.

His earphones came to life again but instead of the crackle of voices from nearby planes and the tower, this time he heard one voice, loud and clear. It was Schlegelberger again, as though he sat in the empty copilot's seat right next to him. "I'm in control now. It will be over soon."

CHAPTER 11

Washington, DC

President O'Brien had first seen the secret Armageddon-proof bunker shortly before his inauguration.

Although there were no windows to the outside world, the world outside appeared around them on wall-sized video monitors displaying maps, images of the White House, seemingly every national monument, Air Force base, airport, missile installation, and 7-Eleven in the country.

O'Brien, like several presidents before him, knew they'd be safe here—even if the monitors went black. And, just in case, there was always a big supply of the favorite beverage of whoever was in power in the fridge. For O'Brien, it meant a year's supply of Maker's Mark bourbon.

The President and his men filed inside, taking their seats. Seated around the long rectangular wood conference table were the key members of the President's staff and uniformed military aides, all hurriedly swept from their desks inside the White House and herded into the secure bunker.

Seated directly across the table from the President, and perhaps the most ill at ease person in the room—other than President Payard—was Johnny Bennett, who appeared to have just concluded a conversation on one of the series of telephones placed around the table. As he hung up the phone, he looked at the President.

"Sir, we are going to shoot it down," Bennett said, loudly enough for the entire room to hear. "God bless those on board."

Dick Dolins's grip would have crushed the high-powered binoculars had they been made of a softer steel. While he watched the airliner approach, he listened through his earpiece as multiple voices, static, and the clicking on and off of the participants' microphones set the backdrop of what he knew was a looming disaster.

"What's the ETA?"

"Minutes, three, at the most."

"What?"

"Sir, it has accelerated and is on a direct path to the White House."

"Are the Stingers ready?"

The White House was surrounded by several portable, shoulder-mounted Stinger anti-aircraft surface-to-air missiles hard-mounted and hidden on the roofs of surrounding buildings up and down Pennsylvania Avenue. It was meant as a last resort or to fight off rogue aircraft and, most recently, drones. Dolins could imagine men dropping their cups of coffee and scurrying to arm and prepare them.

"Location North, ready, sir."

"West, yes, sir."

"East, ready, sir."

"South, ready, sir."

But Dolins had a growing sense that they wouldn't be necessary as, in the distance at the periphery of his binoculars sight lines, he saw the F-16s from nearby Andrews Air Force Base had arrived. Trailing behind them were two Homeland Security helicopters armed with .50 caliber machine guns.

Suddenly the sky lit up as a series of flares and laser lights surrounded the airliner in an illuminated fog and strobe-light show. It was the protocol designed by NORAD to occur moments before they shot an intruder down.

Dolins listened as the communications continued.

"What's the ETA? I repeat, give me the ETA."

"Two minutes, maybe less."

"*How the fuck* did he get through our radar?"

"Interceptor One ready, sir." Dolins watched as one of the F-16s caught up with the plane, appearing to pull up alongside it. The chatter increased, intensifying as NORAD, JADOC, the FAA, the Secret Service, and the other overlapping agencies responsible for the security of the airspace above the capital. Things were happening so quickly, he wasn't sure who was speaking to whom, at least until the first F-16 pilot broke into the conversation.

"Where is the President?" a voice said.

"He's secure," another responded, "all personnel have been evacuated."

Except one, Dolins thought to himself, wondering what his own protocol would be.

"This is Interceptor One, in position, prepared to engage, sir."

"This is NORAD Commander Connors. Shoot it down."

"Interceptor One, sir, I have a visual. It's a commercial airliner. Please confirm instructions."

"Instructions confirmed, shoot it down Interceptor One.

"But, sir—"

"*Shoot it down, now*. Do you read? Shoot it down."

"Acknowledge, sir. Affirmative."

Dolins wasn't sure how many seconds passed, but there was no more chatter and only silence from the F-16 pilot. Had he been disconnected from the exchange?

Finally, the pilot responded, and Dolins couldn't believe the words coming through his earpiece.

"I can't, sir."

"Interceptor One, this is an *order*. Shoot it down, *now*. What do you mean, *you can't*? Shoot it out of the goddamned sky, *now!*"

"Sir, this is Interceptor One. I have a visual on the aircraft, it's a passenger airliner. I can see *faces* in the windows."

"Interceptor One, I repeat, *fire*.

"Sir, this is Interceptor One, I have a close visual on the aircraft, it's a passenger airliner. I can see the passenger's *faces* in the windows. They're looking at me."

CHAPTER 12

Michael tried to take a nap. The flight from New York to Nice and the six-hour time difference had taken its toll. But he couldn't get the image of Schlegelberger out of his mind, or Alex's chilling words: *There's two of us.*

Michael sensed that Alex simply wanted to continue to live his life as though he was alive. If he could, he'd leave everyone alone except maybe for some good-looking women on the Internet and maybe try to have sex with his ex-wife, Donna. To the rest of the world, Alex was, as he had been in life, harmless. But what was Schlegelberger's purpose? What was he trying to do—besides eliminate Michael and his brother? Was Alex a potential obstacle to whatever he had in mind? Schlegelberger was evil in life; now, with his virtual powers and access to everything in the ether, he'd be up to something horrific.

He was tempted to call the authorities, but how could he explain what was happening? Two dead men in the cloud, one of them planning world domination? It beggared the imagination. Samantha still didn't buy into the virtual Alex, although seeing him on the computer screen months earlier had made her reconsider her position.

His iPhone vibrated, reverberating through the bedside table. Michael picked it up and read the text notification. It was a CNN news flash: *Missing mystery airliner appears over the Atlantic headed for Washington, DC. Authorities on alert for potential attack on the city. The Pentagon, Capitol and the White House are being evacuated.*

He texted Alex:

Michael: Could the airliner be connected to Schlegel-berger?

Alex: It is. I just discovered it. I hacked into him. It's bad.

Michael: What's the plane going to do?

Alex: I can't tell. All I know is that S's involved. I'm trying to get in deeper into his systems but he's set up pretty good defenses. He's got an accomplice, some guy in Germany.

Michael: A *real* person? Or...

Alex: I'll ignore that dig, but, yeah, some guy who I can see is having dinner at a restaurant in Germany while this thing with the plane is going down.

Michael: What did they do with the plane for the last few days? And where are all the passengers? Why haven't they been on their cell phones? This is so strange.

Alex: I don't know, the hijackers might have a cell blocker or maybe they took the phones away. It sounds like the passengers are on the plane. The pilot's made announcements over the intercom to the passengers. I don't think they know what is happening exactly or that they may be heading into some building.

Michael: They have to be wondering, especially after 9/11.

Alex: Who knows what they've been told or what they believe.

Michael: But what's S's stake in this? Why would he do this? Can't you stop him?

Alex: No, at least not yet. There's some connectivity between his software and mine but I can't penetrate it enough to control or destroy him. I think he's trying to do that to me but our software systems are designed to fight off and defend against these things, even, I guess, from each other. Without expert help, I can only go so far, and he's probably ahead of me."

Michael: Well, we'll find out more once we see what happens with the airliner.

Alex: From what I've discovered so far, the plane is what S. referred to as the appetizer.

Michael: What do you mean?

Alex: He's trying to hack into systems that go way beyond a single airliner. I think his "main course" is gonna be much worse. I found this e-mail he sent to Dietrich months ago:

> Now that I'm on *the other side,* I'm convinced that the internet, aided by artificial intelligence, can bring about changes so profound their only parallel is the discovery of fire.
>
> The computer and its interaction with the virtual world is no longer precisely constructed, its every action no longer measured for potential ramifications. The machines are running out of control. They are advancing in intelligence beyond a human or a government's ability to control them or understand their capabilities.
>
> They now intuitively bypass security systems and controls. Cameras and listening devices are everywhere. Most of the billions of devices that have been connected to the internet over the past few years were done so with little concern for security. No one is responsible for securing them.
>
> The smell of smoke drifts out of the overheated computer rooms. The security walls are crumbling

from the weight of it all. The machines are on fire.
The world will soon be, too.

Michael: Jesus, what are we going to do? I don't even know
what it means but it isn't good.

Alex: All I know is we've got to kill him before he kills
us—and God knows how many other people."

CHAPTER 13

As though looking over Kruger's shoulder, Schlegelberger had a full view of the cockpit. For a moment, he couldn't help but admire the sleek stage of symmetrical dials and gauges, illuminated in soft hues of green and blue. During the jet's two days on the ground, Dietrich had his men install the necessary cameras and electronics in order to easily allow Schlegelberger to oversee and, if necessary, take control of the aircraft.

"It's unfortunate things have to end this way, Kruger. You could have been a useful asset for us moving forward."

Kruger was frantically attacking the controls and instrument panel, flicking switches. At first, he appeared to be trying to override the flight management system. The system would bring the aircraft to within a few feet of the location that had been input, in this case, remotely by Schlegelberger. Kruger kept pushing the system's disconnect button, to no avail. He then tried to retake control using the sidestick control column on his right.

"None of your efforts will work, Captain. There is no override on my power. I am in control. In other times, I would have offered you my prayers but I'm afraid religion is of no use to me anymore. Nor, I'm afraid, will yours be to you.

As the plane began its final descent, and with the capital's landmarks visible now through the cockpit windshield, Kruger appeared to be ignoring him, working every switch and device within his reach.

"Welcome to the White House," Schlegelberger whispered.

Still on the roof, Dolins watched through his binoculars as the plane drew closer. He wondered what was on it besides passengers. Was this a 9/11-type attack using the airliner as a missile to kill passengers and people on the ground? That would be bad enough. But if this was the missing airliner, there had to be a reason it wasn't simply hijacked and flown directly into a building here in DC. What had the hijackers done to the jet during those two days? Did some terrorist group finally get its hands on a nuclear device and plant it inside the plane? If so, it was already too late to avert a disaster.

The sounds of the unsuspecting capital city below and the hiss of static were all he could hear through his earpiece. It was an incomprehensible silence considering the last exchange from the intercepting pilot. But, after several seconds, the voices came alive, the stress and tension coming through as clearly as the words.

"Interceptor One, I need for you to execute my command, as difficult as it may—"

"Oh my God. Shit!" the captain shrieked.

"Captain Connor, what is it? Interceptor One do you read me?"

"Yes, sir. I'm looking through the rest of the passenger windows, in the main cabin, sir. They're all open..."

"The window shades?"

"No, their *mouths*. Oh God. Oh man, this is—"

"What is it? Connors, what's happening?"

"They're dead. They're *all* dead, rows of them. They're in their seats, no one's moving, their mouths are open. It's all dead bodies, hundreds of them, one row after another. They're corpses."

CHAPTER 14

Claus Dietrich had chosen to stay the night at the Schloss Bensberg castle, now a luxurious hotel outside of Cologne. The city had been virtually destroyed by Allied bombers in World War II. Someday soon, he would see the photographs of the great American cities, New York, Chicago, and others destroyed, just as his beloved German cites had been during the war. He fantasized a Hiroshima-like version of Manhattan, only the spires of Saint Patrick's Cathedral still standing amid the flattened ruins.

Tonight's mission would be only the prelude, the first step toward the mass destruction of the United States and Russia, the two countries that destroyed his beloved Germany.

Not in the mood for the hotel's German signature Michelin-starred restaurant, he chose to dine in the hotel's more casual Italian trattoria.

In his seventies and like his uncle, Hitler's minister of propaganda, Joseph Goebbels, Claus Dietrich was a slight man. He placed his mobile phone by the side of his plate, waiting for word from Schlegelberger that the airliner had reached its target.

Dining on simple spaghetti with clams and fresh tomatoes, he thought of the beauty, the perfect symmetry of the revenge he was about to deliver. Just as the Allies had invaded Hitler's bunker, he would invade and destroy America's own bunker, the White House.

His thoughts went to the vivid newspaper image of his Uncle Joseph, his burned, blackened body, his prominent and unmistakable facial features still recognizable, an arm reaching out yet frozen in death, lying just outside the entrance to Hitler's bunker as the victorious Russian troops displayed the charred corpse for all the world to see.

Dietrich envisioned the similarly charred figure of President O'Brien, perhaps on the South Lawn, on CNN.

He also remembered earlier images of his uncle, his deep-set eyes, the unusual way his mouth contorted, his tongue twisted and often visible, as he spoke in front of the huge crowds, his right arm straight, thrust forward in a Nazi salute. Of all of the photos of his uncle, Dietrich cherished the one of Goebbels seated in the garden of the Carlton Hotel in Geneva, glaring darkly into the camera a moment after an aide whispered in his ear that the photographer, Alfred Eisenstaedt, was a Jew. Dietrich kept a framed version by his bed.

As he waited for word of the airliner, his thoughts went to the next step in their mission. The destruction of the plane and the White House would set the stage for a much greater apocalypse, made possible by the technology Alex Nicholas had introduced. The same technology that had saved Schlegelberger.

He was just beginning to feel a welcome lightness coming over him as he finished the half-bottle of dry Austrian Grüner Veltliner, when he saw the text message from Schlegelberger flash on his phone's screen: *All obstacles evaded. Victory is moments away. The gates of Hell are opening.*

CHAPTER 15

"Interceptor Two, are you in position?"

The first jet had swung away sharply from the jetliner. Now, a second F-16 approached the lumbering aircraft from behind.

A new voice: "Yes, sir. Preparing to fire."

The voice interrupted, "Permission to fire."

Dolins watched the cloud stream tail after the release of the missile from the second F-16 as it headed straight for the airliner. He could feel his whole body tense up, anticipating the horror about to explode before him.

"God help them," he whispered.

But a split second before the missile would have reached its target, it made a sharp turn away from the airliner, falling harmlessly away into the clouds.

"Target's got an anti-missile system, probably a laser," a voice from the F-16 said.

Dolins remembered a briefing, months ago about an anti-missile laser defense system being utilized by Israeli airliners. It was designed to operate autonomously, without input from the flight crew. An array of sensors detected a missile approaching the aircraft and transmitted this information to an infrared tracking camera. The system's computer analyzed the input signals and then directed a laser at the incoming missile. The laser projected a false target into the incoming missile's guidance system, causing it to turn away from the aircraft. The process only took two to three seconds, the system fully contained in a small box mounted on the underside of the plane's fuselage.

He watched as a red laser beam streamed into the sky and locked onto its target, a second missile, which also lurched away before reaching the airliner. The plane appeared unfazed, continuing on its course directly toward him.

More F-16s were now approaching from the left. They broke formation, stalking the airliner, crossing in front of it, directly in its path, incredibly close, then almost in unison, pulling back as another missile was fired, this time from launchers on the nearby rooftops.

"Fire…fire!"

"Negative, sir."

"Negative."

"Negative, sir, it's still coming," said a voice on the ground.

"Dolins—are you there?"

"Yes, sir, it's closing in."

He remembered a scene from a reenactment movie about 9/11, an office worker in the World Trade Center happened to look out of his big glass window moments before the giant airliner crashed into the building. The nose of the plane was almost upon him, its nose and expanse dominating his view, so close he could see the faces of the hijackers.

"Get off the roof, get out of there, now!"

Dolins turned and dashed for the door, knowing he wouldn't make it in time.

He could feel the old building tremble beneath his feet as he reached for the door. The roar of the engines filled his ears. He fought his instinct to jump through the open door and instead took one last look back at the oncoming plane. As he did, he heard an unusual whistling sound and saw the telltale trail of a missile heading for the plane. In a split second, a massive fireball erupted in front of him, blowing the airliner out of the sky.

The missile's explosion ruptured the cockpit, separating it from the rest of the fuselage as debris blanketed the White House roof and the entire surrounding area. Dolins was thrown to the ground. Lying on his back, an intense wave of heat passed over him and in those few seconds Dolins thought he would surely die. But the heat quickly subsided, replaced by a black cloud and a storm of objects raining down from the sky. A piece of the airliner's landing gear and wheel came hurtling at him, missing him by inches, slamming into the roof's solar panels and shattering one of the chimneys jutting out.

He quickly got up on his feet, looked around the cityscape beyond the White House, the airliner's debris peppering the surrounding area and creating pockets of smoke and fire on the rooftops of buildings and on the streets below. Even from where he stood on the roof, he could hear the screams of people and the wail of sirens coming from every direction on the streets below.

Gasoline fumes and burning rubber filled the air. He focused now on the area around him. The White House roof was littered with fragments of the plane, torn metal, pieces of what appeared to be the plane's interior, upholstery and plastic still burning, smoldering, pieces of luggage, some still intact, others on fire, and then the pieces…of remains, passengers who, until moments ago, had been whole.

He turned away from them.

But, as he did, one thing caught his eye. It looked familiar, safe, standing upright, an image he'd seen a thousand times before. Letting his defenses down, he allowed himself to move toward it, his mind needing a moment to process the image. It was…out of context, standing like a piece of a modernist sculpture he'd seen in a museum.

It was an airline seat with its passenger still strapped in, seemingly untouched and in perfect condition, oblivious to the disaster all around him.

Wanting to help, Dolins took several rapid steps toward the passenger. As he came closer, he saw the man, casually dressed, dark trousers and a light blue open collared shirt, his hands gripping the arm rests as though he was still waiting for what was to come, his feet on the ground, brown wing-tipped shoes still tied. His mouth was partly open but his eyes were open wide, staring straight ahead, as though frozen or in shock, eerily still.

Having served in the Middle East, Dolins recognized the look of a dead man. He turned away and went inside.

CHAPTER 16

Hours later, back in the Oval Office after seeing Payard off, President Harry O'Brien watched as the chief of White House security, Johnny Bennett, and CIA Director Jim Goodrich, Chairman of the Joint Chiefs of Staff John Sculley, and National Security Adviser Darryl MacPherson tried to explain how a large airliner could avoid detection, evade oncoming missiles and penetrate the secure airspace perimeter around the Capitol and the White House.

"Sir, we've had the benefit of only a few hours now to investigate this and make at least a cursory analysis of the wreckage." Bennett appeared, once again, nervous. "This plane had the shell and fittings of the original Airbus, but in the days it was missing it was significantly modified for the attack."

The President's eyes narrowed. "Modified?"

Bennett looked over at Goodrich. "Yes, sir," Bennett he, sitting upright in his chair. "The missile-defense system was added on between its disappearance and the attack."

"But how did it get that far? How did it get past us and all our sophisticated radar?"

"First, sir, the aircraft's transponder had been disconnected. Second, our radars *did* show the plane. But only briefly before it disappeared in a flood of literally thousands of additional false blips that overwhelmed our systems. We were unable to pick out the airliner from all the other legitimate aircraft and false signals."

O'Brien looked at him, stunned. "Do we have any idea who was behind this? Have we come across this type of thing before?"

"The answer to your first question is we do not know who did this. We have our usual suspects but no real evidence or even any claims yet from groups taking responsibility."

"And what about whether we've seen this sort of thing before?"

"I'm afraid so, sir. We're not only familiar with this type of radar jamming, we actually created it ourselves."

"Of course," said O'Brien. "How did I know that was coming?"

"Several years ago, we commissioned a company based out of Austin that had been doing cutting-edge work for the Air Force on data mining in large-scale computer systems. We actually gave them a facility in the basement of the FAA head-quarters to create and simulate exactly what was deployed here to disguise the incoming airliner. It was intended to be used by *us* to cripple an enemy's air defenses in the event we needed to disguise our own attack or undercover air operations."

"So you're telling me that someone got their hands on our own technology and used it against us in order to get the airliner past our defenses?"

"Yes, sir, it appears that way."

"Meaning, essentially, that we got hacked?"

Bennett nodded. "Almost certainly. Either someone inside gave it up or, more likely, someone from outside hacked into our systems and copied it."

The President leaned back in his chair, digesting what he'd heard. "I see." He turned to Goodrich, "So, what does this mean? Was this some terrorist group? Do we have a clue who might be behind this thing? Or what their point was?"

Goodrich shook his head. "Like Johnny said, we have no clue on the identity of the perpetrator or perpetrators—or what their point or cause was, exactly." He turned to Bennett, who nodded as though to say, Go ahead. "There is one other thing, sir, but we can't verify or prove it."

"And what's that?"

"We found traces, but only traces, nothing conclusive, of some type of source code that may have been used to infiltrate and hack into our Air Force computer systems. We're still studying the data, trying to trace what occurred inside our systems and, I have to admit, our information is fragmented. It appears that whatever was left of the code used to hack in disintegrated, probably designed to be erased once the attack was completed."

"Jim, Johnny, what are you trying to say?" O'Brien was impatient now.

Bennett looked at Goodrich.

"We've traced the hack to an individual, a man. He's of German descent but worked inside the Vatican as a close aide to the last two popes. He was a monsignor."

O'Brien's eyes widened. "You're kidding me. Do you mean *Monsignor 007*?

Goodrich and Bennett exchanged shocked glances.

"You've heard of him?" Goodrich asked.

"Just before the rogue jet came, President Payard brought him up. I think the French were about to brief our security services on what they had uncovered." O'Brien shared what Payard had told them in the Oval Office. "So how does this all fit together? The hijacking, the hacking into our systems to get to the radar-flooding software, and a dead Vatican spy?"

Goodrich shook his head. "We don't know where the dead guy fits into this yet, if at all—but my sense is this wasn't the work of an individual person or even a private group. It was too sophisticated, too complex, and would have required extravagant resources. It had to be *state*-sponsored."

O'Brien learned over the table. "A *country*? Which one?"

"It's an educated hunch but, in view of who was on that plane, I believe it was Russia," Goodrich said. "And there's only one man behind Russia. Vladimir Putin."

CHAPTER 17

Berlin, Germany

Looking out the large glass windows of his corner office onto Unter den Linden, the main boulevard in Berlin's central Mitte district, Claus Dietrich picked up the newspaper from his desk and turned to face his visitor.

"Have you read the news? *Mein Kampf* is, once again, a best seller here in Germany." He turned away again, looking out the windows. "The Americans have taken the bait. They are convinced Putin is behind the airliner attack. Having Putin's chief political rival on the flight along with so many other Russians and Americans was pure genius, my friend. Only you could have orchestrated it."

"Once I saw his name on the passenger list, I knew we had to take *that* plane," the visitor responded. "Our next mission will destroy the world order."

Still staring out the window, Dietrich nodded and mused aloud, "Now the American citizenry and news services will create the needed atmosphere of threats and taunts. All helped along, of course, with your work manipulating their social media. We have formally reopened the Cold War. The Americans will blame everything that happens next on the Russians. And Putin will be awaiting American retaliation."

Dietrich sighed. "This office stands on the site of the office of the greatest architect of all time, the *Fuhrer's* architect, Herr Albert Speer. Today, we are the architects of a new world order."

Still facing away from to his visitor, he viewed the Hotel Adlon on his right, long a favorite of the Nazi elite and at the heart of its social center during their glory days. To his left stood the Brandenburg Gate.

"The Russians are almost as naive as the Americans. Putin will do anything to undermine his rivals, and no one's more paranoid than he is. We will use that to our advantage. As the world descends into chaos, we will gather strength."

He pulled away from the window and turned to face his visitor. "And you, my dear friend, Kurt, will be instrumental."

Kurt Schlegelberger, dressed in his black priest's jacket and white clerical collar, looked back at him through the computer screen. "Remember, we must be intelligent and calculating in all of our actions. No swastikas or talk of the Reich."

Dietrich looked back out the window. "We are witnessing the creation of the first *virtual* superpower. We have no land, no capital city, nothing the traditional powers can attack. Soon we will transition from a virtual power to one with control not only of the virtual world—but also the physical one."

Dietrich turned around, his cold, deep-set eyes staring at Schlegelberger, "But before we can fully implement our plan, we must destroy any obstacles, anyone who can interfere or cause us...difficulties."

Schlegelberger gave him a knowing nod, "Yes, the two brothers. The living one and the *dead* one. I have already made arrangements to deal with Michael Nicholas. We are following his every move. He will be dead within the week. Unlike his brother, he will only live once."

"But it's the *dead* one I fear the most." Dietrich sat in his black leather and steel desk chair, pulled it in close to his sleek glass desk, and leaned in inches from the desktop monitor. "My dear Kurt," he said, peering into the computer screen where Schlegelberger lived, "you are more alive, more powerful than any other human. You are man and machine, together as one, a superhuman, a specimen of a new master race even our fathers could never have envisioned."

Schlegelberger nodded solemnly. "I stand ready to serve."

"Indeed. But victory requires resources. *Money*. I have an appointment at our mannequin shop around the corner. There is some gold I must attend to. We shall speak again tomorrow."

Claus Dietrich pushed the button on the keyboard and watched as the computer screen turned black. He rose up from his chair and left his office, locking the door behind him.

CHAPTER 18

The White House,
Washington, DC

President O'Brien remembered reading about the "hotline," a direct landline link between the leaders of Russia and the United States. It was set up in the wake of the infamous Cuban Missile Crisis, with the world on the brink of nuclear annihilation. Although barely a teenager then, the images of President Kennedy at his desk at the White House, addressing the nation, were ingrained in O'Brien's mind. Decades later, upon his own election, he had selected JFK's desk for his own use, the same one he now sat at as he picked up the red phone.

Surrounded by his national security advisers, he waited to hear Vladimir Putin's voice.

"Mr. President, I was preparing to call you myself. This situation with the airliner is very disturbing."

Putin, O'Brien thought, was always calculating. Now he was waiting for O'Brien to stake out a position.

"Vlad," O'Brien always addressed Putin by his first name, despite his insistence on addressing him back as Mr. President, "I thought it would be advisable for us to clarify the events behind this airline hijacking and, of course, our need to shoot the jetliner down as it approached the White House."

"Very well. You understand our concerns and...let's say, *suspicions*...over this matter. There were over a hundred Russian citizens on the plane, including Oleg Timchenkov, who was a close friend of mine."

"Yes, I do, and we sincerely regret the loss of all the lives involved and you have my personal condolences for the loss of your friend." O'Brien knew better, Timchenkov was Putin's bitter rival. *What a bunch of BS*, he thought.

"What is your assessment?" Putin was in his former KGB officer curt mode.

Even under the best of circumstances, O'Brien would not have been ready to disclose the existence and apparent involvement of the late Monsignor Schlegelberger or even Alex Nicholas. If the whole thing strained his own credulity, O'Brien could only imagine how it would be received by the ever-suspicious Putin.

"We are still evaluating the evidence, but I can tell you that our internal intelligence agencies have detected highly unusual activities that lead us to believe there are outside parties, not directly attached to either of our countries, potentially at work here."

"Who are these *parties*? And what nation or nations are they from?"

In the pre-call briefings O'Brien had already been warned not to in any way disclose the apparent advances in the AI technology that had created—or recreated—both Schlegelberger and Alex Nicholas. The CIA needed to keep that secret until they had come to understand—and master—it, in the event it proved to be a technological breakthrough. If it was, it would be a game changer in the world's balance of power, and the later Putin found out about it, the better.

"We believe the parties involved were German nationals who have spent time in Italy and other countries."

"And where was this plane during the days it was missing?"

"Unknown, at present."

"I see. You do understand, Mr. President, the shooting down of this airliner, regardless of its supposed course, resulted in the loss of many Russian lives, not only that of my dear friend, Oleg Timchenkov."

Before answering, O'Brien caught the attention of his advisers seated around him. They indicated their approval of what he'd said so far. "Vlad, there is one other piece of information I need to tell you."

"What is that?"

"It appears that everyone on the plane—except for the pilot—was already dead before we shot the aircraft down. Our jet fighter pilots verified this with their own eyes before firing. They could see the dead passengers through the jet's windows. Also, the plane had been outfitted with anti-missile defense systems. We were only able to shoot it down from surface-to-air missiles around the White House. As it was, some of the plane's debris landed on the White House itself. We had no choice but to shoot it out of the air before it hit us. Dead passengers notwithstanding."

There was a momentary silence on the other end. O'Brien figured Putin was discussing the information with his own advisers wherever he was taking the call.

"Mr. President, I respect that your specific actions here may have been necessary. Nevertheless, I am not convinced we have all the accurate information regarding the events leading up to this tragedy—and the correct identification of the conspirators and their motives. There are many around me who feel this was a provocation, whether directly or indirectly, by your country."

"I can assure you—"O'Brien began before being cut short.

"I can assure *you*, Mr. President, we will be investigating this on our own and watching these developments very closely. I hope things are as you say, but your vagueness on the facts is not encouraging. Good day, Mr. President."

O'Brien, his staff, and various US and Russian intelligence agencies listening in on the call heard the distinctive click of Putin hanging up.

But there was another listener.

And as the call ended and the scene dissolved in front of him, Kurt Schlegelberger terminated his own connection.

CHAPTER 19

Saint Tropez, France

It was a magical setting, soft, tiny lights under the trees in a quiet garden terrace. La Ramade was one of Michael and Samantha's favorites. The main courses were arriving, including Michael's filet of beef, pink, perfectly grilled with a thick, charcoaled crust around the edges, and a rainbow of broiled potatoes splayed out around the plate. He'd had this dish before; he could taste it before he even picked up his fork.

He and Samantha discussed the news about the airliner being shot down. Michael knew Schlegelberger had been behind it but was reluctant to tell her since she'd long ago made it clear she didn't believe Alex remained alive in the cloud.

"The world's spinning out of control," Samantha said.

Michael was considering broaching once again the subject of Alex when the proprietor approached and, whispering in his ear, said, "Monsieur Nicholas, I'm sorry to disturb you but one of our Saint Tropez gendarmerie is by the entrance here and has asked for you. He said it would only take a moment of your time."

Michael rose from his seat, "I'll be right back."

"What is it?" Samantha said, instinctively suspicious any time Michael left the table before even tasting his dinner.

"Not sure. Maybe I blocked a car across the street, at the hotel."

He walked around the other tables and to the front entry, which was little more than an open gate to the sidewalk. As he approached the gate, he saw a uniformed gendarme standing in front of a black Citroen, the French wishful-thinking equivalent of a Mercedes.

Once he stepped onto the sidewalk, the officer nodded and left, crossing the street. Michael was only a few feet from the Citroen when the back door opened. As Michael looked inside, the car's front door swung open and a man in a dark suit came out and approached him. In the back seat, another man in a dark suit flashed a gold badge from inside his open wallet.

"Mr. Nicholas. I'm with the Secret Service. Would you please join us for a short discussion?"

Michael wasn't sure whether he had a choice.

The man slid over to make room, and Michael got in while the other man stood outside, as though on alert for anyone approaching the car.

"What's this about?"

"Mr. Nicholas, I have been sent to speak with you personally—by the President of the United States."

"You're kidding."

"I can assure you this is no joke." He handed Michael what
appeared to be a BlackBerry cell phone but felt much heavier.
"The President is on the line."

He placed the phone to his ear. "Hello?"

"Mr. Nicholas. I'm sorry to bother you on your vacation."

It was him, the voice he'd heard on countless television and
radio broadcasts. The man he'd voted for, twice. Calling *him*.

"I understand there've been a lot of very unusual things
happening in your life," said President O'Brien.

"Yes, that's true but—" Michael wasn't sure exactly what the
president was referring to—after all, he had a lot of unusual
things going on, from Tartarus to the Vatican to the Nazis to—

"I'm calling about your brother."

Michael's head was spinning now. "He's dead, you know."

"Mr. Nicholas, I know—everything."

"Everything? Then you know–"

"I know that you speak to him—and he speaks to you—
quite often. It's all as surprising and incredible to me as I'm
sure it has been for you. As a result of this…most recent terrible situation…I'm calling because I need your help."

That was a surprise. "My *help*? Yes, of course, I'll help
however I can. I assume by situation that you mean the airliner?"

"Yes, that is what has brought you and your brother to our
attention. We are exploring the nature of what this *is*. I'm

speaking about your brother and at least one other individual whom, we assume, like your brother, is dead."

"I understand."

"We don't suspect you or your brother of any involvement in the airliner incident, but we believe the person or people who have been hacking your brother are the same ones who hacked into the airliner's systems."

"I see." While he spoke, Michael was trying to process the fact that the President had connected all the dots.

Michael's world had changed, once again.

"How quickly can you get to Washington?" asked the president.

Michael looked back to the restaurant. He would have to leave France and fly back to the States as soon as he could catch a flight.

The president was still speaking, "You understand, of course, these matters must be kept in the strictest confidence. If word were to get out to the press or others, it would mean chaos. We'd lose all control of the situation—and you would likely be in grave danger. So, other than Samantha, you can't tell a soul about this."

He even knew her name.

"I understand," Michael said again.

He could only imagine what Samantha's reaction would be when he told her. She'd never believed the virtual Alex existed. She took his onscreen appearances to be nothing more than a sick game Alex had managed to create before his death. Maybe now she'd believe him...believe it all.

"Thank you. I will make sure you are in the best of hands. Goodbye, for now. I look forward to seeing you here in the White House and, once again, on behalf of your country, thanks."

The connection ended. As though on cue, the back door opened. He stepped out, nodded to the agents, and headed back to the restaurant.

As Michael approached the entrance to La Ramade, his iPhone vibrated, indicating an incoming call.

Jesus, what now?

He pulled the phone out of his pocket, the screen read *The White House*. He stopped just outside the restaurant's garden entrance and placed the phone to his ear. "Hello?"

It was the President again. "One last thing. When you come to Washington—"

"Yes?"

"Don't forget to bring your laptop."

CHAPTER 20

He wasn't the first person to poison a pope.

Monsignor Kurt Schlegelberger would never forget the look in the Pope's eyes. He remembered wondering, as he turned to leave the papal chambers, whether the Holy Father was already feeling the poison coursing through his veins. The poison he'd secretly dropped into the Pope's nighttime Benedictine.

Monsignor Schlegelberger had stopped believing in God soon after entering the priesthood. Quickly, he'd found that without religion, life was easy. No repercussions for one's deeds except on earth, and those consequences had been easy to avoid, especially in his position.

Now he thought about what it would be like if he met the old man again, under these new…circumstances. It was this possibility that told Kurt Schlegelberger he could still feel fear, now more than ever before.

He'd created what should have been the ultimate cover for his crime; he had been, after all, the Pope's consigliore, his protector, confidant, and chief operative. But he had made one major miscalculation…he'd underestimated Michael Nicholas.

He wouldn't make that mistake again. This time he would destroy both brothers, forever, beginning with Michael.

———

It began years earlier, the first of a series of poor judgments. A Bronx bishop was about to be put on trial for molesting young boys. The victims suffered a car "accident" that killed them all hours before they testified. It was the culture, the accepted practice within the church, to protect the cause by covering up the dirty secrets, regardless of the collateral damage. Monsignor Schlegelberger was the fixer, the enforcer of such actions.

In this case, he had owed a low-life Mafia church faithful, Joseph Sharkey a favor, one that would come back to haunt him.

Sharkey had fallen in love with Alex Nicholas's first ex-wife, a woman bent on revenge after a bitter divorce. Sharkey gallantly took up her cause, arranging Alex's murder while he dined at a Queens restaurant. But when Sharkey was quickly named as the person behind the murder, he fled to Rome. In response, Schlegelberger had paid his debt in full, hiding and then protecting Sharkey inside the Vatican complex.

What Schlegelberger had failed to anticipate, however, was the most remarkable discovery: Alex Nicholas, a wealthy underworld figure, had paid millions of dollars to a team of computer geeks who had made a secret technology breakthrough. And so Alex Nicholas had been able to duplicate himself on a specially designed laptop computer—days before he was murdered.

The virtual Alex was breathtaking to observe—it was his exact image, body movements, and facial expressions; his voice had the precise guttural tough-guy sound, complete with the requisite New York accent; he recognized faces and voices and, amazingly, had the same memory and personality as the original, living version, the one Joseph Sharkey had murdered.

This new incarnation had enabled Alex's younger brother Michael to learn the truth about Joseph Sharkey—and then his protector, Schlegelberger.

Michael set off to find Schlegelberger, planning to expose him for the cover-ups of the various church scandals and for Alex's murder. In response, Schlegelberger had lured Michael into the basement of the Hotel Lutetia in Paris, where his plan was to execute Michael Nicholas. But Michael turned the tables and, with the unexpected help of his former female bodyguard Sindy Steele, gained the upper hand, killing Schlegelberger instead.

Ironically, the same discovery that had doomed Schlegelberger saved him. Only weeks before, he had hacked into Michael's computer, discovering the virtual Alex and the new relationship the brothers had established. After locating the software engineers who'd made the AI breakthrough for Alex, Schlegelberger quickly arranged to copy the software and, just like Alex, duplicated himself on a computer.

Also like Alex, he had been murdered shortly after, leaving both of them digitally stranded in the ether.

CHAPTER 21

"The airliner carried nearly a hundred Russian citizens, including a prominent oligarch who happened to be one of Putin's political rivals, numerous members of his entourage and of the Russian press. This has raised tensions between the US and Russia despite unconfirmed rumors that many or most of the passengers may have already been dead before the plane was shot down by US jet fighters."

The television hanging over the bar was tuned to CNN and all the latest reports on the missing airliner that had reappeared only to be shot down before it could hit the White House. Photographs of the pilot, crew, and passengers in happier times flashed by in rapid succession, each face looking back at the camera, unaware their unknowing face would be broadcast on CNN for the world to stare back.

"The irony of this," the announcer said, "is that although the Russians have condemned the US actions, Mr. Putin lost a bitter rival and a group of critical reporters in the process."

Mario's and its owner, Tiger, were a Westport institution. Located across from the commuter train station, in earlier times it had become the watering hole for harried New York City advertising executives looking for a quick martini or two before they headed home to the wife and family. It still served the best homemade meatballs anywhere around.

Mario's was the first restaurant Michael and Samantha ate at twenty years ago when they moved to Connecticut from Manhattan. Since then, they'd shared a lot of events and memories at the restaurant, mostly good ones. Tonight, they shared the table in the front just inside the big picture window overlooking the train station.

"Alex used to love to come here and meet us for dinner," Michael said. "He'd order the veal parmigiana and then a Johnny Walker Red."

"What he really liked, was watching the young ladies at the bar and comparing notes with Tiger," Samantha said. "After eight o'clock, they were like two kids in a candy store."

"Yes, and somehow they always attracted women."

"Some of the ones Alex attracted—or that he was attracted to—weren't the brightest," Samantha said.

Michael wanted to add that intelligence wasn't high on Alex's list of criteria, but he decided to let it pass. It was part of a much bigger issue they would get to shortly, he was sure.

Samantha had thus far resisted all his efforts to demonstrate his brother was—at least in the virtual sense—still alive. It had been right after Alex's murder that he'd taken her down to the wine cellar and brought Alex up on the big screen. But as soon as Alex began speaking to her, she fled the room. And, until yesterday's phone call from President O'Brien, she'd written off any further talk of Alex and artificial intelligence. To her, Alex was simply a sophisticated video game. At one point she'd even suggested that Michael seek counseling. At times, Michael found himself questioning...everything. But he never called Dr. Shapiro, the psychiatrist Samantha had recommended. After all, how would he even begin to explain everything to her?

"I wish," Michael said, "things could go back to the way they were."

"What do you mean, exactly? What *things*?"

Maybe it was the martini. Michael was speaking and thinking simultaneously, something he'd learned from experience could be a mistake when discussing sensitive matters with Samantha. And a stiff drink or two only made it riskier. It was far better to think before speaking; what he really he needed was the five-second delay the television networks used. Nevertheless, he continued.

"I wish our lives were back the way they were before Alex was murdered. Before I agreed to wind down his business for Donna. Before our family became *hunted*."

"And before you had that little fling with your crazy bodyguard? I should have known we had trouble when you hired her. I mean what man hires a good-looking woman as a bodyguard? Especially one with a name like *Sindy Steele*? So I couldn't agree more about wishing we could go back before that." She flashed her brief, tight little smile, the one that was not meant to demonstrate humor.

"Yes, of course…in particular, before *that*." Even if he didn't believe it, he had to say it. But he was pretty sure he did believe it.

"Remember," she said, "you weren't happy then…before. You were bored stiff with your work, you hated the corporate nonsense. You were under constant pressure."

"I know. I never appreciated how nice it was to be bored."

"And then you were entranced, fascinated, enthralled with Alex's business; you were wishing for something different and challenging in your life. Remember?"

"Yes, I do. And back then I *loved* Alex's business. No boards of directors to answer to, no corporate bullshit, no laying people off or firing them. It was freewheeling, no five-year plans, *just go with it*. It was so different, you know?"

She nodded. "And you got to hang out with your brother's old friends, guys you knew since you were a kid. Guys you loved."

"Yes, it brought me a lot of…comfort. Maybe that's the word."

"It apparently did and, maybe at that time, after the trauma of losing Alex, that was what you needed. But you need to remember, you were always different from Alex. You actually had a library from the time you were a teenager; Alex rarely read a book unless it was the Mickey Mantle story. You were respectful of others' feelings; you were gentle, considerate. Alex was a tough guy. You didn't chase women, at least until you walked into your brother's life."

"I still never *chased* women."

"Well then they chased you and you stopped running, at least with Sindy Steele. You were enjoying yourself, old friends, freedom, a little sex on the side, some nightlife, a different cast of characters than in your corporate world. It was refreshing."

"Yeah, it was good…until…it wasn't, and people were trying to kill us."

"That did put a damper on things." Samantha gave him that smile again. "Maybe the lesson for us—for you—is to be careful what you wish for."

Around them, Mario's tables were filled with many familiar faces. "It's hard to believe that just last night we were having dinner in Saint Tropez."

"And even harder to believe," Michael said, "that we'll be in Washington tomorrow—at the White House."

Tiger stepped up to their table with a plate of old-fashioned spaghetti and his famous meatballs. Samantha eyed the dish suspiciously as her own, healthier dish of salmon was placed in front of her. "Don't eat all of that, Michael."

Tiger, in his early seventies, a short, chunky teddy bear of a man with a mischievous twinkle in his eyes, having probably heard this routine a hundred times before, laughed. "Don't worry, Samantha, this is my healthy version, at least for Sicilians."

Michael noticed that Tiger looked tired. "How are you doing tonight?"

"It's one of those nights, you know, when you say, I've got to get out of here."

"Restaurant biz getting old?" Michael said.

"Not just that. I mean Westport, even Connecticut, the town, the freaking weather, the yuppies or whatever the hell you call them now. The town's changed."

"Well, we aren't exactly locals ourselves," Samantha said. "Although, after twenty years, I'm beginning to feel like one."

"You two are good. It's these newer ones, with their freakin' Range Rovers they can't even drive. It's these guys in their jeans and five-hundred-dollar custom shirts. Most of them work for that hedge-fund outfit, Blackstreet or something."

Michael nodded.

"I guess I've been feeling this way for a few years now. It's just now that I've had time to really think. These new people, they're not happy with veal parmigiana, or spaghetti and meat balls, or a stuffed lobster. Now its kale, quinoa, and they don't even say spaghetti anymore, it's *pasta*. They want different things, slick-looking places, fancy drinks. *Craft cocktails*."

"I see you're cranky tonight, Tiger," Samantha said.

"I've got an idea for you," Michael said. "You know that Samantha and I bought a weekend place at the beach down in North Carolina. A restaurant like Mario's might go over real well down there. I'll even be your first investor."

"I do like the weather, and the beach. I don't know how those Southerners would feel about me, though."

"They'd love you, Tiger," Samantha said, laughing now. "And they need a good traditional Italian restaurant at the beach."

"Do you think those older Southern women would go for a little old Italian guy?"

"*Everyone* loves you," Samantha said, placing her hand on Tiger's. "Especially if you can cook. Southerners love good cooking—and they love to drink."

Tiger became serious. "By the way, a guy was in here about an hour ago, looking for you," he told Michael.

"Really? Did you know him?"

Tiger shook his head. "No, I don't think I ever saw the guy before but…you know, I'm not the best at remembering faces, at least not of guys anyway. He said he'd catch up with you later."

Tiger moved on, while Samantha had that look on her face of unfinished business to be discussed. As Michael twirled his first fork of spaghetti, he felt his iPhone vibrate. He pulled it out of his shirt pocket and checked the screen. It was a text from Alex.

Take Samantha and get out of the restaurant NOW!

CHAPTER 22

Michael turned around, looked for Tiger, but he was nowhere to be seen. Across the table, he grabbed Samantha's arm as she was about to nibble at her fish, "We've got to go outside—"

She looked up, pulling back her arm. "What are you doing?"

Michael grabbed her again, more firmly this time. "We've got to go. No time for questions. *Now.*"

Who was that guy Tiger said had been looking for him? He squeezed his wife's hand tightly, leading her out through the front door as he looked back over his shoulder. As they went out, Samantha whispered, "Are you okay? Are you going to be sick? What's wrong?"

"Please, just come with me." They crossed the street to where their car was parked. Michael checked his phone again, hoping for another message.

Watching him, Samantha appeared to reach her own conclusions. "Michael, talk to me. What just happened in there?"

"I just got a text telling me to leave right away and to bring you."

Samantha's eyes narrowed. "A text from whom? Don't tell me..."

"Yes, from Alex, but I don't know why."

"Okay, Michael. Listen, you're not all right. I'm making an appointment for you with Dr. Shapiro and you're going to go if I have to walk you in there myself."

Michael turned away, checking up and down the street for threats. Despite Samantha's critical stare, he held his phone out again and messaged Alex.

What's going on? We're outside Mario's.

He stared at the screen, hoping to see the little dots indicating an answer was on its way.

Nothing.

Samantha was watching him. He looked back at Mario's. Through the picture window, now from outside, he could see the table they'd just left. Through the smaller window on the left, Michael could see Tiger, near the bar, looking out at him, his hands spread apart to ask, *What's going on?*

He turned back to Samantha. "Please, *stay here.* I have to go get Tiger."

He took one step back toward the restaurant as the explosion blew both windows out into the street. Michael felt his body lifted off the ground as he watched in slow motion everything that moments before had been inside Mario's windows come out like a meteor storm hurtling toward them. The hot blast of fire and shards of glass pushed him back against Samantha. They both fell hard to the ground, Samantha pinned beneath him.

It was the last thing he remembered.

CHAPTER 23

"Michael…Michael can you hear me?"

His name was echoing inside his head. He recognized the voice but nothing else seemed right. He knew he was lying down, but not on a bed. He moved his arms, placing his hands around him onto…the ground; it was hard, rough… concrete. There were noises, sirens. He began to remember. The explosion. Samantha…

"Samantha, are you…?"

"Oh, thank God you're alive." It was her voice.

He opened his eyes to see Samantha bending over him, beautiful as ever but her face smudged with ash.

"Are you okay?" he asked.

"Yes, I'm fine, just dirty. You fell on top of me; I hardly felt anything. Are *you* okay? Do you feel any pain?"

He began to move, lifting his head up from the ground. They were still in the street, now surrounded by debris and shards of glass. He saw a body. There were more sirens, in the distance but getting steadily closer. He looked back, over the row of storefronts and the burning gap that had once been Mario's.

Flashing strobe-like red and blue lights began to light up the street as the police cars and fire trucks arrived in unison. The air was filled with the sound of police radios and the grinding of the fire engines. Bodies were being pulled from the wreckage, hoses rolled out. A woman with EMT on her yellow vest ran toward them.

He looked back at Samantha. "What about Tiger? He was still in there."

Michael and Samantha stood in the hospital room doorway. With all the tubes, tanks, and wires surrounding him, it was nearly impossible to recognize their good friend Tiger lying on the bed in front of them.

"The doctor said he's in a coma," Michael said.

"For how long? When do they expect him to wake up?"

"They have no idea. The doctor said *if* he wakes up."

"Oh God, don't even say that."

"They don't know yet. He's lucky to be alive."

"It's hard to believe that less than an hour ago he was joking around and bringing us drinks." Samantha was tearing up.

"I hate to leave him here tomorrow." Michael said.

Samantha looked surprised. "What do you mean?"

"I have to be in Washington, remember?"

"Oh, I know…but with all this—"

"I've still got to go and you should still come with me."

"But what about Tiger?"

"His family's on their way. Right now, there's nothing that can be done anyway. He's out of it until he wakes up, which is probably better."

Michael wondered if Samantha also remembered what had preceded their exit from Mario's. His thoughts were interrupted by a familiar voice coming from down the hall.

"Samantha, Michael." It was Fletcher Fanelli, their close friend and the Westport chief of police. As soon as he approached, Samantha gave him a hug, "Oh, Fletcher, it was horrible."

"I heard you guys had just left when the explosion hit."

"Yeah, we were lucky," Michael said, looking cautiously over at Samantha.

A former semi-pro hockey player, Fletcher looked the part, built like a tank, ideal for his role as a small-town police chief in a wealthy suburban town with virtually no crime, except, on occasion, when someone was trying to kill Michael or Samantha. On the side, he had helped Michael in trying to track down his attackers, traveling with him in pursuit from North Carolina to Paris. Fletcher had little real crime to attend to in Westport so he was thrilled with the chance to do some real crime-fighting, even if it involved some of Michael's more questionable activities, which Fletcher considered to be more or less victimless crimes. Twenty years as a New York City cop had cured him of such ethical distinctions.

"Do you know how many people were...?" Michael asked.

Fletcher looked down, "It looks like at least sixteen are dead and we've got another ten here in the hospital. Word is we might lose another two or three."

"Do they know what happened? Was it a gas explosion?" Samantha asked.

Fletcher hesitated. "Keep this to yourselves for now but I don't think so. It's still premature but the fire chief's already told me that it looks suspicious. Believe it or not, he thinks it was a bomb."

"A *bomb*? In Mario's?" Samantha said, a little too loud.

"Keep it low," Fletcher said as he looked around. "Things'll get crazy once word gets out. We've found what looks like bomb material blown into the street."

"Who would want to plant a bomb inside Mario's?" Samantha said. Michael noticed that her eyes avoided his.

"I don't know. There's so many nuts these days." Shaking his head, he pointed to Tiger. "Let's hope he pulls through… Anyway, I'm glad you two are okay. I've got to get back to work."

As soon as they were alone again, Samantha reached for Michael's hand.

"So it was Alex who told you to get us out of the restaurant? What in the world is going on?"

Michael pulled out his cell phone to show Samantha the text he'd received from Alex just before the explosion. He scrolled through his contacts until he came to Alex.

All of Alex's previous texts, including the ones he'd received inside Mario's, were gone. But as he continued to stare at his phone in disbelief, a new one appeared.

Are you still alive?

CHAPTER 24

onna Nicholas, formerly known as Donna Finkelstein, was the last of Alex Nicholas's three wives. She was sure of that. What she wasn't so sure of was whether she was his widow.

Propped up by three pillows, she sat up in her bed, her perfect 36D silicone breasts—an engagement gift from Alex—peeking out of her black Victoria's Secret nightgown. She snuggled under the crisp white Frette comforter and, after emptying her second glass of chardonnay and pouring a third from the bottle on her nightstand, opened up her laptop. She was ready once again to sign into the iJewishMingle dating site.

Several weeks earlier—in what she was not entirely sure was a coincidence—she had been matched online with a potential date. They'd had several online chats. She had yet to meet him in person. His name was Alex.

Finally feeling a good buzz from her wine, she navigated the site, hoping that Alex would be online tonight. He appeared in seconds.

Alex: *I knew you'd be back.*

Donna: *My husband is dead. He was shot in a restaurant two years ago, in front of a bunch of people, including some cops who were at the bar. He was buried at Saint Michael's Cemetery. So now you're expecting me to believe that this is you—on a dating website, no less?*

Alex: *If you're so sure he's dead, why did you have his body exhumed?*

Maybe, she thought, someone told him about all that and he decided to find her and try some type of scam. It was too bizarre to really *be* Alex, even if he did fake his death somehow. No, this couldn't be real—although she'd always had her doubts—and Alex was certainly capable of anything... when he was alive.

Donna: *Maybe I thought you took some of your precious money with you. It'd be just like you to line your casket with hundred dollar bills. Or, maybe, I had your—his—grave dug up because there were too many odd things happening—*

Alex: *You mean like Michael somehow being able to go from running a boring, legit corporation to running my old business, successfully?*

Donna: *That's one, definitely. But there's been a lot more. Some of his friends have told me about e-mails or messages that appear to have come from Alex's account. And then his closest friend—who now works supposedly for Michael— mentioned that Alex had spent a small fortune on some computer thing, something called—*

Alex: *Artificial intelligence?*

Donna: *Yeah, that's it, so he supposedly could duplicate himself on a computer. I think it was so he could create a diversion or something so he could keep communicating and torturing me even though he was hiding in some nice condo in Las Vegas or Miami.*

Alex: *Really, is that what you think? And what would he be doing there, all alone?*

Donna: *Oh, he's not alone. He's got his cronies that would still be around him somehow and you can be sure he's got a parade of good-looking twenty-one-year-old, big-busted bimbos coming in and out every day. Believe me, he's not alone. The difference, though, is that when his ballgames come on TV, he can send them all away and sit back in one of those recliners with a drink in his hand and enjoy the game. "In fuckin peace," as he always said.*

Alex: *Yeah, well that does sound good. He must be a smart guy.*

Donna: *Actually, Alex is—was—very smart. Not book smart, he hated that stuff, but very smart. That's why he was so good at bookmaking.*

Alex: *I'm curious, was he good in bed?*

Actually, he had been quite good in bed, the best she had ever had, and she'd had quite a few, before and during their marriage. She looked away from her laptop as memories of some of their best nights swept over her. If this was really Alex, it was the type of rhetorical yet provoking question he would ask.

Maybe it was the wine, or just the thought or possibility that this really was Alex, but it was too much right now.

Donna: *I've got to go to sleep.*

Alex: *Yeah, me too.*

She switched off her computer but, just before she did, she saw he had already signed off.

Typical Alex.

CHAPTER 25

Michael knew Samantha enjoyed staying at the Four Seasons Hotel; she loved the indoor pool and Georgetown shopping. Even though the President of the United States had summoned Michael to the White House *because* of Alex, it was apparent that Samantha was still skeptical that Michael's brother was anything more than incredibly good software. So as soon as she left the room for her morning swim, Michael opened up his laptop, clicked onto the ancient gold cross and waited for Alex to appear.

"I've got a letter I want to read to you'" Michael said as soon as Alex appeared on the screen.

"A letter? Who sends letters anymore?"

Michael looked back with a satisfied smile. "The Pope does."

He took the envelope out of his pocket and, after showing Alex the gold embossed Vatican seal on the envelope, removed the letter and read it aloud:

Dear Mister Nicholas, on behalf of the Vatican family and as the spiritual leader of the holy Catholic community, I sincerely apologize to you and your family for the terrible events that were directed at you and your family by members of our clergy...

He looked back up at Alex, "I love this new pope."

But he could see that Alex wasn't impressed. After all, he'd never been a fan of the clergy—or of any religion. Not to mention that, even though they had been rogue priests, the Vatican had still protected Alex's killer and, in trying to cover up the entire affair and silence anyone who could reveal what they'd done, had also tried to murder Michael.

"Schlegelberger," Alex growled. "That son of a bitch tried to penetrate my software. He was trying to get inside it and both duplicate it for his own purposes and eliminate me. It cost me over two million dollars before we made that break-through—and he thought he could just hack in and copy it."

"We don't think the old—and certainly not the new—pope ever knew about what Schlegelberger and the other priests had done."

Alex shook his head, not buying it. "We don't know anything for sure. But Schlegelberger was the right-hand man to the last pope, so you can make your own conclusion."

Michael was nervous about the upcoming meeting with the President. How much did the government know about him? Did they know that besides being a respectable corporate CEO, if there was such a thing, that he was also in charge of the major illegal gambling operation that he'd inherited from Alex?

Worse, did they know that Michael's former bodyguard, the beautiful but certifiably disturbed Sindy Steele, who was now quietly residing on a Greek island, had been hired by the rogue priests to kill Alex's murderer, Joseph Sharkey, after he threatened to reveal what he knew? She had finished him off with a stiletto to the heart inside a Florence leather shop, just one of a string of dead bodies that accompanied Michael's new life. Then there was the hit man the Vatican sent after Sindy Steele to silence her. She blew him away in a North Carolina hotel room.

As Michael began recounting all the things that had happened over the past two years, he wondered how he'd gone from the straight-arrow suburban corporate life he and Samantha had lived, to what now appeared to be a character in a Stephen King novel. But when he looked back at the computer screen, it was clear. Once his brother had been murdered, Michael had wound up living *Alex's* life, too. And that meant being anything but a straight arrow.

Michael knew he was good, too good at times, at compartmentalizing aspects of his life. He had the ability to store his emotions, if not memories, on a shelf in the closet of his brain and close the door until he needed to revisit whatever he'd put there. It was an invaluable trait for someone living, as he now was, two different lives, one of them secretive and hidden from the world.

Today, Michael would find out whether his secrets remained secret or whether they'd been uncovered by the federal government, of all things.

"I'm meeting with President O'Brien in just a few hours—O'Brien told me on the phone that he knew about *everything*. Those were his words. Do you have any idea what that means, exactly, or what he wants with me?"

"No, not really, I don't. I just know there's a lot of activity, like I said, someone's been attacking, hacking into my...site, my cloud accounts, texts, everything. I haven't been able to get on top of it yet except to fight them off."

"You've been able to hack into phone lines, video surveillance feeds, and e-mails, and you can't figure this one out?"

"There are 182 billion e-mails each day, I can't read them all...yet."

Michael sat back, frustrated yet fascinated. "I just hate going into this meeting with the President, and probably all kinds of CIA people, blind."

Alex looked back, expressionless. "I don't think they want much from you. It's *me* they're looking for. It's funny how much more attention people pay to you when you're dead."

CHAPTER 26

Santorini, Greece

She sat alone in the outdoor café, watching the local Greeks and the summer tourists in the square. In her mid-thirties, tall, long black hair, a slender yet athletic build, and mildly drunk, Sindy Steele was a male tourist's dream. Or so they might think. Some of the locals knew better.

She had been a promising medical student at Stanford until she was suddenly expelled as part of a sealed arrangement with prosecutors following the not-so-mysterious-but-impossible-to-prove poisoning death of the lover who'd just jilted her.

Disgraced and shamed, banned from ever reentering medical school, she put her talents to work, first in the service of a Russian oligarch who approached her after reading about her case, and then other organizations. Murder for hire, it turns out, is a tight, close-knit community, in which an assassin capable of avoiding detection by forensic science is a valued commodity.

After a few years, Sindy Steele had established a reputation and a loyal clientele, leaving a trail of dead bodies whose autopsies, if looked at together, would have indicated an epidemic of sleep apnea, alcoholic binge poisoning, opioid overdose, and heart attacks in upscale hotels, restaurants, and bars, her venues of choice.

As the Greek ouzos warmed their way down her to her stomach, her mind flashed back again to each *assignment,* the ones she was paid to do, and paid well. Her favorite weapons were both silent ones: exotic, impossible-to-detect poisons—a result of her excellent pharmacology training at Stanford— and her stiletto.

She preferred the intimacy of the stiletto, which felt much like sex…in that other place…where you know it hurts but you want it deeper. Except this time, she was the one doing the thrusting, the gentle piercing. She remembered each face as they looked into her eyes, their mouths always slightly open, searching for clues. *Who was she? Did they know her? Who sent her? Why was she doing this?* Their eyes pleading for answers, their voices already stunned into silence.

And then, after the initial shock and after they'd gotten used to the pain, they'd plead silently: *Put it in again, deeper… please. Once more.*

Tonight, Sindy Steele was growing increasingly restless. Her anxiety had been building for months.

The tourists sitting near and far in the café, a mix mostly of Brits, Germans, and Americans, seemed to focus on her, the men trying to catch her attention, perhaps dreaming of a liaison with a stunning Greek woman—they had no way of knowing she was an American in exile, in voluntary retirement, compliments of her last employer. Instead of having her eliminated because of what she'd done for them and what she knew, those dirty priests had paid her a lot of money, as long as she went away, forever, far away. Like Santorini.

The locals here were still talking about what she said to the Greek Orthodox priest, Father Changaris. He accosted her one night at another outdoor café when she was drunk, telling her she should come to church on Sunday and get on her knees to ask for forgiveness for her sins. She took another swig of her ouzo and said, loud enough for all of Santorini to hear, "Father, when I'm on my knees, I'm not praying."

There was trouble coming. She wasn't sure what it was but, like the dogs who instinctively know when to flee before anyone else sees the tsunami arriving at the shore, she knew the signs, those feelings when the drugs the doctors prescribed were no longer keeping her impulses in check. That dangerous combination of restlessness mixed with loneliness.

She had a dark history with her lovers. Of the two in her life of any consequence, one was in a cemetery not far from Stanford. The other was in Connecticut, very much alive. She'd been his bodyguard, then his mistress, and, when he'd abandoned her for his wife, she'd nearly murdered him, too. But they'd reconciled, speaking occasionally; she'd even helped him once since then, an incident in Paris where he'd gotten in trouble. Fortunately, she'd been stalking him and rushed to his rescue when some combination of old Nazis and corrupt Vatican priests had tried to kill him. In her mind, she remained, in a sense, his bodyguard. She knew that he still thought of her and that, deep down, when he put his wife aside, he would still want her. She had not given up.

She missed Michael Nicholas.

CHAPTER 27

Berlin, Germany

Claus Dietrich went down the elevator and out of the modern glass building that housed his office. He headed toward the Brandenburg Gate but, just before he reached it, he turned left onto a series of quiet streets and then reached Wilhelmstrasse. He paused when he reached the site of Hitler's bunker, where the Fuhrer and Dietrich's uncle had spent their last moments, marked now by a simple information placard for tourists.

He kept walking and in just a few minutes arrived at the shop, a relic of old Berlin, virtually untouched since the war. The painted wooden sign above the window read *Heinrich's Mannequin Shop*.

It was long past closing time, so the store windows were dark. Despite being rarely open, the strangely life-like appearance of the mannequins visible through the shop window always seemed to attract the attention of passersby. Mothers could be seen pulling away their children—whose faces were glued to the window—as they themselves sneaked a curious look back.

Although Dietrich was technically one of the owners of the Heinrich Mannequin Shop, he rarely entered it and wasn't active in the mannequin business that was transacted in the store. In fact, Dietrich found it disconcerting to be there alone. The latest, electronically enhanced mannequins put him particularly ill at ease. In fact, his stomach knotted as he anticipated entering the building.

He checked behind him and up and down the street and then placed his key into the old brass lock and entered through the front door. Once inside, he took a moment to get his bearings. The only light came from the street lamps outside—and from two tiny red LED lights about twenty feet away farther inside the shop. He had seen them before and it still unnerved him.

As he stepped further into the shop the red rights turned blue. She had seen him. He continued toward the stairwell on the right but she rose up from her couch. He wouldn't be able to avoid her. She came toward him.

"Is that you, Herr Dietrich?" Her eyes, like lasers, bore down on him as she came within inches of his body, invading his private space. Always unsure of himself around her, he stopped. "Yes, it's me. I need to go downstairs."

His partners had briefed him on Heidi. She was the latest in smart mannequins, also known as gemenoids, powered by the most advanced artificial intelligence, voice and facial recognition software. Her face and body, patterned after a famous

German supermodel, were made of a special silicone, giving her a hyper-realistic human appearance, thereby making her even more unnatural.

"You don't like me, Herr Dietrich."

Although he resented doing so, he knew it would expedite things if he called her by her given name. "Heidi, I don't dislike you, I'm just in a hurry. I must go downstairs. Please, go back to your couch...or my partners will sell you to the Russians, like your friends."

She was beautiful, tall, shapely, her white skin peeking through her black silk negligee. As he pushed past her, her breasts, strangely warm, grazed his arm.

"You don't understand me...but, eventually, you will." She moved back, allowing him to pass. He was further disconcerted when, as he walked briskly away, she murmured, "We're more alike than you realize."

He continued to the stairway, down the flight of steep concrete steps and into the basement. He went past three steel-caged storage bins, pressed open a disguised light switch plate, entered the numerical passcode on the hidden keyboard, and watched as the adjacent wall panel rose up to the ceiling, exposing another keyboard panel. He pressed in a different series of numbers and was relieved to finally hear the sound of the metal locks as one after another they opened. He stayed back until the heavy steel door slid open, revealing the vault and switching on the light inside.

In the same instant it took for his eyes to take in the scene in front him, he felt a pressing pain in his chest for, instead of rows of gold bricks stacked from the floor to the ceiling, he saw an empty room, its walls exposed for perhaps the first time since 1944.

CHAPTER 28

Washington, DC

It felt strange to drive up to the West Wing of the White House in his Lexus SUV, the same car Michael drove almost every day in the most ordinary places. After passing through the gatehouse checkpoint, he drove up the circular driveway to the front entrance. The lawn, shrubs, and pathways were perfectly manicured, an ordered still life. He left his car with the waiting military attendant, entered through the portico, showed his ID once again, and was ushered into the entry hall.

Maybe it was the uncertainty, or the somber surroundings, or the gravity of everything that had gone on and was yet to come but, for whatever reason, he felt nervous.

As he walked, escorted, through the Chippendale- and Queen Anne-furnished lobby, he was struck by two thoughts. The first was trying to imagine the history and the great historical characters that had walked these halls, seeing the same view he now was taking in. His presence here, at this moment, seemed so undeserved.

His second thought was how much the furnishings and decorating resembled places he'd seen before, such as the Ritz Carlton in San Juan or the Short Hills Hilton in New Jersey.

Following close behind his escort, he continued a short distance before making a left turn and then down the hall to the entrance to the Roosevelt Room on his right. The heavy dark oak door with polished brass fittings was opened for him as he made his entrance into the chamber he'd seen on television so many times.

Once inside, any thoughts of the Ritz Carlton or other hotels vanished. He'd sat in many boardrooms before, but none that felt like this one. FDR, JFK, LBJ, Nixon…their images flashed through his brain.

His escort carefully directed him to a seat in the middle of the long row of chairs on one side of the conference table. He assumed the President would be seated opposite him, facing him, on the other side. From his own boardroom experience, Michael knew those were the two seats of power, the centers of attention.

The door closed almost silently behind him. He took a deep breath and looked around. The room was probably thirty-five feet long; he sat at the large rectangular mahogany conference table and counted fifteen other tan leather chairs. To his right, the wall was a large semicircle, centered by a fireplace, a portrait of Teddy Roosevelt as a Rough Rider hanging right above it. One of FDR hung at the other end of the room. There were no windows, but a large artificial skylight right above him added a natural lighting effect. Surrounding the skylight in the ceiling were maybe fifty small, recessed lights.

He sat, even more uneasy than before, alone, wondering when the door would open and the show would begin. He wondered what they wanted and whether his life would ever be the same after he walked out.

How could he begin to explain Alex, who, despite his underworld past, was more trustworthy than most of the politicians who had ever sat in this room?

This wasn't the world Michael wished to inhabit. He loved his life, cherished his friends, family, and his privacy. He doubted that anything that would happen in the next hour would do anything but threaten everything that mattered to him.

And, deeper down in his thoughts, lurked that nagging little question: Was it possible that Alex was still *alive*?

After all this, if he is still alive…I'll kill him.

He laughed at the thought, his first chuckle in quite a while and—he feared—his last for a long time after today.

He heard movement and men with deep voices speaking outside the door and now he could feel his heart pumping. In his last few seconds alone, he wondered how Alex, of all people, had led him to this table in the White House.

The door opened and in walked a procession of suits and military uniforms, followed by President Harry O'Brien.

No one was smiling.

CHAPTER 29

Berlin, Germany

As Dietrich stared at the empty shelves where the gold bricks had been stored, he knew immediately who had taken them. The only question was how to get them back—and how exactly he'd kill the man who took them.

He reached for his cell phone but before he could dial, he heard footsteps: someone was coming down the stairs. He moved, hiding behind the door, and waited. There was only one other…person…in the shop capable of walking, and she was a mannequin. He doubted whether Heidi could even walk down steps. He hid behind the partially open door as the footsteps approached the doorway. As the person entered, he squinted to see through the sliver of light in the narrow space between the side of the door and the wall until he saw her clearly.

It was Heidi.

Annoyed, he swung the door nearly shut so he had a clear and full view. She turned around to face him, apparently unperturbed.

"Herr Dietrich," she said.

"Since you appear to be so knowledgeable, where is my gold? Who took it?"

She moved closer to him, until they were only a few feet apart.

"How could I possibly answer your question? Isn't that what you think? Isn't that what you are thinking at this very moment…*Herr Dietrich*?"

She said his name as though to make a point. She was right. His gold was gone and a smart mannequin was carrying on a conversation with him.

"You see everything, Heidi. Tell me who took it."

He noticed a change, a flicker of acknowledgment, her eyes suddenly more expressive. She took two steps closer to him, once again entering a space he considered his own.

"Jonathan Goldstein was here, with many others."

It was what he'd suspected and feared. He reached again for his cell phone. Jonathan Goldstein answered immediately.

"I was wondering how long before you called me," Goldstein said by way of a greeting.

"The gold was not to be moved until next month, when the proper plans had been agreed to. We had an arrangement. This is unexpected. It's disconcerting. You were not to remove the gold or begin our investments until everything was formalized. You were to invest this only *then*. We haven't even—"

"I don't think you understand, Claus. Your gold is on its way to a place you'd least expect."

"What are you talking about? Where is it?"

A long silence followed, until Dietrich wondered whether Goldstein had disconnected him.

"*Where is my gold?*" he screamed.

Seconds later, however, he heard Goldstein's voice, nasally and weak, so typical, he thought, of an American Jew.

"The Benjamin Solomon Center for Holocaust Victims is appreciative of your support."

———

After leaving the mannequin shop, Dietrich rushed back to his office, turned on his computer, and summoned Schlegelberger.

"You must find Jonathan Goldstein," he said as soon as Schlegelberger came on the screen. "Now."

He explained the scene at the shop, the missing gold, and his call with Goldstein.

"So is it lost?" Schlegelberger asked.

"Goldstein made it sound like it belonged to the foundation already but I'm not so sure. The gold has to be transported, unloaded, counted, and then converted into euros or dollars before it can be wired to any account. Their offices are in New York and Tel Aviv but all of this could be done virtually anywhere. No one can move so many bricks quickly or easily."

"How much does he know about our plans?"

"Fortunately, he knows nothing beyond the existence of our fortune. But even that's too much. We were foolish to have trusted him."

For a moment, Schlegelberger appeared to be frozen on the computer screen. Dietrich wondered whether he'd lost the Wi-Fi connection. He turned away, only to hear Schlegelberger's voice once again.

"Jonathan Goldstein is in his car, on something called the New Jersey Turnpike."

CHAPTER 30

Washington, DC

Eight men walked into the Roosevelt Room, most of whom he'd seen over the years on the evening news or *Meet the Press*.

President Harry O'Brien came over, extended his hand. As they shook hands, he held Michael's other arm. It was a warm gesture that put Michael at ease.

"Let's all sit down and then we can introduce everyone. It'll save us some time," O'Brien said. They went around the table.

"Welcome, Mr. Nicholas, I'm Jim Goodrich, CIA Director"

"General John Sculley, Chairman of the Joint Chiefs of Staff."

"Darryl MacPherson, National Security Adviser to the President."

At least those were the ones Michael remembered or recognized. The last one who introduced himself mumbled his name. John Benoit? Michael wasn't sure but it sounded like he was a computer geek working for one of the intelligence agencies.

President O'Brien started things off. "I want to be the first to thank you and express our appreciation for your being here today, especially on such short notice." He turned to the others at the table, "I only spoke with Mr. Nicholas two nights ago when we caught up with him having dinner in Saint-Tropez. It was right after my meeting with President Payard and... the airliner situation."

"I'm happy to help my country in any way that I can," Michael said firmly in his best, boardroom-confident voice.

A man at the far end of the table spoke up. "Mr. Nicholas, your attorney and I have spoken and we have executed a broad grant of immunity for you regarding anything surrounding what you tell us or, for that matter, anything found on your laptop, assuming you give us permission to look at it. I believe you're already aware of this."

"Yes, I am and I appreciate your confidence in me."

"Okay," the President said, "now that we got that stuff out of the way, let's get down to business. Tell us about your brother Alex."

General Sculley spoke up. He was a big man with what looked like a permanent scowl, dressed in a uniform full of medals. To Michael, he simply looked like a son of a bitch. "Refresh my memory, if you will. Was..." he stopped, then let out a laugh, "I guess I mean, *is* his name Alex? Alex Nicholas?"

"Yes," Michael answered, annoyed either by the general's lack of knowledge or, more likely, sarcasm. "It's Alex Nicholas. But, why don't you tell me exactly what you want to know?"

"Listen, gentlemen," O'Brien said, again addressing both ends of the table, "we're the ones who asked Mr. Nicholas to be here. My guess is he'd prefer to be back in the south of France right now. So let's keep an open mind. Remember, the French are convinced there is something happening here, something big. So this is our opportunity to find out what's real and what isn't."

"Thank you, Mr. President," Michael said, staring at Sculley. "You all can believe what you want to believe. I'm not here to convince any of you of anything. I'll gladly tell you what I know and show you what I can. You can reach your own conclusions."

"Why don't you begin by telling us a bit about who you brother was? What was he like?" O'Brien said.

Michael took a deep breath. "My brother was—and still is—a character. We both grew up in Queens, New York. Same house, same parents, he was ten years older than me. In many ways we were very different. He was a tough kid, a big-time jock, a great high school athlete. The Cardinals tried to sign him to a minor league baseball contract but my parents forced him to go to college—where he banged up his knees. So that was the end of his athletic career—and then his college career, too."

The attorney interrupted, "Mr. Nicholas, your brother was a bookmaker and loan shark, was he not? In fact, our information is that he ran and owned one of the largest illegal gambling operations on the East Coast, employing upward of fifty full-time people. Is that correct?"

Here we go, Michael thought. "That's basically correct, although I suspect it's somewhat of an exaggeration. He loved sports and he wasn't someone who could work for anyone else or hold down a nine-to-five job. He was a rebel, and a generally nonconformist personality. He was really smart, great at math, at setting odds, working the numbers, kind of like a human casino. It's the same skill a great stock trader has. It's what made him so successful in his business and that, along with his love of sports, is what led him into sports betting or, as you would say, *bookmaking*."

The attorney seemed impatient. "Nevertheless, your brother wasn't exactly an upstanding citizen, was he?"

"I guess that depends on your definition," Michael said. "If by upstanding you mean a good person whom you could trust and who was loyal, yes he was upstanding. He had a big heart, many of his biggest and oldest customers had been his friends, for years. Most of them had a good amount of money, some were prominent figures whose names you would recognize. He wasn't feeding off people who couldn't afford to bet, like the *legal* casinos and off-track betting parlors do. My brother also took care of a lot of people in need, many who had problems, drug, alcohol issues. He's not the stereotype you probably have in mind."

"So," O'Brien interjected, "you're saying he was a liberal Democrat?"

The room broke up with good-hearted laughter.

"No," Michael said. "Actually, he was more of a conservative. But, the truth is, he disliked—dislikes—most politicians with a passion, whatever their political party."

"Interesting," O'Brien said. "I can't say that I blame him."

"But he was a tough guy, wasn't he?" CIA Director Jim Goodrich asked. "I mean, it appeared that he wasn't someone to be messed with. He was a fighter, not a killer, perhaps, but a man who wouldn't hesitate to hurt you on some level if you crossed him."

"Yes, that's true. But I'll tell you, often when he got angry or went after someone, it was because that person was going after a weaker individual who couldn't defend himself."

"It sounds like Alex was afraid of nothing and no one," O'Brien said.

Michael thought for a moment before answering. "Actually, he was afraid of only one thing."

Everyone around the table leaned forward appeared, almost in unison.

"And what was that?" O'Brien said.

"He was afraid of…dying."

Now, you could hear a pin drop.

There was a lull, a break in the conversation. Michael had the sense there was a plan and he had a good idea what it was. Glances were being exchanged, most of them aimed at O'Brien. Finally, O'Brien addressed him.

"Michael, I think you can understand the skepticism around this table."

"Sure, I understand it. At times, I even question…everything myself."

"Since you've been good enough to bring your laptop there," O'Brien said, pointing to Michael's computer case on the conference table, "maybe it's time to cut to the chase. How about if we get to meet…Alex?"

Michael unzipped his laptop case, pulled the aluminum laptop out, opened the lid, pressed the power button, waited for the home screen to appear. He looked up, everyone around the table watching him closely, particularly the geek who actually got up and stood over Michael's shoulder to get a closer look at what he was doing. Michael certainly had their attention now. This would be the moment of truth.

As soon as the gold cross icon appeared, Michael double-clicked on it. The geek leaned in even closer. No longer wanting to look up at the others and feeling nervous, Michael stared at the laptop screen. He could hear the sounds of throats being cleared, then a cough, then another throat clearing. It reminded him of business presentations when the technology wasn't working and the PowerPoint slides from his laptop failed to show up on the boardroom's screen. Each second of waiting—wondering if it was going to work and doubting it more as each second passed—felt like an eternity.

Where are *you, damn it?*

CHAPTER 31

Minutes passed, each second marked by the ticking of an antique clock that, until the room fell silent in anticipation, Michael had not heard before. He kept trying to summon Alex, retyping in the password, then old passwords, asking the tech guy to check the White House Wi-Fi connection, but Alex was a no-show.

He glanced over at President O'Brien, who was looking back at him and no longer smiling. He could feel the mood around the table turning against him.

Finally, a laughing General Sculley broke the silence. "Sometimes it helps if you turn the computer off and then on again."

There was a burst of laughter, then several simultaneous conversations, none of which had anything to do with the subject at hand. He'd lost them and nothing he could say now would change things. Already, it seemed was as though he were no longer in the room.

It was time to pack up and go home. He should have known better than to expect Alex to show up, even though he'd told him about this possibility for the meeting.

President O'Brien stood. "I think it's best to adjourn, we've all got busy calendars." Then, looking at Michael, "I confess I'm baffled at what's going on here. I love the French but sometimes their intelligence can get carried away. I need to regroup with our own intelligence folks here on this to see how things got this far. Clearly, they should have vetted the matter more thoroughly before bringing it to this level. I wish you the very best. Someone will escort you out. We'll be in touch."

Michael nodded, closed the lid on his laptop, and got up to leave. An aide appeared by his side and they both headed out. The room seemed to be in a controlled commotion, with several of the men cracking jokes while preparing to leave. There were thinly disguised recriminations going back and forth, "…So whose crazy idea *was* this?"

Michael looked over at President O'Brien, who seemed absorbed in his own thoughts, not angry like most of the others around him. If anything, Michael thought as he walked away, the president appeared confused. Michael thought of Samantha and how she'd react once he told her what had happened. Any chance of her believing in Alex—and perhaps Michael's own psychological stability—had been dashed.

But just before Michael reached the door, Alex's husky voice with its familiar Queens accent bellowed loudly from the closed computer's speakers and throughout the room.

"Where the fuck are you?"

CHAPTER 32

Jonathan Goldstein loved being rich. It was who he was. More than his newborn and grown children and certainly more than any of his wives, money made him tick. He rarely found reason to bother reflecting upon it.

Recently, a lump under his armpit, and the resulting malignant tumor diagnosis brought into his psyche the harsh intrusion of his mortality. Briefly, he'd wondered if his priorities had been misplaced. But the most recent prognosis, assuring him of many more years of business as usual, had restored his faith in his...material world.

Several years ago, he'd dumped his wife of forty years to marry a young woman forty years his junior whom he'd met in a Chinese restaurant. The story was later reported in the business and social rags, how he'd slipped her his business card as she was leaving with her General Tso's Chicken takeout, telling her, "Google me."

As soon as she signed a generous prenup and not long after his latest facelift, and only two days after his divorce was finalized, they married.

As he drove out of the Newark airport parking lot in his new Talia, the latest model with an optional self-piloting feature, he glanced at his image in the rearview mirror and wondered if he'd overdone the facial surgery. Never handsome, he nevertheless barely recognized the face that looked back at him in the mirror. Was it better than it would have been if he'd left it alone? His deep-set, hollowed eyes and the dark circles from lack of sleep stared starkly back at him.

The long flight from Berlin had given him time to reflect. Perhaps too long, but he'd been unable to sleep. He longed to drive up to his Short Hills mansion and get into his own bed.

It had taken him fifty years to accumulate his first billion, hard work at major investment banks, setting the stage for his final triumphs as a takeover artist, buying distressed—and sometimes healthy—companies, then cutting out every last ounce of fat, plus muscle if not bone, in order to create a favorable bottom line before flipping those businesses to other investors, each time earning himself millions, often hundreds of millions in profit and fees. Who cared if the business was left crippled with debt and lost talent?

Yes, the trip from Berlin had given him time to think. He briefly engaged the autopilot switch, enabling the self-driving function of his car so he could open his iPhone. He clicked on the First Bank of Aruba app, pointed the screen to his face, allowing the facial recognition feature to recognize him, clicked on the balance in his account. *$5,048,776, 222.70.* Yes, that was five *billion* in his account. He laughed out loud, placing his hands on the steering wheel and regaining control over the sleek automobile.

Moments ago, Dietrich's Nazi gold had just been converted to euros and then to dollars and then wired to his account. He had secretly promised the money to the Benjamin Solomon Center for Holocaust Victims, an organization he had donated to over the years in memory of his grandfather, who had died in the Sachsenhausen camp. An old family friend who represented the Solomon Center, Saul Silverberg, had been working in concert with him after Jonathan told him he'd met a prominent Vatican monsignor and suspected Nazi sympathizer who wanted him to convert his gold and invest it for him.

He pushed the button on his smooth polished mahogany steering wheel. "Call Saul Silverberg," he said.

"Jonathan, do you have good news?"

"Yes, I've just received the funds and will be arranging the transfer into your bank this afternoon as soon as I arrive home."

"Splendid, we are so grateful to you. You have done good work. Your grandfather would be so proud of you."

"Thank you, I'm honored to be of help."

"Jonathan…before you hang up, may I ask how much we will be receiving? I need to let our bankers know what to expect and I'm curious as to how much gold these people were able to hide all these years."

"Yes, of course," Jonathan said. "It came to just over a billion dollars."

To Jonathan, that seemed more than fair.

"God bless you, my friend."

CHAPTER 33

Everyone in the room stopped, frozen in their places, some seated, others standing or, like Michael, heading for the door. It was like that game where, on a command, everyone has to stop what they're doing and freeze.

They were all staring, their eyes fixated on Michael's laptop still under his arm. He too stopped in his tracks, feeling a wave of relief and newfound confidence flow through him.

Alex's gruff voice resounded once again through the laptop's speakers. "There was a lot of traffic. Computer traffic, you know. Internet, not car traffic. I got delayed. I'm not big on meetings, either, in case my brother hasn't told you."

Michael turned around, returned to his seat and, after carefully placing his laptop on the antique conference table, opened the lid. The mood in the room had changed.

The computer geek got up and, once again, looked over Michael's shoulder at the laptop screen. His head jerked back slightly when he saw Alex, apparently live and well, whatever that meant.

"Can you flip that thing around so I can see?" President O'Brien said.

Michael turned the laptop away from him and toward the President so O'Brien and Alex could see each other.

"Harry O'Brien, huh? Who'd have thought?" Alex said. "I voted for you, by the way. Not sure why, though."

Although O'Brien, apparently speechless, appeared somewhat surprised at what he was seeing and hearing, Michael could see that he—and others around the table—were not only confused but, once again, skeptical.

O'Brien looked up, first at the computer guy and then at Goodrich. "Jim, can you have someone take a close look at this? I mean, I see someone here on the screen that looks like the man in the photos you showed me a few days ago, Alex Nicholas, the *late* Alex Nicholas, I guess, right? But how do we know...? I mean, if it's real, this is remarkable."

"Listen," Alex said, in his thick, throaty voice, "I didn't want to be here in the first place. I'm here because my brother asked me to show up. I don't like it when you guys talk as though I'm not in the room."

O'Brien's mouth dropped. The computer guy scrambled back to his own laptop and started furiously typing.

General Sculley laughed, loud and hard. "This is goddamned ridiculous, folks. Y'all can't be serious about this."

Michael knew that Alex was going to go nuts over Sculley's comment. This was where their personalities differed, not so much in what they felt, but certainly in how they reacted to their emotions. Where Michael was usually easygoing, Alex could be brusque and blunt. Both had tempers, but Alex's was lethal and hung on a hair trigger. Michael was more calculating. Alex was a risk-taker, defying the odds, acting on instinct.

Alex had no patience for subtlety, whereas Michael could dwell in the gray areas of life.

Even though Michael couldn't see Alex's face, he knew what was coming, and Alex didn't disappoint him.

"Go fuck yourselves."

The screen went dark.

CHAPTER 34

Washington, DC

CIA Director Goodrich looked to his computer geek. "Talk to me. What do we know?"

"Well, it could be good software, you know, some combination of AI, voice-duplication and recognition software; someone could have loaded in a lot of his personal history, done an algorithm to model his basic attitudes and decision-making or personality. But, assuming Michael here is being straight with us, it's also true that no one has been ever able to duplicate a person in software."

"What about IBM's Watson?"

"Let me be more precise, no one has ever been able to duplicate a particular, *actual* person on a computer. It's one thing to mimic human reasoning or thinking. It's another to take an actual human being and literally recreate them, their look, their voice, their recognition capabilities, their memory, their beliefs and attitudes, their...very consciousness."

"You must have been able to trace this to something?"

"No, sir...we haven't."

Goodrich cocked his head, reminding Michael of a confused puppy. "How's that possible?" He looked over at the President, then back at Michael. "What in the world is going on here?"

The President also looked at Michael, his expression somber, serious. "I guess I didn't know what to expect but I didn't expect *this*. Was that really your brother? And, if it was, is he dead or...could he be alive? And I only ask if he could be alive because, other than Jesus Christ, I've never heard of someone who was dead ever coming back to this life and, at the risk of my political future, in the case of Christ, I'm not even convinced of that. So, help me out here."

Michael tried to come up with an explanation that would make sense. "Alex was gunned down in a Queens bar two years ago in front of a room full of off-duty New York cops. He was carried out of that place in a body bag and taken to the city morgue. At least this is what I've been told by the people who were there and, officially, by the NYPD. I happened to be in Paris when it all happened, actually speaking with Alex by phone when he was shot. I heard him die. After the morgue, his body was delivered to a funeral home, where he was embalmed, placed in a casket and, after his funeral three days later, buried at Saint Michael's Cemetery in Astoria. If there is more to this than that, the burden, gentlemen, is now on *you* with all your resources to find it. I haven't been able to uncover any other scenario, despite what Alex's widow and some others seem to want to believe."

"So," the President said, "the person we saw and heard talking to you on your computer was...really..."

"*That* was Alex," Michael said.

The President looked at his computer expert, who was typing away on his laptop while listening to someone through his earbuds. "Can we verify this?"

"The CIA techs are still analyzing it. I...I'm not sure yet. But this looks...legitimate. It's a sophisticated program that appears to be running on artificial intelligence software but... it's not just software...I don't have the correct words for it...it's more advanced than anything we or I have ever seen before. It's almost...or is...real, a real independent entity or being... It may have been software once but now has taken on a life of its own...I've never seen anything like this before, except in the movies."

Goodrich turned away and looked back at Michael. "Wasn't your brother's body exhumed a few months ago?"

"Yes, his widow Donna Finkelstein had his body exhumed. I was there, of course. But as the casket was brought out of the ground, a helicopter swooped down and...hijacked...the casket. It was later delivered to a church on the Lower East Side in New York City. When we opened the casket, there was another man's body inside."

"I must be living in a bubble," the President said. "How is all this stuff happening around us and we don't hear about it?"

"Well, then," Goodrich said, speaking to Michael, "in the absence of a body, shouldn't we first assume that Alex Nicholas is *not* dead and that his murder was an act of some sort, you know, blanks for bullets, ketchup for blood, Hollywood style, and that he is, in reality, hiding out somewhere watching baseball games in a Las Vegas condo—as, I understand, his wife suspects?"

"I don't think so," Michael said. "I think he's dead, that his body was stolen by rogue priests inside the Catholic Church who felt threatened by what his reemergence could represent."

"Oh, this is great." Sculley said, as though he had just woken up again. "It just keeps getting better."

"Can you prove this?" O'Brien said to Michael.

"Possibly, it depends what level of proof you're looking for."

Michael had a lot of information in the form of e-mails, much of it from Alex himself but not the type of proof he knew these people would be looking for. The truth of it was, only Alex himself, the virtual Alex, could *prove* any of it. And Alex didn't appear to want to cooperate with this bunch.

"No, I can't prove it with absolute certainty, at least not without my brother's help."

Michael could feel the tempo of the room shifting again.

The President lowered his head and placed his hand over his forehead. "This is…crazy. I don't know what the hell to make of this." He looked around the table. "Well, you guys are the experts here, what *is* this?"

Darryl MacPherson, the national security adviser spoke up for the first time. "Well, either we have a very clever, elusive man who is savoring his freedom somewhere in the world and laughing at us—or…"

"Or? Or *what*?" the President said.

"Or, we have a *game changer*...in which case we here at this table have witnessed a monumental occurrence in the history of mankind. Right now, I have no idea which one we're dealing with. But we need to remember why we asked Mr. Nicholas to be here in the first place. It was because we have a problem. A big one. And, if his brother really does exist in the Internet or cyberspace or whatever the hell it is, we need to know that because...well, we need his help."

Everyone seemed to look now at the FBI director, Jesse Graham. "Mr. Nicholas, with all due respect, first of all, from what we've seen here today, we're not convinced your brother actually exists in the form you've suggested—a human being recreated by artificial intelligence. Second, assuming that he *does* exist, that somehow your brother and his hired tech experts were truly able to crack the code of—let's call it immortality through technology—he doesn't appear willing to be of help or even to speak with us."

The room fell silent. After an awkward pause, O'Brien spoke. "Michael, I appreciate what you've done to be here and share what you know with us. I don't doubt your honesty but it appears that none of us—including yourself—are really sure what we have here. As I mentioned in our call the other night, we came upon this during our investigation of the airliner, that's how we got to Schlegelberger and then you and... your brother."

O'Brien looked around the table. The expressions on the faces of his advisers ranged from skeptical to confused. "Listen, I'm going to be as honest with you as I can. We believe that this Schlegelberger—whoever and whatever he or it is—

was behind the hijacking and ultimate destruction of that airplane. But, there's more to our concern than just that. Much more. I'm afraid that's as far as I can go right now."

"Well," Michael said, "where do we go from here?"

O'Brien checked again around the table. No one else had anything to offer. He looked back at Michael, "I'm afraid we'll have to get back in touch with you…soon."

CHAPTER 35

Newark, New Jersey

As he headed home to Short Hills, Jonathan knew it wasn't over. They would come after him. Everything had happened so quickly and his first priority had been to get out of Berlin and back to the US, but he knew he had to put a ring of protection around him.

He had a brief window, although he wasn't sure how brief, before anyone would discover that he'd taken the gold ahead of schedule and left Germany. He would have to take extraordinary precautions from now on.

He was about to call his private security service to set up a round-the-clock surveillance and bodyguard service when his back and shoulders were suddenly jolted as his seat belt tightened around him so hard that it slammed his body tightly against the driver's seat and pinned his neck and head to the headrest. He heard the doors click locked. He struggled to keep his hands on the steering wheel when he realized the wheel was turning…without him. The self-drive function must have accidentally been reactivated. The car was driving itself.

He struggled to get his arm extended out of the seat belt but it wouldn't give, the taut nylon pressing against his neck and shoulders like a steel vise. He could barely touch the steering wheel with his fingers. The autopilot function was designed to disengage, forcing the car to pull over and park if the driver's hands left the wheel for too long. But the car wasn't pulling over. In fact, it sped up, moving in and out of lanes on the New Jersey Turnpike like a race car. He could see the faces inside the cars he was passing as they turned their heads, some expressing anger, others…perhaps surprise, maybe even, admiration, as they recognized the state-of-the-art Talia. He needed to move his arms to make some gesture signaling he was in trouble but, with his head and shoulders securely locked in place, he could only move his eyes, a terrified prisoner captive to the Talia's incredible technology.

He had loaded the GPS with his home address when he entered the car at the airport. At least he *hoped* it was taking him home. But that hope faded when the car exited the turnpike and changed directions, seemingly headed back, but not to the airport. The exit sign read: *Staten Island.*

Jonathan had never even been to that borough of New York City and couldn't imagine why the car would head in that direction. He knew of it only as a blue-collar working-class part of the city, Italians, Irish, not his type of people. In addition, to get there, they'd have to cross a complex tangle of roads and bridges.

He looked ahead, a steady hard rain had begun to fall, making it hard to see out the windows as the glare of oncoming headlights streaked across the windshield, the wind-swept rain blurring the view. It would be perilous driving now, even for him. But the Talia was equipped with radar and eight cameras, each with a 250-foot range, providing whoever was driving with a 360-degree view. He saw strange lights up head, a bridge, dark and foreboding looming in the near distance and, to the right, an expanse of black. They were approaching a sign; he strained his eyes to see through the rain and reflections: *Goethals Bridge.*

Did the car have a mind of its own? He wondered as he sat, helplessly watching the controls, the highway ahead of him, and the cars all around, if there was something…or someone…behind the Talia's artificial intelligence-driven computer systems.

His question was answered when a voice spoke, sounding so clear it seemed to come from someone sitting right beside him.

"Good evening, Jonathan."

It had to be the emergency helpline integrated into the Talia's systems, although the voice and the German accent suggested his worst fears.

"Who is this? Help me. The car's out of control and I'm trapped…"

"I'm afraid you're much worse than trapped. You're almost dead."

"Who is this?" But he knew.

"Surely you were expecting my visit."

The Talia picked up speed. Jonathan checked the speedometer: he was traveling seventy-eight miles an hour, through decent traffic. At least before, the car appeared to be moving with the traffic but now it had separated itself from the other vehicles and was going dangerously faster, pulling up too close to the rear of other cars before passing them and then leaving them behind until the next car appeared in its way.

"What do you want?" Jonathan was terrified. He tried to hide his fear but his voice was weak, trembling. It was so unlike him, and he hated himself for letting it show.

"What do I want? I think you know. You will either return the money that was transferred into your offshore account or in the next sixty seconds I will send you and your car to the bottom of the most polluted water that man has ever created. Do you see the Goethals Bridge ahead of you?"

He said nothing, staring at the bridge that looked now like a monster rising up from the dark.

"I asked, do you see it, Jonathan?"

"Yes, yes, I see it."

"The drop from the bridge into the water is the equivalent of fifteen stories. You'll have plenty of time to think about whether you will die from the impact or drowning as the polluted water enters your car. An impact death would be quickest."

Through the evening fog and rain, the lights of the old 1920s bridge, its cantilever span and old steel cables passing over a strait known, fittingly, as Arthur Kill. The bridge, ancient-looking now, connected Elizabeth, New Jersey, and Staten Island, names that conjured up dumping grounds for Jimmy Hoffa and other Mafia-inspired nightmares.

"I'll do whatever you want. Just get me out of this."

"I hoped you would say that," the voice said.

Immediately, Jonathan felt a sudden change inside the car as the voice apparently responded to his desperate agreement.

He took a deep breath as the car slowed down, its right turn signal went on, and it moved from the right lane onto the shoulder of the road, finally coming to a full, controlled stop.

Jonathan pressed against the seat belt, hoping it would disengage and release him, allowing to him to flee the car and take his chances outside. But the belt would not release, continuing to hold him tightly in place, nor did the engine shut off.

"You won't be able to escape or leave your car until you return our money."

"I can't even reach my phone," he said. "I can't do anything if I can't get my hands free."

"Very well, I will loosen your seat belt so you may retrieve your phone. I assure you, however, you won't be able to leave your car, it is under my complete control. Don't test me, or you will immediately be on your way…to the bridge."

At that moment the belt loosened up, just enough so that Jonathan was able to reach for his cell phone. He turned his head to look out the window: he had to get out or at least get someone's attention. All he could see were the lines of cars speeding by with dizzying speed; on his right, through the passenger window, lay only darkness.

Through the Talia's speakers, the voice returned.

"Surely you are aware that I can see you and every movement you make. Unless you happen to have an ax, you will not be able to leave your car until I unlock your doors. So, I see you have reached your phone. I have just texted you with my banking account information. Copy it, and then log into your account and transfer the same amount that was deposited to you from the gold—into my account."

His hands were shaking as his fingers struggled to copy and paste in the series of numbers.

"What happens after I do this?" he said.

"I will return control of the car to you and you will be free to go. As rich as you were before you stole our money."

"How do I know that you'll let me go?"

"What choice do you have? You should realize, however, that I will likely be able to retrieve the funds with or without you. It will be quicker with your help, and you have the added benefit of saving your life in the process."

He stared down at his phone. All he needed to do now was click on the "Transfer Funds" button and the money would be on its way back to the Nazis. He looked up again through the water-streaked windshield at the bridge, lurking, beckoning, threatening.

As his finger reached for the button, he hesitated.

CHAPTER 36

Whitestone, Queens, New York

It was that time of night when Donna's thoughts inevitably came back to Alex. As hard as she tried to put him out of her mind, she couldn't resist succumbing to the torment he was now inflicting upon her. It was as though he'd never left. He'd dominated her thoughts when he was alive—and, whatever or wherever he was now, he still did. Nothing had changed except now, he was totally in control and he'd added an incredible mystery to their relationship, the mystery of his very existence.

She took a long swig of her wine, opened up her laptop, and signed into iJewishMingle. She clicked on "Alex," took another long sip and, while she waited, pulled her bedcovers over her breasts. There was no way he could see her since they'd simply be texting, but it felt better this way. In a few seconds, she could see the little dots appearing on the screen. He was texting.

Alex: *Hi.*

Donna: *Okay, smart-ass, Let's get back to when I had your body—or grave, at least I guess it is or was yours—dug up.*

Alex: *You mean the disinterment you put everyone through?*

Donna: *Not everyone. Just you. Everyone else watching was alive, which is more than I can say for you.*

"At least," she whispered to herself, "I think so."

Donna: *Anyway, how about if you explain how a black man showed up in your casket?*

Alex: *I got a good tan. They have Photoshop in heaven.*

Donna: *I can believe the tan part, since I'm sure when you died you went straight to hell.*

Alex: *I know you miss me. Why don't you just have another bottle of wine and get the nerve to admit it?*

Donna: *Another bottle of wine, what the hell is that supposed to mean?*

Alex: *You drink too much.*

Donna: *Now I know you're dead because you couldn't be this stupid.*

Alex: *Yeah, well, there's an empty bottle of wine right by your bed there and it's only eight-thirty at night where you are, so I'm betting you're going to get up shortly and go to the portable fridge and open up a second bottle.*

How could he know *that*? One thing was sure: she needed another glass of wine.

Donna: *Let's cut the bullshit. Who the hell are you?*

Alex: *You know who I am.*

Donna: *Let me be fucking honest with you now. I never had any idea who you were, even when I was married to you and was pretty sure you were alive. And where exactly are you? Where are you sitting or standing or whatever the hell you're doing at the moment?*

She placed her laptop on the side, got up out of her bed, walked a few feet to the portable fridge they had built into the master bedroom cabinets along the wall, and pulled out another bottle of chardonnay. When she returned to bed and looked back at her laptop, Alex's picture suddenly appeared. He was laughing.

Alex: *Where am I? I'm watching you. From afar, but closer than you think.*

Donna: *I'm sick of this shit.*

Alex: *I can see the wine's having its usual effect.*

Now he had that devious smile on his face. She remembered the look well.

Donna: *How did that happen? This is supposed to be a text-only conversation. Can you see me?*

Alex: *In case you haven't figured it out, I can always see you.*

She looked up at the top of her laptop screen. It looked like she wasn't on the iJewishMingle website anymore. His video image had disappeared, as well.

Donna: *What happened to iJewishMingle? What did you do?*

Alex: *Donna—*

Donna: *Yes, what?*

Alex: *Where's your little toy?*

Donna: *My little toy?*

Alex: *You know, your vibrator?*

Donna: *You're sick.*

Alex: *How can I be sick if I'm dead?*

Donna: *If you're so real, let's meet. Like you always said to me, Put up or shut up.*

Alex: *Actually, I think it was "put out or shut up." But I agree. Let's meet.*

Donna: *No, I mean in person, for real.*

She watched the screen, waiting. For the first time, his response wasn't immediate…Was he gone? She checked her connection; nothing had changed. She knew he was there, somewhere. Had she called his bluff? What did that even mean? She began typing.

Donna: *Are you there? Having a problem???*

Still nothing.
And then she saw the dots. He was there.

Alex: *Sounds good.*

Donna: *Okay, name the time and place.*

Was this possible? And if he was alive, how could he show up now and expose himself? There were practical complications of which Alex, of all people would be well aware—starting with the insurance settlement of a million dollars she'd received upon his "death." If nothing else, Alex was no fool. How could he possibly risk showing up in public? If he were really alive, that is.

Donna: *How about Joe's Garage Bar in Astoria?*

Alex: *Sounds good. I can't meet for two weeks.*

Why? she wondered. Was this a stall? Or was it typical Alex? Make me wait, keep me guessing? And how could he possibly agree to meet at Joe's Bar of all places, where everyone would know him as soon as he walked in the door? She finally had him—whoever he was—by the balls.

Donna: *Busy these days?*

Alex: *Not really. Let's just say I may have to fly in.*

Donna: *That shouldn't be a problem. La Guardia's just five minutes away.*

Donna stared blindly into the screen until she could see he'd signed off. She closed her laptop, reached for the bottle of wine, wondering if, perhaps, she'd had too much already.

CHAPTER 37

"**P**ress the button, Jonathan, or I'll do it myself when you're at the bottom of the Arthur Kill."

He needed time to think, to delay, maybe someone, maybe a state trooper would pull up behind him to see if he needed assistance. Anything.

"First, tell me who exactly you are," he said.

"You already know the answer to that. Push the button or I will kill you now."

The car left the shoulder and reentered the highway. It began picking up speed, moving rapidly into the left lane.

"Your time is up."

"Okay!" Jonathan shouted. "I'm doing it." He clicked the button and, after a second, he received the notice, *Transfer Completed*. He knew he would still die tonight, and it was in that moment that Jonathan, for the first time in his adult life, realized money didn't matter.

The car continued picking up speed. The bridge lay just ahead.

"Very well. I'll play a final opera for you, Jonathan. This was Herr Hitler's favorite."

Music began filling the cabin.

"I *did* it! What else do you want?"

"Nothing that you can give me. But, since you were so cooperative, I'll give you a choice."

"A choice? Just let me out."

"Before you go over the side, you have a choice. Windows up or down?"

This was sick; nevertheless, he shouted, "*Up*, leave them up."

The car was now moving so fast it was seemingly out of control, although Jonathan knew it was just the opposite. He was virtually flying from the far-left lane, maneuvering past and in between two other vehicles before veering right, almost turning, straight for a low barrier ahead, the only thing standing between the bridge and the fifteen-story plunge into the water.

Jonathan prayed against all logic that the car would bounce off the gate and back onto the road.

But the six-thousand-pound Talia, hurtling at ninety miles an hour, was no match for the barrier. In a split second, the car crashed right through it; Jonathan barely felt even a bump.

Suddenly, the grinding of the tires against the bridge's steel and concrete roadway, the soft purring of the engine, and the faint sounds of the city and passing vehicles were gone. Inside the Talia's luxurious cabin there was near-perfect silence, broken only by the rich harmonies and elaborate orchestration of Wagner's opera *Tristan and Isolde*, giving Jonathan's precious last moments a surreal, operatic flair.

He was torn between two emotions, utter panic and complete peace. He felt comforted that at least the windows and doors were sealed, and the white leather and exotic burled wood interior gave him a semblance of luxury and security from the fast-approaching end. At least he wouldn't feel the cold water below.

Jonathan was still securely pinned against the seat even as the car began its rapidly accelerating descent. He could only see darkness in front of him now as the car pointed headfirst toward the water. He'd read about how, in the last moments of someone's life, time slows down, turning days into years, seconds into minutes. Now, as his time slowed down, he felt oddly grateful to be in such an expensive, luxurious, and comfortable car. He knew it would be his tomb, but at least its airtight cabin would shield him from the harsh elements he feared the most. He would die in comfort and silence, in the calm that would surround him until the end. And perhaps the well-engineered car would protect him just long enough for help to arrive. He imagined still being pinned behind the seat belt but dry and secure, listening to Wagner, as the underwater searchlights ranged through the muck, the divers behind them, arriving to rescue him.

But his composure wilted when he suddenly heard the sounds of the bridge traffic above and felt a rush of cold, damp, odorous air entering the car.

All four of the windows were opening.

"Son of a bitch," were his last words as his Talia hit the hard water. He felt the jolt of the finely polished wood steering wheel crushing into his chest and the rush of black water holding him in its icy embrace.

CHAPTER 38

The White House
Washington, DC

President O'Brien sat in a large comfortable club chair just in front of his desk in the Oval Office. General John Sculley, seated on a couch alongside O'Brien, sat upright, his imposing large frame in full uniform and medals.

Each was nursing an early evening scotch on the rocks. O'Brien had purposely set up the casual meeting alone with his chairman of the Joint Chiefs of Staff. He wanted to watch him without the eyes of the others, particularly the other military brass whom, he suspected, caused Sculley to demonstrate a certain aggressiveness. Of all his military advisers, Sculley was the most dogmatic, authoritarian in his approach, often making O'Brien feel uneasy in seeking his counsel and even more personally uncomfortable rejecting it. Perhaps alone together, he would find a more measured, contemplative adviser.

"I believe the Russians were behind this, sir. It has all the markings of Vladimir Putin. It was an attempt to stir fear and conflict here, to show to the world our vulnerability and, if they were successful, to kill an American president and at least some of the leadership team. The symbolic value of destroying the White House, exposing our vulnerability, would have been priceless."

"They—if it was the Russians—came pretty damn close," President O'Brien said, agreeing, despite having grown skeptical of Sculley's judgments.

"I know you guys see me as a hawk on anything having to do with the Russians—and I'm proud to say, *I am*—but, I know these people and I know Putin. This was a cleverly designed attack made to appear to be the work of some rogue right-wing terrorists in order to deflect attention from the obvious—which was that Putin killed two birds with one stone. He embarrassed us by flying that aircraft right through our defenses and at the same time got rid of one of his biggest opponents."

"If that's true, why would he have allowed this to happen on a flight with so many other Russians on board? I mean, despite eliminating Timchenkov and maybe some unfriendly reporters, he sacrificed a lot of innocent Russians in the process."

"Just for the reason you're giving me now. No one would believe that Putin was behind the hijacking of a flight with so many Russians on board. But you must understand his mentality. Putin would sacrifice his own mother to advance his power and his agenda."

"And what about everything we have learned about Monsignor Schlegelberger and his virtual, so to speak…reemergence…through this Alex Nicholas, AI breakthrough? I gather you don't think that had anything to do with this?"

"You know, sir, that I never believed any of that nonsense. If anything, it's a clever ploy, maybe even a plant, a diversionary tactic of the Russians in order to throw us off their scent."

O'Brien pondered that idea, taking a long sip of his drink. "I guess nothing is out of the question."

"Seriously, sir, do you really believe computers can recreate a human life?"

O'Brien wasn't anxious to go too deep with Sculley into that more abstract realm, and he was hesitant to reveal his own religious skepticism to someone who, he knew, was a devout Catholic. The thought even crossed his mind that anything he said about his religious beliefs could be used against him in his reelection campaign, especially if he ever formally broke with his general. Perhaps it was the scotch, but he decided to throw caution aside.

"Do I believe a computer can recreate a human being, bring him back to life?…Let's put it this way, John, maybe I believe it's as likely as us waking up in heaven or hell after we die."

Sculley was clearly taken aback. "Sir, I have to say I'm surprised at that. I always thought you were a rather religious man."

"Maybe I am, in my own way. I'm sorry to disappoint you, John. I *do* believe there's more out there than we know. I'm just not sure that it's what we're taught in church."

Sculley looked resigned, "Fair enough."

"So," O'Brien said, relieved to be off the topic of his spiritual beliefs, "if you're correct and the Russians are behind this, what would you recommend we do?"

"Sir, with all due respect, I believe we need to send them a message and let them know that we believe—or suspect—they attempted to fly an airliner into the White House and that, if proven correct, we will take retaliatory action against them. That's the only language Vladimir Putin respects."

"And, if it *is* proven to be correct, what type of retaliatory actions would be appropriate in your view, General?"

"If I'm proven correct, sir, we're talking about nothing less than an act of war perpetrated the Russians."

CHAPTER 39

Donna was tired, exhausted. Alex had, once again, worn her out. How could she wait for two weeks to see him? She opened up her laptop and signed in again to iJewishMingle. Alex came on immediately, as though he'd been waiting.

Alex: *Can't sleep?*

Donna: *Two weeks is a long time. I don't understand the wait.*

Alex: *I told you.*

Donna: *What does that mean? You might have to fly in or whatever the hell you said?*

Alex: *Just what I said. Leave it alone.*

Donna: *Maybe I don't want to see you.*

Alex: *Maybe I don't want to see you either. You're the one who asked.*

Donna: *You're the one who went onto my dating site to find me.*

Alex: *Maybe I was looking for a nice Jewish girl and found you instead.*

Donna: *You shouldn't even be allowed on iJewishMingle. You're not even Jewish.*

Alex: *I don't think there's an iGreekOrthodoxMingle.*

Donna: *By the way, who can I tell?*

Alex: *I don't give a crap who you tell but...Michael will go nuts.*

Donna: *I'm going to call him.*

Alex: *Good, it'll save me the trouble.*

Donna: *You talk to him? He knows?*

Alex: *Call him. Let him tell you.*

Donna: *Oh my God, this is crazy. You're crazy.*

Alex: *You'll see.*

Donna: *I'm tired now. I'm going to sleep. I'll call Michael in the morning. I think.*

She didn't wait for a response but signed out and had just begun to push down the lid of her laptop when a pop-up on her laptop's screen caught her attention:

Warning: Security Breach

Hacking Detected

INTRUDER

CHAPTER 40

Michael had just landed at New York's LaGuardia Airport; he had some time to kill before his dinner with Donna. The black Cadillac limousine pulled up at the terminal with his name written on a sign in the window.

"Before we go to the restaurant, I'd like you take me to 149th Street and 34th Avenue in Flushing."

"Here, in Queens?" the driver said, obviously surprised. Michael knew that the driver had him pegged for a Manhattan-only type who'd probably never seen a Queens neighborhood except for landing at LaGuardia or maybe attending a Mets game. He couldn't blame him. His custom-tailored pin-striped suit, gold cufflinks, and Charvet tie from Paris didn't help. Somehow, unlike Alex, Michael had never acquired a true Queens or even a particularly New York accent. But Queens was Michael's home, the place he and Alex grew up.

A place he had only the fondest memories of, and not a bad place to return to, or at least to remember.

There are areas in Queens that are less than desirable—just as in Manhattan or Paris. The world is full of subtleties, and Michael saw layers and layers of them in his old neighborhoods. They seemed so much more interesting than the places he called home now. Michael and Samantha's daughter, Sofia, could never have imagined living in Queens, her years growing up in toney Westport, Connecticut, having prejudiced her with the stereotypes of the city's outer boroughs; she was blind to their warmth, diversity and beauty. Michael had never taken the time to show her the aspects of the area that he still believed he could enjoy.

"Yeah, it's only about fifteen minutes from here," Michael said.

"Sure thing."

This guy was wondering what he was up to, Michael thought. In truth, he simply wanted to return, however briefly, to a time when things, life, seemed simpler and less complicated and, yes, happier.

Since Alex's death, Michael's life had spun out of control. The allure of Alex's entrepreneurial—and seductively illegal—business, working with Alex's older lifelong friends, the lack of corporate boards looking over his shoulder, the colorful people Alex had surrounded himself with instead of Michael's corporate, risk-averse ones on Madison Avenue, and, simply, the freewheeling lifestyle, all had created a perfect storm of attraction to lure Michael into taking over his brother's business while retaining his own corporate CEO role.

But running two professional lives—even with a loving and supportive wife—was draining him. He knew he wasn't able to give everything anymore to Gibraltar Financial yet, just as Alex had needed to be a licensed insurance broker, Michael needed to retain his corporate position if, for no other reason, than to keep up a legal front and source of legitimate income. And Alex had strained his relationship with Samantha who, until he was called into the White House, believed that he was delusional about Alex's ongoing existence.

After several minutes, the car came to a stop. From the back seat, Michael looked out the car window and saw a familiar sight: a long, tan, brick building, a school, the one he'd attended as a teenager. But, more importantly, his eyes went to the clean concrete extending from the building, with a dark green fence enclosing it from the surrounding homes. At one end were two basketball courts, at the other the wall of the school, JHS 185, Bleecker Junior High School.

The concrete was perfectly marked out as a softball field, the bases sixty feet apart, with home plate at the base of the building. The surface was true but fast. This was where Michael perfected the skills and thoroughly enjoyed the game that Alex had initially taught him. This is where Alex had been the true big brother, protecting, teaching…a young man Alex and his friends looked up to and admired.

Ten years older than Michael and his friends, Alex had coached Michael's softball and baseball teams. In fact, Alex would retain those relationships with Michael's friends and teammates long after Michael himself abandoned them.

Where Michael lived a life dictated by intellect and reasoning, Alex lived according to his heart and his instinct. Where Michael was measured, Alex was loyal. Michael always felt a sense of cool or cold detachment with others, whereas his brother became deeply attached to people, friends, family.

Michael had always lived more inside his own head than in the outside world. He was used to—and comfortable with—being alone, even to this day. It was sports, school, and later business that, fortunately, pushed him into the world outside his mind and imagination. Unlike Michael, Alex partook naturally of the larger world around him. It was a fundamental difference between them.

He gazed at the spot on the ballfield where an older, bigger opposing player had threatened him—backing off as soon as he saw Alex approach.

He had been so proud of his big brother.

The driver looked at Michael in the rearview mirror, "Is there somewhere in particular here you wanted to go?"

Michael took one last look outside. He grasped, but he couldn't find, that sense, the emotion, the certain feeling he was sure was somewhere inside him. He kept reaching—for exactly what, he wasn't sure. Maybe it was some sense of greater meaning, maybe...happiness. Or was it the security of those times and a family that, at least from the eyes of a child, would be there forever?

He knew what he wanted. It was to get out of the car and walk the four blocks to his old home, and then to sit down to dinner again, surrounded by a family that was gone.

"No, I'm done here."

CHAPTER 41

Whitestone, Queens, New York

The Clinton was a throwback to the old-fashioned neighborhood restaurants and bars of Queens. Tin ceiling, pine paneled walls, red and white checkered tablecloths, a long, wooden well-stocked bar with a mirrored wall of bottles behind it; bartenders older than fifty and liquor not measured with an eye dropper, maybe not even measured at all. At the end of the meal, your check comes from one of those standard green check pads—the ones that say "Guest Check" at the top, not the computerized printout with your server's name.

This wasn't the Queens where Donald Trump grew up but the stolid New York City borough of suburban, middle-class, working people. It had been a favorite meeting place for Michael and Alex and the other assorted friends and relatives who revolved around Alex…when he was alive.

Michael sat at a table in the bar area, facing the front door. As he looked around, sipping his martini, he realized that The Clinton reminded him of his beloved Mario's in Westport. The one that had just burned to the ground. Briefly, Michael's thoughts turned to Tiger, still in the hospital, somewhere between life and death, much like Alex.

Michael was just feeling the warm buzz of the gin when Donna blew through the door. She glanced at Michael's drink and then, before she had even sat down, called out to the bartender, "I'll have what he's having but skip the vermouth and the olives."

"Drinking straight gin these days?" Michael said.

"I hate olives," she said as she settled in her chair. "Your brother always liked these freaking neighborhood joints. I never understood it. He'd come here and have the pizza or the veal parm. That's what he was eating, you know, when they shot him at Grimaldi's. Veal parm. Knowing him, he's still pissed he couldn't finish his meal. If he'd hung out at classier restaurants, he might still be alive…if he isn't already."

"It's good to see you, Donna," Michael said. "So, tell me, what's going on? I'm anxious to hear."

He wasn't of course. In fact, what he wanted more than anything right then was to be seated alone at this table and enjoying his martini and a serving of The Clinton's veal parmigiana, watching the neighborhood world go by and just thinking.

"Okay, well let me tell you. Last night I was on my computer, my laptop and, when I was done, right after I signed off, I got this message that there was an intruder, that's what it said, *intruder*. It said I'd been hacked."

"What were you on, a porn site?" Michael was well aware of Donna's late-night habit of going on the Internet while in bed with a bottle of wine.

"Actually, yes, more or less. I'd say speaking with your brother on the Internet is pretty much like watching porn. Being married to him was like living on a porn site."

"Oh, no," Michael leaned back, sighed, he could feel his blood pressure shooting up. "You weren't on the dating site again, were you?"

"You mean iJewishMingle?"

"No, Temple Israel. Of course, I meant your dating site."

"Don't make fun of it, Michael. It happens to be highly rated. It's brought a lot of couples together. And these dating sites are how this generation hooks up."

"I don't know where to start. First, you're not part of *this* generation. Second, what's this about *hooking up*?"

"It's like getting married but with sex."

"Okay, I'm sorry I asked. Anyway, you should change your password as soon as you get home. Not only on that site but on your computer and whatever search engine you use to get online."

Michael didn't want to let on but he wondered...*intruder*? Being hacked while supposedly communicating with Alex? The possible causes were too much even to contemplate.

"I have some news," she said. "You and I are going to meet Alex in two weeks, at Joe's Bar."

Donna went on to relate as much of her iJewishMingle conversation with Alex as she could recall.

"You're not serious, are you?"

"Yes, of course I am…Well, at least we'll find out…*something*. Hey, don't look at me like I'm nuts. I'm not the one responsible for his missing body, his hijacked casket, and all these strange communications. You know there's been a lot of crap going on since the day your brother…died, or whatever the hell he did."

Michael had to admit, at least to himself, that she was right. Who was he to make her feel ridiculous? After all, somehow Alex had made his story into a cross between a murder mystery and science fiction. Except none of it was fiction. Maybe now he'd find out, but he found it hard to believe he'd ever find an answer. Even the government seemed stymied.

"Okay, you're right. I'll be there with you."

"Good," she said with a mischievous little smile. "I'll let him know."

CHAPTER 42

New York City

Monte's Trattoria never appeared in *The Godfather* movies but it should have. In the heart of New York's fabled Greenwich Village on MacDougal Street, it was filled with the special buzz of that rebellious part of town known to every city, a cross between a grown-up Bob Dylan and the late John Gotti.

Monte's waiters were just that, waiters. Not servers. They were black-suited old guys who could be gruff but who knew what they were doing and brought you exactly what you ordered in good time with no speeches, unsolicited small talk, or nonsense. They could be cold, but all it took was one well-placed joke and they warmed right up. They just need to know that you were human and not a jerk. Michael watched as they carried out a steady stream of savory dishes from the kitchen and onto the tables of conversation-engrossed patrons around him.

As he and Karen DiNardo were enjoying glasses of Gavi di Gavi and finishing their salads, their waiter placed the plate of Monte's homemade Tagliatini Pesto on the table in front of Michael.

"I love this dish; the green pesto and pasta makes it look like the whole thing was just picked fresh from the garden."

"I agree," Karen said, as the waiter grated fresh Parmesan onto her Fettuccini Bolognese, "it looks delicious. Too bad it's not Saint Patrick's Day."

Karen had a well-tuned and well-timed sense of humor. If there was one person in the corporate world whom Michael could trust, it was Karen DiNardo. She was much more than her title of executive assistant implied. She had a solid logical and analytical mind, a great memory, and she got things done: more than ninety-nine percent of the execs—earning ten times what she did—out there could do. She could be a senior executive in any company if that was what she wanted to do. It wasn't.

She was the only one in his corporate world who knew of his other, secret life, specifically that he owned and operated Alex's illegal business, Tartarus. She covered for Michael when the inevitable conflicts arose. He also relied on her to educate and periodically update him on the subject of artificial intelligence. It was a role she appeared to relish, especially since he would always have her do it outside of the office, usually over lunch.

"When are you going to tell me what all this AI curiosity is all about?" she asked. "I've known you for over ten years. You trust me with some of your…secrets. Why not this one?"

She knew there was more to his AI interest than he let on but she did not know about Alex, so she couldn't—yet—connect the dots between Michael's curiosities about the technology. And because of that, she was obviously going crazy trying to figure out why Michael was so interested in AI. It had become a game they played each time they discussed it.

Someday, Michael would tell her, but not today. He wasn't ready to have this secret spread any further than it had already.

He repeated the question he had put to her over the phone, "So, tell me, can a computer ever duplicate a person's brain—and their very consciousness?"

"Okay, from everything I've researched—and I have a written report here with all the backup but I know you're not going to plow through it all now, or probably ever—it looks like we're not quite there yet. The technology is advancing quickly but it's still pretty limited…although there are some indications that breakthroughs may have occurred. But those are only rumors."

"What does that mean? What kind of rumors are we talking about?"

"Well, it's strange and I hate to even bring it up since it's totally unsubstantiated."

"Tell me."

"There's, how should I put it? Have you ever heard of the *dark web*?"

"Oh, here we go. Yes, but only slightly. Is it even real?"

"Yes, it's a special encrypted network that can't easily be accessed on the Internet. I won't bore you with the details but it's a source of a lot of underground things going on in the world, particularly the technology underworld, a lot of it rather dark, hence the name dark web."

"Okay, keep going."

"Well, this is where I've seen some activity around AI and a potential breakthrough. The rumors are that some Silicon Valley geeks—real outliers, you know, not the ones working for Google or anything—were able to actually *duplicate* someone. And, when I say duplicate, I mean the whole enchilada."

"The whole enchilada? What the hell is that?"

"It means *the person*—everything—his brain, mind, consciousness, memory, reasoning, personality, and more."

"More? What else is there?"

"Well, if there's anything to this, these guys used a breakthrough in AI to duplicate the mind and then combined that with more established technologies like computer imaging, facial recognition, voice duplication and recognition, and things like that to also duplicate the look, appearance, mannerisms, voice, tone, everything that made up this human being, so that when 'he' showed up on a computer screen, it seemed exactly like the real person, including his ability to recognize others, the ones he knew."

"But, come on, if this is true, and these geeks really did that, how could they possibly keep it a secret?"

"I don't know. That's one reason it may *not* be true. But one rumor is that these guys were hired by some rich underworld figure who paid them a fortune and they had to sign some lock-tight nondisclosure agreement. But, wait, there's more...if you want to believe it."

"What's that?"

Karen took her time, clearly knowing she had Michael right where she wanted him.

"The man they duplicated was murdered just days after they completed the project for him."

Michael felt his control over his life beginning to slip away even further. How could this be? How could Karen stumble onto this, coming so close? It would only be a matter of time until all hell broke loose.

"You're kidding." He didn't know how else to react.

"I knew you'd get a kick out of this. It's all probably fantasy, of course. It's pretty far-fetched, don't you think?"

Michael twirled a fork full of his spaghetti and placed it in his mouth, buying time.

"*Far-fetched?* I don't know. Who knows these days?"

"Maybe," Karen continued, eying him closely, "but here's something else I read, too. It relates to the part of your question about whether they can recreate consciousness. That same rumor says that they did. It turns out—again, if it's true at all—that the personality, the consciousness, of the guy they apparently duplicated...well, let's say they were afraid he could be dangerous."

"So, what's that got to do with why the word wouldn't have gotten out?"

"Because despite whatever contract they signed with this guy to stay silent, they were deathly afraid of him."

"Despite him being dead?"

She shrugged. "Seems like they were even more afraid of him dead."

CHAPTER 43

New York City

The doorbell rang in Suite 801 of the St. Regis Hotel, Michael's corporate apartment, a perk from his role as CEO of Gibraltar Financial. He and Samantha used it whenever they were in New York. Since she was spending a few days at their new weekend home in North Carolina, he was alone this evening.

"Mr. Nicholas, I believe you're expecting me. I'm Suzy Wong."

"Yes, my wife just texted me that you were coming. This was quite a surprise, an early birthday present, she said."

Michael took in the view and her sensuous jasmine scent. She was gorgeous, too beautiful to be a straight masseuse. Yet he couldn't imagine that Samantha would send a gorgeous woman up to his room for anything more.

"I understand you've been uptight. I can see it in your face already and how you're moving your shoulders. I'm going to help you relax. Do you mind if I call you Michael?"

"Sure…of course. Did you bring a special table?" he asked as she walked by him while he held the door open. Her long straight black hair was in a ponytail, sitting high up and bouncing as she moved, making her appear even younger than her looks reflected. Michael guessed that she was in her late thirties. He couldn't help but admire her from the back as she passed through the long hallway and into the living room, leading the way, as though she'd been in the suite before.

"Normally I would, but since this suite is so well appointed, I think we can do it on your bed, if that's all right with you. That's how I do it with your wife. She assured me you were safe and wouldn't misinterpret things."

The way she said *do it* made Michael think of something more than a massage. "So you've given her massages, too? I didn't know that. I thought—"

"My guess is that there's a lot you don't know." She turned around and flashed him a mischievous smile. "Nothing too bad, of course. All very innocent."

Her well-worn skin-tight jeans, halter top, and the gold chain around her bare slim waist sent Michael a different message.

She had a soft voice, soothing in itself, with a slight British accent and perfect diction.

"I detect an accent. Are you from the UK?" He knew he was just making things up to say as he tried to figure out what was really happening.

"Actually, Jackson Heights, in Queens."

"I grew up in Queens too."

"I know," she said. "I'd suggest you pour yourself a glass of wine and then we move to your bed for the massage."

"You want me to have a glass of wine?"

"You're going to need one." Her tone was soft and innocent sounding, yet firm, matter of fact.

He knew he had a decision to make. Clearly this was no legitimate massage session. Was Samantha testing him—or sharing him? Or did she perhaps really believe that he needed something extra, with no emotional attachments, to help relax his nerves? To ease the strain of the recent events?

Before everything with Alex happened, he would have escorted Suzy Wong out the door. But now, things were already screwed up, at least physically, with Samantha. He'd had a tryst of sorts with Alex's mistress, Jennifer, and her friend, Catherine Saint-Laurent. And then there was Sindy Steele. So, the great divide of monogamy had been crossed.

But how could he ever uncover the complexities of Samantha's motivations here, particularly when it came to sex? And what could she possibly expect from him by sending this woman to his bedroom? He made up his mind.

"And how about a glass of wine for *you*?" he offered.

"A decent size glass of your good Scotch, straight up, if you don't mind," she called from the bedroom.

"Oh, God" Michael whispered out loud.

Samantha was up to something. Was it simply a *gift*? A wish fulfilled, for most men. No, it had to be more than just providing him with an evening of sex with a beautiful stranger. And what exactly was Samantha's relationship with Suzy Wong? Prior to texting him a few hours ago to expect the masseuse, her special gift to him, she'd never mentioned her name.

He poured her a healthy few jiggers of his Johnnie Walker Blue. He noted that the bottle was nearly empty—even though there was no one he could recall who'd been in the suite who actually drank Scotch.

Before heading to the bedroom, he took a sip of his chilled Riesling and wondered how something that was supposed to be an hour of simple relaxation had turned out to be so filled with anticipation—and stress.

He heard music coming from the suite's stereo system. "I hope you like the music, it's the soundtrack from *Memoirs of a Geisha*. I see you have it in your iTunes system—did you see the movie?"

"No," he called out, "I may now, though."

As soon as he entered the bedroom and handed her the glass of Scotch, she took a long swig and placed the glass on the bed stand. "Okay, while I get a fresh towel from your bathroom, why don't you take your clothes off—all of them—and then lie facedown on your bed. Don't worry, I'm going to place the towel over your rear—although they have a tendency to slip off."

"Speaking of movies, wasn't there one with a character, Suzy Wong?" he asked.

"Yes, way before my time—and yours, I hope. It was called *The World of Suzie Wong*. We're not related."

Michael emptied his glass and then followed her instructions.

In a few minutes, she had climbed on top, straddling, nearly riding him. He could feel her soft bare legs alongside him on either side, gently squeezing him. She was nude.

"I couldn't find a towel by the way," she said as she pressed herself against him. He could feel her warm breasts on his back and her sex grinding against his rear as she managed to expertly massage his shoulders. "I want you to just close your eyes now and let me give you the massage of your life. Don't say another word."

But before long her hands stopped massaging and exploring his body. He felt her hands gently holding his head back slightly—as she covered his eyes with a silk blindfold. "I want you to turn over now, Michael. Lie on your back. I'll do everything."

And she did.

He had tried hard to make it last but he knew he couldn't hold off much longer.

"I can't believe Samantha sent you," he whispered.

He was at the point of no return when he heard her.

"Samantha?" she repeated softly, "who's Samantha? I thought your wife's name was *Sindy*, Sindy Steele."

As he finished, he ripped the blindfold from his eyes and looked into Suzy Wong's eyes, her long legs wrapped around him, lost in her own ecstasy as she watched him in his.

He knew it was crazy; his mind was scrambled with a myriad of conflicting emotions, yet this was possibly the single most intense moment of pleasure he had ever experienced. And so he knew it was just a matter of time until Sindy Steele reappeared in his life.

CHAPTER 44

Berlin, Germany

The specter of Michael Nicholas was eating away at Klaus Dietrich. Sitting at his computer, Dietrich watched old video of Michael leaving the White House the day after the Connecticut bombing. Anxious and angry, he switched onto a screen with icons, found the one with a cross overlaid over a swastika, tapped on the keyboard, let the facial recognition feature recognize him, and entered into Schlegelberger's world.

"I don't understand how Michael Nicholas is still out there—and talking. He is a danger to our plans."

"He left the restaurant just before the bomb went off," Schlegelberger said, solemnly. "Our man did everything right. No one could anticipate that he'd leave when he did."

"I'll say this for him: he's elusive, and lucky. Perhaps."

"Neither. He had help. His brother intercepted messages, mine perhaps, or our man's when he told me the bomb was in place. Either way, he and his wife ran out just before the device detonated. There was loss of life."

Dietrich absorbed the message, *loss of life*. He let it sink in. For some inexplicable reason even he didn't understand, his mind stayed on it, dwelling on the phrase. There had been so much already, what difference did more make? he wondered. Yet, he was curious.

"Loss of life?" he said, then repeated it, this time as a statement of fact. "Loss of life."

"Several, at least, sixteen to be precise," Schlegelberger said. "It was a restaurant at dinnertime. There are several in the hospital too, some critical."

"Who do the authorities or the press think did this?" Dietrich said.

"The local police chief speculated it could be the mob, organized crime, a failed attempt at extortion. He said on television that the restaurant owner—a friend of Michael Nicholas—had been the target of a pay-for-protection scheme that he had evidently refused on several occasions."

"Interesting. There's always someone willing to kill you, isn't there? If it's not one group or person it's another, or a war, a bullet, a bomb, a blade, a piece of bad fish. Did the owner survive?"

"Yes, he's one of the ones in the hospital."

Bridgeport, Connecticut

Tiger opened his eyes. Everything was a blur, but he had the sense everything was wrong.

"Can you hear me?"

The voice was familiar but out of place here at his bedside.

"Can you hear me? How are you, buddy?"

What in the f'ing world was Fletcher doing here? Tiger could feel his mind slowly waking up, slower than usual. What had he been drinking last night? Why was he so…sluggish? He stretched his eyes open, wider, trying to focus. Fletcher's head loomed large, a giant blur slowly coming into focus.

"What the hell are you doing in my damned bedroom?"

"You're in the *hospital*. Do you remember…what happened?"

His eyes kept working, harder now, as the room around Fletcher came into view. It wasn't his bedroom.

"Where am I?"

"You're in Bridgeport Hospital. You're going to be okay."

"What happened? Did I have a heart attack?" But, as he said it, Tiger began to remember the restaurant…a loud boom, and red, so much, red…blood…blood everywhere. "Did something happen at Mario's last night?"

"It wasn't last night, Tiger. It was a few nights ago. I'll tell you later, when you're more awake."

"Who got hurt? What—"

But before Tiger could say more, a nurse arrived, rushing through the door toward his bed. Seeing him awake, she turned to Fletcher.

"Sir, I'm afraid you'll have to leave now. He's too weak for any questioning."

"I'm not just the police chief," Fletcher said, "I'm his close friend."

The nurse didn't appear to be listening or interested as she tested a needle and then injected it into Tiger's limp arm. His eyes were open, although he seemed to be struggling to stay awake.

The nurse turned to Fletcher. "I just gave him a sedative, the doctor wants him to continue to rest. He's still very fragile. This will knock him out. You'd best come back in several hours."

Fletcher got up to leave. "I've got to go now, Tiger. Get some more sleep. You need to get your strength back, buddy. Everything'll be all right." He gently touched Tiger's arm and left.

Tiger felt a warm comfort come over his body. He could feel the oncoming sleep. The nurse had left, the room was silent except for the beeping of machinery, oxygen, a heart monitor, whatever else it was that seemed to be in every hospital room, everywhere. As long as he could hear these noises, he knew he was alive.

As his eyes began to close, he saw movement, someone walked into his room. He saw the shadow from the corner of his eye, the door…shut. It was a man, but not Fletcher. He struggled, fighting with his eyes to keep them open. The man approached him. He knew the face.

"Danny," Tiger said, unsure if he could even be heard. Danny Delorenzo, a local kid, middle-aged now and a small-time but lifelong criminal he'd once helped out. "What are you—"

"I'm sorry," Danny said, whispering into his ear. "I'm sorry."

"Sorry?" Tiger could hardly pronounce the words, he was falling off, falling away, darkness was taking over the light. "Sorry…about…what?"

He struggled to open his eyes one more time. He saw a cloud, a white cloud…but he was inside…No, now he recognized it as it came closer, about to envelop him. A pillow, pressing hard against his mouth. He could feel Danny's hand through the pillow, a fist barely cushioned as it pressed into his mouth and down his throat. His eyes opened easily now, wide open. He saw his face, above the top of the pillow, Danny's eyes flared, staring back at him like a wild man.

Tiger wanted to say just one more thing, but he knew it was too late. He was never going to speak again. It was over.

He tried to speak the words with his eyes before they closed. *You son of a bitch.*

CHAPTER 45

As the elevator doors opened, Michael was momentarily surprised by a man, a male nurse in pale green hospital garb rushing to get on before he and Samantha had even exited. He had seen him before but, out of context, he couldn't place the face.

They walked down the halls, searching for Tiger's room. As they approached, they saw a commotion outside of one of the rooms.

"That's got to be his room," Michael said, checking the numbers on the doors.

"Oh my God," Samantha said. "Something's happened."

They froze outside the partly opened door.

"Don't go in there," a nurse called out to them.

They stood nearby, anxiously watching the rush of aides, nurses, and then doctors in and out. Michael had already called Fletcher, saying only, "Something's happened," and the sheriff was hurrying back to the hospital.

And then, as though synchronized, an orchestra whose concert was finished, the room emptied. The tone changed, the bustle of activity slowing to a sudden stop.

There appeared to be only one nurse left in the room. She gently shut the door.

Just a few minutes later, the doctor reappeared from down the hall. He spoke to Michael and Samantha, telling them news they already expected.

He left, leaving them outside Tiger's door, alone. They held each other's hand.

As they stood there, the door opened and the nurse came out.

"If you'd like, you can...see him now."

"Why don't you wait out here?" Michael whispered to Samantha.

Relieved, she turned away.

Michael walked in, and there, dominating the room, was Tiger, looking calm, very still. And dead.

Days later, as Michael and Samantha walked up the steps to the church, Michael thought of his own father's funeral. As at that ceremony, the church today was standing room only, mourners from all walks of life, janitors to CEOs, filling the pews. Tiger had been a friend to them all, treating them with equal respect regardless of how much money they had or how big a house, if any, they lived in.

"He was murdered," Fletcher said, approaching Michael as he entered. "Suffocated with a pillow."

"Do you have any idea who did it?"

"We found a surveillance photo from the cameras in the lobby so we got a picture, a male nurse seen in the hospital lobby going in and out within fifteen minutes. None of the staff recognized him as an employee at the hospital." Fletcher pulled out his cell phone. "Do you recognize this guy?"

"Yeah, I'm pretty sure it's the guy we saw pushing his way on the elevator when we got to Tiger's floor at the hospital. I even remember thinking he looked familiar, but I couldn't place him. I still can't."

"Well, we've got him. He's known as Danny D, pretty much a lifelong criminal. His real name is Danny Delorenzo. We've arrested him several times in town over the years. He's a local, grew up in Westport, in and out prison, started small but then major felonies, child porn, drugs, larceny, theft. He's been known to attach himself to legitimate people with money, ingratiate himself with them, and then take whatever he can steal. He's clever and was broke.

"Murder sounds like a big step up," Michael said, wondering now if this was a crime of convenience, coincidental to the bombing.

"Yeah, but he's had steady progression upward already. And he's a druggie, they get desperate."

Michael nodded.

"Someone clearly offered him money—which he needed—to kill Tiger. It's ironic."

Michael raised his eyebrows, skeptical; on the other hand, there was no reason he could think of for Schlegelberger to go after Tiger.

"Tiger helped Danny many years back, got him his first job." Fletcher chuckled sadly. "A job he quickly lost for stealing cash out of the register. You've probably seen him around town."

"I guess that's why he looked familiar. Do we know who hired him?"

"No, and he's not talking, yet. I get the impression he's scared of them and, if it's who we think it is, he should be. Danny wasn't exactly the type to screen his employers."

CHAPTER 46

As Michael walked into Joe's Garage Bar, he couldn't help thinking, *Is this the night the mystery of Alex's life or death will be solved?*

Located on an industrial-strength Astoria side street right next to Joe's Auto Body Shop, Joe's Garage Bar was a cross between the gritty blue-collar industrial and quickly gentrifying parts of Astoria. Joe Sal, the owner and a close friend of Alex's, was a sturdy, tough, motorcycle-riding Robert De Niro-type mythic figure, another tough guy but with a heart of gold, similar in many ways to what Alex had been. Michael, too, had known him, through his brother, for years and had always liked him.

Michael was glad, however, that Joe Sal wasn't around tonight. He didn't want to have to explain to the hard-nosed auto-body king of Queens that Alex might be coming back from the dead in his bar tonight.

The bar had a classic neighborhood-bar look and had already been used in a number of film sets: Pool table illuminated by a low red hanging lamp on the right as you walk in, an old subway sign, *Main Street, Flushing*, above the entrance to the bathrooms, a dimly lit Guinness display, a dartboard, an old Pac-Man machine, a real motorcycle, and a long steel bar stretching maybe fifty feet long across the back wall, complete with a fit young female bartender with wild don't-mess-with-me black hair.

Michael sat where he could see the door, waiting for Donna. A Blue Sapphire gin martini accelerated his already heightened sense of drama, if not dread. Simply meeting Donna for dinner was enough to send his blood pressure soaring. The incalculable possibility that Alex might join them was, despite Michael's regular conversations with him, like an overdose of adrenaline. He watched the young couple at the next table as they devoured a pizza. He was dying to order one, it looked so good, but the idea of chowing on a sausage and meatball pizza while waiting for Donna—not to mention Alex—didn't sit right.

As usual, Donna was late. She would surely blame it on the thunderstorm or the traffic even though she lived twenty blocks away.

Only two other tables were occupied, and the bar was almost empty. It was a quiet night. The storm outside had kept many people indoors and it was early yet for Astoria's nightlife. In the background, coming from the television hanging above the bar, Michael heard the Yankees game, interrupted periodically by flashes of lightning and claps of thunder. He'd focused so intently on the front door that he neglected to even glance back at the television, despite being a die-hard Yankees fan, something he'd learned in childhood from his brother. He remembered the many times he'd had dinner with Alex and how Alex's eyes would inevitably drift away from the table and up to the game.

"Who're you meeting tonight, Michael?" the bartender called out from halfway across the bar. Teresa had known Alex well. In fact, Michael recalled, she had attended his funeral at the Greek Orthodox church, three blocks from here. "I'm meeting Donna, Alex's…wife."

"Oh, sorry about that. How's she doing?"

Great question. "Pretty good, I think."

"It's gotta be tough, you know, losing your husband that way. I feel for her. Your brother was a great guy, always nice, took care of people, you know? He was a good tipper, too. I miss him."

"So do I. Thanks."

Michael looked up at the television. Severino was on the mound for the Yankees and they were already up, 1-0.

If Alex does show, he'll be loving it.

Michael resumed his watch of the front door. It was about thirty feet away, right in his line of sight. He checked his watch, the one Alex had given him years ago. Back when they used to get together, Alex always checked to see if he was wearing it. This wasn't the night he wanted to let him down.

He finished his first martini and could feel the buzz. It was odd no one had walked in the door for at least twenty minutes. The Orioles tied the game. A server walked by with a pizza from the kitchen. It looked even better than before; Alex would want one.

Who'll walk in first? Donna or Alex?

Neither of them was ever on time.

He got his answer almost immediately as the door swung open.

CHAPTER 47

As the front door opened, Michael could feel his chest tighten. The possibility—however remote—that Alex might be alive and walk through the door in front of him froze him in place. But his hopes—or fears—were quickly dashed as Donna came storming in, her enhanced breasts encased in a tight faux leopard skin blouse, her long legs and high heels seemingly arriving an hour before she did.

"I would have been on time but this freakin' lightning screwed up the traffic lights. It took forever to get through the streets," she said, throwing her Hermès Birkin bag on the table. "Jesus, I know you and your brother like this place but this is like something out of Archie Bunker, you know."

"Hey, Donna, it's good to see you."

Michael was lying. Michael had never enjoyed being around any of Alex's wives. It was odd, he had always liked the women

Alex *didn't* marry. But, actually, Donna wasn't the worst of the lot. That honor went to Alex's second wife, Greta, who put several bullets into a wall trying to kill Michael because she thought Alex had screwed her in his will. The NYPD had arrived just in time to save his life before a bullet hit its mark. When the cops ordered Greta to drop her gun, she whirled around at them instead, never the sharpest crayon in the box. They shot her dead as they were trained to do when a crazed person points a gun at them.

Alex's life—and now Michael's—would have made a great novel. Tonight, he'd find out whether it would be a crime thriller or science fiction. Or...nonfiction.

Donna was finally seated right across the table from him. Michael tried not to notice her enhanced breasts and the scent of her Chanel No. 9, the crazy but surefire way to identify one of Alex's wives.

Teresa quickly brought Donna a drink, a straight vodka on the rocks.

"I thought you were a wine drinker," Michael said.

"I am, but I've already had my fill of wine for the night. I need a quick hit right now. Alex could walk in any minute."

Michael said nothing. He had nothing to say.

"He's coming, isn't he?"

"I have no idea. Either way, this whole thing with Alex is incredible. The truth is, if he doesn't show and it turns out he's a product of artificial intelligence, then it's actually even more amazing."

Donna clearly didn't get it or didn't care. Probably both. "All I care about is if he's alive and if he's been faking all this time, hiding out and doing whatever the hell he wants to do and, you know, ultimately screwing me out of a lot of money. That's what I think will be the most freakin' amazing."

"When did you stop cursing?" Michael said, noticing the lack of profanities that usually littered Donna's every sentence.

She ignored the jibe. "He's *your* brother and you've been supposedly speaking with him. What did he say to you? Is he showing up or not?"

"You know Alex, he can be stubborn. He wouldn't tell me. If anything, he's gotten even more cagey with…all this. He said I'd know when the time came. I think it was his way of making sure you didn't go and invite a whole bunch of people to be here. As long as you couldn't be sure one way or another, you wouldn't risk being embarrassed."

"He hasn't changed; he's always thinking, plotting, such a pain in the ass. He was probably afraid he'd have to pick up the fucking—freakin'—tab if they all came to see him."

Since Michael had never fully leveled with Donna as to the extent of his interactions with Alex, it wasn't surprising that she failed to grasp the significance of the virtual Alex, if indeed, that's what his brother was.

Michael checked his watch, it was almost 8:30. Another boom of thunder and a flash of light caused the bar's lights to flicker. The television went off. Moments later, Michael glanced at the screen, hoping to catch the score, but it simply said, *No Signal.*

"Storm must have knocked out the cable," Teresa called out. "This hasn't happened in years."

"Hm," said Donna. "It reminds me of when I got the *intruder* message on my computer the other night when I got hacked." She looked a little nervous now.

As another bolt of lightning lit the windows, Michael saw a tall dark figure go by, approaching the bar's entrance. Whoever or whatever it was, it swept by, strangely illuminated by the lightning. Then the door swung open.

The figure who walked through the door was draped in a long flowing black robe with a hood covering his head, obscuring the face. Teresa, who was closest to the door, froze; the wine glass she'd been holding fell to the floor, shattering.

The figure lifted the hood from its head, revealing a familiar face.

As he advanced toward their table, Michael heard Donna breathe, "Oh my God."

The man's eyes immediately locked onto Michael's.

CHAPTER 48

Maybe it was the long black robes, the beards, the inevitable heavy gold cross, the ever-present European accent, but Greek priests always seemed to have a presence, an aura that hinted of something beyond this world. Father John Papageorge was no exception. The old man slowly stepped inside, somehow seeming dry despite the driving rain he'd just left outside. He walked directly to their table. Michael and Donna both rose to greet him. Father Papageorge first took Donna's hand in his, but Michael could see that she lacked the innate reverence that came from growing up in the ancient church.

The priest turned to Michael, gripping his arm, "I have come with news and perhaps the answers you have both been seeking."

"I thought Alex was coming," Donna said as the priest sat.

Father Papageorge, sighed, his eyes unblinking, his manner calm yet self-assured, in the way of a man who is sure of things the rest of us would love to believe. "My dear, Alex *is* here tonight."

Michael watched the exchange, feeling more like an observer than a participant.

Teresa interrupted the drama as she approached the table, "Can I get you something to drink, Father?"

He looked at Michael's and Donna's glasses. "Yes, I think we may all need drinks. Would you happen to have ouzo?"

Teresa smiled. "Actually, we do. I'll have it right up for you."

As she left for the bar, Father Papageorge whispered, "Perhaps it would be wise for me to wait until she returns so we are not interrupted."

They sat through a strained silence until Teresa returned with a large jigger glass filled to the top with the clear but potent liquid. She placed it on the table in front of the priest who, without a moment's delay, drank it down in one practiced motion, gently placing the glass back on the table.

"Can I get you another one?" Teresa asked.

"No, one will suffice, thank you."

"Would you all like to see menus?"

Impatient now, Michael said, "No, I think we're good for now. Thanks."

Teresa scooted away.

"Father, you said Alex is here tonight?"

"Yeah, what do you mean?" Donna asked. "Are you saying he's *coming*?"

"No, my dear, he is here. Here, now. He is with us."

"Oh Jesus." Donna said, looking like she was about to lose it. "You're not going to give me this spiritual stuff now, are you? I mean, come on, what do we need here, a rabbi to keep things real?"

Michael leaned over, gently touching her arm. "Let's just listen."

"Jesus, Michael, I am listening. Do you hear what he's saying?" she said, pointing her glass at Papageorge. "This is ridiculous. I'm looking around and I don't see Alex Nicholas. I don't see him anywhere. Unless you've got the bastard in your pocket."

Father Papageorge reached down to his side, below the table. It was then that Michael noticed the Bloomingdale's shopping bag that must have been hidden in the priest's robes. Papageorge reached into the bag and pulled out a brown cardboard container the size of a shoebox. It appeared to be heavy for its size and was sealed with typical-looking packing tape. With great deliberation, he placed the box on the table. He looked straight at Donna.

"This is Alex."

CHAPTER 49

Michael couldn't take his eyes off the box. It brought back the same feelings he'd had when, at Alex's funeral two years ago, he'd stared at the mahogany casket, tortured by the thought that the brother he'd grown up with, the one he loved from his first day of life, was inside it.

True to her persona, Donna seemed unfazed.

"What the hell is this?" she said, regarding the box as though it was radioactive.

Father Papageorge, a man obviously practiced in the art of soothing a grieving widow, seemed perplexed but patient.

"My dear Donna, your beloved husband is inside this box. He was cremated." He turned to Michael now, "Cremation, as you may know is against the strictures of the Greek Orthodox Church. After all, the body is God's property. Nevertheless, my esteemed predecessor, the late Father Papadopoulos, had an arrangement with Alex, one that I did not discover until quite recently when I had the opportunity to read his diary."

Donna looked confused or annoyed, or both. "Papadopoulos, Papageorge," she said, not quite loud enough for the priest to hear, "all you Greeks are papa-something."

Teresa appeared at the table and set down another round of drinks. "These are on the house," she said, then stopped and pointed at the box, "What's in the box, Father?"

Before the priest could utter a word, Donna did.

"It's Alex," she said.

"Oh, shit. Really? I'm…sorry. I just thought…" She turned and left, walking quickly.

Father Papageorge resumed his story. "As I was explaining, I discovered in Father Papadopoulos's diary a notation that he and Alex had an arrangement."

"An arrangement?" Michael said.

"Yes, an *agreement* it appears. You see, they had grown quite close. Michael, as you know, Father Papadopoulos was your family priest from the time you were all quite young."

Donna appeared to be losing patience. "But Alex didn't give a crap about religion."

"Your husband was, perhaps, a more complex man than you were aware. It is not unusual for men, tough men, to conceal their true feelings about God and the spirit. Alex had deep fears, ones he didn't easily admit to or confide in others."

"Deep fears? *Alex*?"

"Yes, like most of us."

"And what were those fears?" Donna said. "Because the Alex I knew wasn't afraid of anything. Even the things he should've been afraid of."

Michael knew the answer but kept silent.

Father Papageorge leaned in closer to Donna. "Alex was petrified of death, of dying. He couldn't accept that his life would end and he was never secure enough in his faith to feel assured that the moment he died would not be the last moment of his life. He did not believe in eternity."

Donna still seemed confused but Michael felt only relief. Deep inside, despite occasional doubts, he had always believed that his brother was dead. He was thankful to have him now as a virtual human, a virtual brother who looked, acted, sounded the same, who knew their mutual history, remembered their parents and the places they grew up. It wasn't perfect, but it hadn't been perfect when Alex was alive, either.

And now, years after Alex died, Michael had discovered they both shared the same fear: death. The absence of life. That was what eternity meant to Michael. Yet, for him, it was less a fear of dying than simply missing all that was so good about living, the ones he loved, the places, the food, the wine. Even if Father Papageorge's heaven did exist, it couldn't be better than the life Michael lived here on earth.

"Okay," Donna told the priest. "I get it. He wasn't a believer. I don't believe in all this voodoo either. And let me tell you, I don't think he was so afraid of dying as he was thinking that the freakin' world would still go on without him in it. He was *selfish*, get it? And, anyway, what's it got to do with all this stuff that's gone on since he died? I mean, his business is still going, he's on my dating site talking to me and trying to pick me up. You tell me, what's this all about? I mean, what the hell am I supposed to do with this box?"

"Maybe," said Michael, "it would be helpful if Father Papageorge finished telling us the what he learned from Father Papadopoulos's diary."

Michael caught Donna's eye roll.

Papageorge nodded graciously. "As I was saying, Alex had a close spiritual relationship with Father Papadopoulos, despite his lack of faith. I'm sure for Father Papadopoulos it was a matter of trying to reach him, to help him...believe. Nevertheless, they built a bond together. Alex confided in him."

"Alex confided in no one," Donna said.

Unrattled, the priest ignored her and continued. "It appears that they had an arrangement, one that the church would never officially sanction, by the way. But these things occur; after all, we are all mortals."

"So," Michael said, "what was this *arrangement*?"

"Yes, the arrangement. It was simple, really. Alex, as both you know, was somewhat vain. He wanted to be sure no one saw him, as he said to the Father, *stiff*. So, he planned ahead. He made Father Papadopoulos promise that, when he died, his remains—against the dictates of the church—be cremated. Further, he wanted his casket sealed immediately and his ashes eventually spread at...Yankee Stadium."

"Oh, for heck's sake," Donna said. "That's what all this shit was about?"

"Not completely, my dear. There is more. You see, his mind was, perhaps, one might say, devious. He told Father Papadopoulos about this artificial intelligence breakthrough that people he'd hired had made. He knew that, even if he died, he would be back, back among the living. He suspected that, at some point, people would try to determine whether he had truly passed on—or whether he had staged his death. He wanted to prevent anyone from truly knowing, for sure. He loved the suspense. I suppose it was another way, in his mind, of staying alive, even beyond the reaches of artificial intelligence."

"And whose idea was it to put a black man's body in his casket?" Michael said.

"Oh, that was Alex's idea. He stipulated it in his agreement with Father Papdopoulos, even directed him to where he could obtain such a body."

"And what was the point of that?"

"I believe it was twofold. First, to ensure that, even before any testing, it would be immediately clear that the body in his casket was not his and—"

"I can only imagine," Donna said.

"This was quite innocent, I must say. He simply thought it was…" The priest shrugged. "Funny."

It all sounded plausible, but solving one mystery only led to a bigger one, the original one. What exactly *was* this new Alex? Did he really still live on in cyberspace, a real, living, growing, thinking hybrid of human and technology? Did this new Alex not only think, but love and hate? Did he have a conscience, a soul? Was he…immortal?

And more to the point, how much did the Greek priest know? Michael watched and waited as Donna left the table and entered the ladies' room. There was one important question he had to ask Father Papageorge.

"The only ones who knew we were to be meeting Alex tonight were Donna and myself. So tell me, Father, how did you know to be here with Alex's ashes?"

CHAPTER 50

Michael kept his eye on the ladies' room door, hoping Donna would take her time. He knew that Father Papageorge would speak more freely if it were only the two of them.

"How did I know about your planned meeting with Alex?" he said. "Michael, let me say, there is still so much I do not know or understand. But I was aware from my talks with Father Papadopoulos and then from reading his journal of Alex's great experiment, his breakthrough."

"Did he confide in you during his discussions with my brother?"

"He did, but toward the end, before Father Papadopoulos' heart attack, he seemed to keep more to himself. I believe he warned Alex that this technology was a threat to many people, that he had to be careful."

"A threat?"

"Yes, the promise of immortality, of the everlasting spirit, it is the particular domain of the established—and not-so-established—religions. It feeds the spirit of the believers and those who seek to believe. It is the power of the church; it is how they exert control, keep the flock, and perhaps how they fill the coffers, too. But Alex and this new computer breakthrough had one big advantage over the church's version of the hereafter."

"What was that?" Michael said.

"Unlike the church, he could *prove* it. If his version of immortality got out, the world could see it—on every computer, perhaps every mobile device. And worse, no one had to believe, or go to mass, or fast, or give to charity, or to the church at all. No one even had to be…good. Don't you see the threat? It's a wonder that this new Alex hasn't also been murdered, obliterated, *crucified*—symbolically of course—or, shall we say, *deleted*? Once the Catholics got wind of it, they were truly threatened. Or at least some in the Vatican were… perhaps not this Pope."

"You still haven't answered my question. How did you know that Donna and I would be here, waiting to meet Alex?"

"Fair enough. You are, like your brother, good at extracting information from those who prefer not to share it. So, I will tell you more than I would prefer—for both our sakes, I might add."

Michael looked toward the ladies' room, "Tell me before Donna returns."

"Despite the fact that this technology—the Internet, cyberspace, computers, cell phones, iPhones, whatever—are all relatively new, certainly compared to our religions, there are definite similarities between the two phenomena."

"How do you mean?" Similarities between the Greek Orthodox or Catholic Church—and Apple, for example?"

Papageorge laughed. "I wouldn't phrase it quite like that but, yes, between the *cyberspace* that Alex inhabits and the *spiritual* space that all religions live in. "They both exist in the *invisible* world. There are no wires, yet 'the cloud' is all around us. The Holy Spirit and the Internet are everywhere and yet nowhere to be seen. They both travel through the unknown, the invisible roads of the human mind and spirit."

"And how does this explain how you came to be here, tonight?"

Father Papageorge lifted the second glass of ouzo to his lips, this time slowly sipping it. Michael observed a slight shiver in the old priest as the liquid slipped down this throat.

"I confess to you that I myself am somewhat in shock. How did I know to come here tonight? I seldom check my computer, as I still do most of my work with pen and paper. Nevertheless, as I sat at my desk the other night, I heard an unusual sound, a chime coming from the computer. At first, I ignored it, thinking it was just another idiosyncrasy of a box…a technology…I don't understand. But the chime kept repeating, first every minute or so, then more frequently until I could no longer ignore it. So I turned the computer on and there, before my eyes on the computer screen, was your brother."

Michael glanced at the restroom, then motioned for the priest to continue.

"I recognized him immediately; Father Papadopoulos had introduced us years back. There he was, on my computer screen. He seemed to be sitting somewhere, *where* I have no idea. At first, I said nothing; I didn't know what to make of it. And then…he spoke. He spoke directly to me."

"What did he say?"

"Well, actually, he laughed. I couldn't believe what I was seeing. And his laughter made it all the more difficult to comprehend what was happening before my eyes. But then he spoke. He asked if I recognized him. I said, yes, of course. And then he told me he had a favor to ask of me. He offered no explanation of how it was that he was able to be in front of me, to be present. Perhaps he assumed that I knew more than I did. He asked if I had his ashes. I told him that yes, I did, and he instructed me to meet you and Donna here at this time. And, before I could ask him questions, to inquire about his very presence, he thanked me and…disappeared. That is all I know."

Donna returned but, instead of sitting down, extended her hand to Papageorge, "I've got to get back home. It was nice to see you, Father." She then turned to Michael, "I gotta go, I can't take this any longer. It's too much."

But just as she turned to leave, Father Papageorge held up the box with Alex's ashes and offered it. "I believe you forgot this."

She stopped, appearing uncertain for a rare moment, then said, "No, I didn't forget it. I don't want his ashes. I want Alex but not a box of his ashes, and I'm not about to go to a Yankees game and throw his ashes out on the field. Hell, I don't even like baseball."

And with that, she walked away and out the door.

Michael took the box from the priest's hands, gently cradling it in his own, "I'll take care of this."

CHAPTER 51

Bronx, New York

"You've heard of Stephen Hawking, haven't you?" Karen DiNardo asked, pulling out her thick manila file labeled "Artificial Intelligence."

They sat at the far end of long wooden communal table that they had to themselves. When Michael had called and requested another meeting about AI technology, Karen had reminded him that he'd promised to take her to Arthur Avenue, a series of tree-lined streets in the Bronx that had become a well-known enclave of Italian restaurants, bakeries, butchers, and other purveyors of old-world Italian food. It was a haven of safe streets, enforced by Italian culture itself, often stereotypically referred to as the Mafia, despite being in the midst of a high-crime quadrant of the Bronx.

Michael had a plate of linguine with marinara sauce and sausage; Karen had the linguine with meatballs. The dishes were works of art: creamy, textured linguine, a bright red sauce barely concealing the meatballs and the sausage, all served on a white plate with jars of grated cheese, crushed red peppers, silverware you could bend with your hand. No one even noticed the decor or the atmosphere.

No one dined at Dominick's with people they didn't enjoy and trust. The atmosphere in the restaurant was oddly formal—old-fashioned, schizophrenic waiters who could be formal yet friendly or brusque and impatient—the decor simple and rustic, fake wood wainscoting and cream-colored walls. A fan gently spun on the ceiling, presiding over a photo of Yankee Stadium and paintings of old Italy on the walls.

You knew if the serving staff liked you, and they probably didn't, especially if you weren't a local or a regular, or if you embarrassed yourself by placing a credit card on the table when the bill came. Dominick's was all cash, naturally. But the food was plentiful and great.

It was packed on weekend evenings and any time before a ball game at Yankee Stadium, just fifteen minutes away. Michael would never have come there then. But since this was an early Monday lunch with no game going on, they had the place to themselves.

"Hawking, yes, of course, the guy...the physicist," Michael said. "Died of Lou Gehrig's disease."

"Yes, *the guy*, as you call him, was known for his work on black holes and relativity and was regarded as one of the most brilliant theoretical physicists since Albert Einstein."

"He was still a guy."

"Fine, point taken." Karen rolled her eyes and looked down at her report. "Nevertheless, in an interview published by a German magazine, Hawking argues that the increasing sophistication of computer technology is likely to outstrip human intelligence in the future and that unlike our brains, computers double their performance every eighteen months."

"Jesus," Michael said. Alex was already smart, though in his own chosen ways, but it was hard to imagine him with some sort of superintelligence.

Karen continued to read from her file, "So," he said, "the danger is real that such superior artificial intelligences could take over the world."

Michael tried to picture Alex as some master-of-the-universe-type character. It was almost funny. Almost...And what would the government—or a church—do with Alex once they got their hands on him or his technology? That was an even scarier thought.

"Hawking was studying the universe, right? Not AI?" Michael said.

"True," Karen said, reading from the report, "but before he died, he warned that the efforts to develop artificial intelligence and create thinking machines could spell the end of the human race. Personally, I'm afraid AI may replace humans altogether. Someone will design AI that improves and replicates itself. It would be a new form of life that outperforms humans."

She pulled another page out of her file and looked up at Michael. "There's something else, too."

Karen had a way of leading up to things, her good-natured way, Michael thought, of torturing him.

"I'm sure this is unrelated but while doing my research I read about the suspicious death of two people down in Raleigh, North Carolina, a Brett and Laura Adams. This happened just a year ago. They supposedly were two of the top researchers in the field of artificial intelligence."

"What happened to them?"

"They burned to death when their house caught fire—but it was ruled suspicious. The police found evidence of some sort of a bomb that they believe started the fire."

"Interesting. That's it?"

She pulled out more documents, news clippings. "They had moved to the Research Triangle area, then suddenly, seemingly, retired. No one around them was sure even where they'd made the money to do that. All of this came out after their deaths, when the police started looking into their background."

"So, what do you think?" he said, trying to appear simply curious. "How is this related to anything?"

"You're asking *me*?" Karen said. "This red sauce and the meatballs are incredible, by the way." She eyed a plate of lasagna on its way to the next table, then stared directly into Michael's eyes. "This is probably none of my business and, obviously, that's how you're still treating it. I'm sure you have your reasons but, as a *friend*, I need to tell you that, whatever is going on, from all that I've researched on this, you'd better be careful. There appear to be some very dangerous alleys in the dark web, more than meet the eye. And dead bodies as well.

"As long as we're on this subject, I stumbled upon something else during my research. Again, it may not even be pertinent to anything you're using this information for, but it fascinated me." She paused. "Actually, it scared me to death."

Michael put down his silverware. It was unusual for anything to frighten Karen.

"It's from a UK report out of Oxford. I found it on Google but it's a legitimate source." She put down her fork and pulled another magazine article out of her file. "Listen to this:"

> Nuclear weapons systems are at threat from hostile states, criminal groups and terrorist organizations exploiting cyber vulnerabilities. The likelihood of attempted cyberattacks on nuclear weapons systems is relatively high and increasing from advanced persistent threats from states and non-state groups.
>
> It is believed, for example, that the US infiltrated the supply chain of North Korea's missile system, thereby causing a test failure last year.
>
> The silos of US nuclear-tipped Minuteman intercontinental ballistic missiles are reported to be particularly vulnerable to cyberattacks. Presently, this is a relatively ungoverned space and these vulnerabilities could serve to undermine the overall integrity of national nuclear weapons systems.

She looked up at Michael. "Here's what *you* might be particularly interested in:"

DEATH IN THE CLOUD

Potential *artificial intelligence* applications, while creating new opportunities for cybersecurity, add another layer of vulnerability to nuclear weapons that could be exploited. The United States military, in particular, has led the way in utilizing artificial intelligence software to select and guide missiles to their targets. Although proven to be highly effective in missile guidance tests, its introduction into sophisticated missile systems also opens the door to cyber-attacks and the threat of hackers taking control of them, overriding current safeguards.

Michael pushed his plate away, a new sense of unease flooding his mind.

CHAPTER 52

He had been a priest once. Monsignor Kurt Schlegelberger, protector and confidant of the pope. Two of them, actually. One of whom he'd poisoned when that pope found out the things he'd done, protecting dirty priests and hiding Alex Nicholas's killer.

When he'd first been ordained, he had believed almost everything. But the further he advanced within the church and the closer he got to the spiritual elders, the more he doubted. At first, he found himself challenging peripheral church beliefs or dictates, a conflict he ascribed to the difference between church dogma—that which was divinely revealed—and doctrine, the church's teachings and interpretations. Between what is God-given, handed down by Jesus and the apostles, and what is man-made. But the closer he got to the flame, the more cynical he became, about all of it.

In time, surrounded by the loosening of church mores, financial and moral corruption at all levels of the Vatican, right and wrong seemed to overlap, then blend together, open to interpretation and the exigencies of circumstance.

Each step away from the church, from the concept of the supreme divine being, was incremental. Schlegelberger's loss of his faith seemed to progress from one stage to the next, almost unnoticed, until he found that he no longer believed in the concept of sin. There was no all-knowing, all-seeing judge in heaven, no final judgment, there was no afterlife… there was only this world.

In his new, disembodied form, Schlegelberger was conscious of having a conscience. Confused, searching for more definitive data, he scrolled through his mind, computer-like now, until he found an article that caught his attention:

At the extreme end of this phenomenon, we have the concept of artificial intelligence, which strikes immediately at questions about the extent of human power, and whether intelligence is distinct from a soul. Meanwhile, some transhumanists foresee a period when the human mind will be uploaded onto a deathless computer. As religion scholar Robert Geraci has argued, this vision of people shedding their imperfect bodies and achieving immortality sounds an awful lot like the Rapture, that time, evangelicals say, when all believers will rise into the sky and join Christ.

Was there more to come? Was this stage he was in simply another step on the road to the very same place where the church was going? Was this artificial intelligence, this virtual existence, simply another step along the way, a progression—not a replacement—designed by the same God Schlegelberger had worshiped as a young man?

He continued reading, looking for answers. He scanned the Internet for related information until he found a documentary on YouTube. He wondered how many others paid attention. For him, it was fascinating. He didn't recognize the face of the narrator; the piece was probably meant more for academics than the general viewing public. He watched and listened:

"In his book, *A Brief History of Time*, Dr. Hawking concluded that 'if we do discover a complete theory' of the universe, 'it should in time be understandable in broad principle by everyone, not just a few scientists. Then we shall all, philosophers, scientists and just ordinary people, be able to take part in the discussion of why it is that we and the universe exist.' 'If we find the answer to that,' he continued, 'it would be the ultimate triumph of human reason—for then we would know the mind of God.'"

The mind of...*God*?

His AI brain battled against his human mind...or was it his conscience? Battled between what he'd been and what he had become. But that old voice was still there. How was that possible? How could he still be confronting the same inner voices, the familiar conflict between the mind and the soul, the head and the heart, the brain and the...conscience? If he were ever going to be free, unencumbered by ethics, morality, and conscience, it should be *now*, when he was no longer attached to a human body or any pretense of a spiritual God.

Yet, here he was, confronted by those old inner voices. How could that be possible? Unless…

No, it was too late to reconsider his path. And since there was no higher power, no God, no inherent right or wrong, the quest for *power* would rule his new life as it had his old one.

Still, a deep sense of dread, a sharp pain, ran through his chest.

What, he wondered, *have I done?*

CHAPTER 53

Kure Beach, North Carolina

It was the end of summer, which, on the North Carolina shore, was still quite hot; a time of shorts, tans, loafers, the smell of coconut suntan lotion mixing with the salty scent of the ocean, and the sounds of the waves breaking on the shore while cocktails and ice were being briskly shaken in the ever-present cocktail shaker behind the bar.

But for Michael and Samantha, those were the only care-free reminders of summer.

Sitting in one of the restaurant's old dark wooden booths, Michael poured the remainder of his martini from the steel cocktail shaker into his glass. "I love a bartender who gives you your drink along with a little extra in the shaker. It's a lost courtesy, left over from a bygone time."

Since the bomb destroyed Mario's, Michael's new favorite comfort food Italian restaurant was located next to their vacation home on the North Carolina coast. It had a similar feel, red check tablecloths, a great bar with generous drinks, traditional uncomplicated Italian dishes, a laid-back, unpretentious atmosphere, and a warm, friendly staff. Samantha, too, enjoyed it, despite her penchant for healthier, lighter food.

"Michael," Samantha said, "I'm sorry I doubted you, but who could possibly believe this whole AI thing with Alex, and now, of course, *Monsignor* of all things, Schlegelberger? After seeing you actually called into the White House, and then everything with the Greek priest and his diary, I finally came to accept what you were trying to tell me about Alex. I honestly thought you needed psychological help."

An apology from Samantha was a huge deal. Michael wanted to say that, but he feared she'd take it back if he did. Better to just graciously tuck it away in his head for safekeeping, never ever to be acknowledged or brought up again.

"I know, but you think *everyone* needs psychological help," he said with a mischievous smile.

"And they usually do," she replied, perfectly serious.

"I rest my case."

For Michael it was a relief to be able to talk openly with Samantha again about Alex and the bizarre happenings that had occurred since his...initial...death. He was no longer alone. And, since Samantha and he had a very close relationship in most other aspects of their lives, he looked forward to being able to share his experiences—and his brother—once again with her.

The relationship between the humanly alive Alex and Samantha had, at times been testy. Alex's view of women wasn't the most progressive, to say the least, which rightfully offended Samantha. They were both strong willed, too, which led to infrequent but explosive fireworks, leaving Michael with the thankless task of trying to play peacemaker between his wife and his brother without getting bloodied in the process. It usually didn't work out like that.

"You know the last time we sat down to dinner out like this, the restaurant blew up," Michael said, looking around. "I'll miss Mario's—and Tiger. He was a good man and a generous friend."

Perhaps it was the similarity of the restaurants, or just reasonable paranoia in view of what had already occurred, but Michael felt a premonition, a disquieting anxiety that, despite the comfort and familiarity of his surroundings, something wasn't right. He didn't want to mention it to Samantha since it would only stoke even greater anxiety on her part, which would then create even more for him and, after all, he could find no tangible sign of danger.

"I heard from Fletcher," Michael said. "It appears the Westport police and the FBI know who was behind Tiger's murder."

"You mean who hired that local guy, what was his name?"

"Danny D—aka Danny Delorenzo, the guy we saw in the hospital elevator. Yes, it appears to have been a 'crime of opportunity,' as Fletcher quoted from the report."

"I don't get it."

"In other words, the bombing was *unrelated* to Tiger's murder. It just provided a convenient cover for the local Mafia group that was already threatening Tiger because he wouldn't pay protection money for the restaurant. I guess he'd also been pretty vocal telling other business owners that they shouldn't pay off these guys. So, they needed to set an example with Tiger; otherwise, they'd be out of business. When the bombing happened, they figured they could eliminate him without having the authorities looking for them and instead the attention would go to whoever was responsible for the bomb."

"So," Samantha said, "who was responsible for the bomb?"

"*That* they still don't know, or at least the FBI isn't saying. They appear though to have eliminated that local Mafia group. And no one is interested in what Alex may have known, or Schlegelberger, of course."

"Well, it *is* pretty far outside the usual cast of characters, especially if you're law enforcement. I don't think they easily go down such obscure alleys when they're looking for suspects."

The server arrived and placed one of Freddie's specialties on the table for Michael, a flame-grilled pork chop sautéed in butter and brown sugar and topped with sliced peaches and pecans.

Michael looked over at Samantha before cutting into the pork chop. He knew what was coming.

"That looks so good," Samantha said as she prepared to cut into her simple grilled lemon salmon. "Don't eat it all, take some of it home for lunch tomorrow." Samantha, protective of Michael's health, was constantly trying to watch over his diet, despite his best efforts to the contrary. His dinner would soon become a negotiation over how much Michael would save for another day and how much of the chop he would actually eat tonight.

"Schlegelberger is planning something *big*," Michael said, trying to eat as much of the pork chop as he could before Samantha caught up to him.

"You mean like flying a plane with two hundred dead passengers into the White House?"

"Bigger. I'm afraid much bigger. When you and I were in Uzes, at the resort, Alex and I had a three-way conversation with him online."

Samantha looked shocked. "You're kidding me, aren't you? When did you do this?"

"I couldn't tell you. You were asleep and you would have thought…"

"Okay, I know, Yes, I would have thought whatever it is you think I would have thought. Probably worse."

"Okay, so anyway, at first Schlegelberger seemed interested in getting Alex to work *with* him."

"Seriously? What did Alex say?"

"You can imagine, something like 'go to hell,' to put it mildly."

"Well, that's good…I guess. What happened then?"

"This is what I'm so worried about. He said something like, the plane thing was simply the appetizer and that it was too bad but we were going to miss the main course."

Samantha finished what was left of her wine.

"What could he possibly have planned that's so…big? He's just a computer or something."

"Yeah, just a computer—look what he's done already. We can only begin to imagine the power that—oddly enough—*Alex* has unleashed. This is all uncharted territory. Alex just wanted to keep living and enjoy his life; he never tried to tap into the real power that this artificial intelligence unleashed."

"But Schlegelberger—"

"Schelegelberger," Michael said, "is Hitler on steroids. Like Hitler with the atom bomb, except no one believes it yet. They don't even think the AI Schlegelberger exists."

"And where does that leave us—you, me, and I guess, Alex, too?"

"Because of our connection with Alex, who is the only other…person…with the AI powers that Schlegelberger has, we are a potential threat to Schlegelberger and whatever plan he has up his sleeve."

"So…he needs to…"

Michael finished the last of his martini. "Schlegelberger needs to get rid of us, all of us."

He kept watching the front door each time it opened, looking for a suspicious or familiar face, perhaps one that he remembered leaving Mario's just before the bomb exploded. Or the bystander watching from the street after the explosion, mingling in the crowd, like the pyromaniacs who set a building on fire and then stay on the scene to watch the aftermath. There were faces from that night in Westport lodged forever in his memory bank, ones that he couldn't quite picture or identify but that he sensed he *would* remember if he ever saw them again. Or so he thought.

But now, as one stranger after another walked in Freddie's door, Michael scrutinized each face, aware that, tonight at least, everyone was a potential killer.

CHAPTER 54

New York City

They were an unlikely pair, two cousins, Fat Lester and Skinny Lester, two of Alex Nicholas's closest friends from childhood right up until his murder. Both had become his trusted employees in Tartarus, the name signifying the ancient Greek underworld that Alex had bestowed upon his massive illegal gambling and loan-sharking operation in Queens.

Both were delighted when Michael took over the business and retained them in their roles as the brain and brawn of Tartarus. Despite the trauma of losing Alex, it had been an easy transition.

They were as their nicknames described them. Skinny Lester, tall and fit, with a basketball player's frame and the look of someone who struggles to fill out his loose-hanging clothes. A college dropout, he was a mathematical genius, a critical skill for setting the right odds on the games each day, sufficient to give the house the edge.

Fat Lester was built like a tank, half his cousin's height but double his weight, and appearing to be bursting out of his sport coat, which he obviously never buttoned. Although in his fifties, he was an intimidating presence who had been useful to Alex when a client got behind on his debts.

Donna sat facing out at the plush but discreet dining room, a vodka martini and a copy of the *Hollywood Reporter* on the table in front of her. Passing by the gleaming bar on the way to her table, she had soaked up the attention as her wild blond hair, slim figure, low-cut blouse, and short skirt turned the head of every man in the restaurant, many of whom were young enough to be her son.

The Lesters were sharing a bottle of Contesa Montepulciano. Skinny Lester longed for a cigarette, Fat Lester his cheap cigar.

"This is the type of place I like to eat at," Donna said. "First of all, it's in the *city*, not in Queens, and it has a nice-looking clientele." She gazed around Felidia's handsome dining room filled with men in suits and women in smart outfits. "Alex was always taking me to his hangouts, the freakin' Clinton, Joe's Garage. Jesus, I am so sick of Queens. I belong here, the Upper East side, eating spaghetti with truffles instead of meatballs."

"The food's good there, too," Fat Lester said defensively before Donna stared him down as though he was crazy.

"Did you read this?" Donna held up the front page of the *Hollywood Reporter.*

"Ah, I don't think so," Skinny Lester said. "We don't exactly subscribe to that…particular newspaper. We read the *Post* and the racing form. Real news."

"I should have known. Anyway, listen to this, it's right on the front page, for God's sake." Donna proceeded to read the story out loud:

> French legend Catherine Saint-Laurent is reportedly seeking financing for her newest pet project, a story about an underworld figure who fakes his murder in a New York restaurant and runs away to Las Vegas, where he starts a new gambling empire, surrounded by strippers and show girls, and leaving his silicone-enhanced, bitchy wife millions in hidden cash and a huge life insurance payout. The story revolves around their separate lives and her revenge-fueled search to find him.

"Wow," Fat Lester said, "That sounds like a great movie."

His cousin gave him a look, discreetly shaking his head, as though to say, "Don't go there."

"This is just one more piece of proof that Alex is alive somewhere. I know he was screwing around with that French actress and, by the way, her girlfriend, separately and together. Two lesbians…that's the only heaven Alex is in."

"Yeah," Fat Lester said, "he was cheating on them, with each other, together." He gave a little chuckle. "You know what I mean?"

"No, I don't. And, really, is that who he was cheating on? What about his fucking *wife*? *Me*? *That's* who he was cheating on."

"Yeah, that too, I guess." Fat Lester picked up the article and whispered while he read portions of it. He looked up at Donna. "And, by the way, I happen to like silicone-enhanced and bitchy—"

She cut him off. "Only the part about being a bitch is real. The rest is fake."

"Exactly," said Fat Lester.

Skinny Lester tried to suppress a smile.

"Oh my God," Donna said, "I'm going to blow my brains out here." She shook her head, "Anyway, boys, I'm going to find your old friend."

"Find him? He's…dead," Skinny Lester said.

"Maybe, maybe not. I think, probably not. Either way, but if and when I find him, he'll wish he *was* dead."

"Well, if he *is* alive, how do you plan on finding him?" Skinny Lester said.

"I've just hired Sherlock Holmes."

"Is he still alive, too?" Fat Lester asked.

"No, you idiot. Don't take everything so literally. Holmes is dead."

"And fictional, by the way," Skinny Lester said.

"Really?" Donna said.

"Yeah, he never existed. He's a character in a book…or a movie. Maybe both."

"Columbo?" Fat Lester said, excitedly. "I love him."

"Now, he's dead." Skinny Lester said. "That was Peter Falk, the actor."

Fat Lester stopped eating his tagliatelle. "I'm so confused on who's dead and who's still alive."

"Isn't *that* the truth," Skinny Lester said with a straight face.

"Oh, for fuck's sake," Donna said, "it's impossible to carry on a conversation with you two. No wonder you and Alex got along so well. Am I the only intelligent person at this table? Please, just shut up and listen: I've hired one of the biggest-name private detectives in the country."

"Inspector Clouseau?" Fat Lester asked. "He was funny. You need someone with a sense of humor to find Alex, especially if he's dead."

"Jesus," Donna moaned. "This is what I'm talking about. No, I hired Vito Colucci."

"Colucci," Skinny Lenny said. "I know *he's* alive, I just saw him on CNN."

CHAPTER 55

Kure Beach, North Carolina

Michael and Samantha finished dinner at Freddie's and drove back to their house down a quiet two-lane beach road, less than a mile away.

During the short ride, Michael kept on eye on his rearview mirror, searching for headlights that might be following, but he saw none. In front of him were two cars, one in front of the other, two sets of red taillights. Despite the lack of any signs of danger, his anxiety only deepened.

After a few minutes, in the rearview mirror, he noticed the first headlights approach, a car steadily gaining on him. He sped up slightly but the car continued to close in from behind until it was a car length away. The cars ahead had moved on. There was no one else visible on the road except the vehicle behind him.

It was late, the homes were dark, no street lights, no moon, just the road ahead, the dark ocean on the right—and the set of headlights on his tail casting a glare inside their car. He looked back and forth from the side mirror to the rearview, trying to get a peek at the driver, but the glare of the headlights made seeing anything behind them impossible.

He glanced over at Samantha.

"Is something wrong?" she said.

"No, it's just dark and this car is following a bit too close behind us."

She began to turn around to look out the rear window.

"Don't," he said.

She did anyway. "He is close. Is he following us?"

Just then the car closed in even tighter. Michael tapped the brakes lightly, watching through the mirror for a reaction. But instead of staying close behind, the car pulled into the oncoming lane and passed, speeding ahead of them.

There was nothing he could put his finger on to substantiate his growing certainty that something bad was about to happen; if it weren't here on the dark beach road, it would be later, at home, during the long night ahead of them. He was sure of it.

Once inside the house, Michael walked out through the French doors onto the deck, watching and listening to the waves crashing onto the darkened beach. He felt a...presence...someone or some*thing* watching him. He felt a restlessness, an unease. Was he being paranoid? Perhaps, but he knew *something* was out there, maybe in the sea, or closer, on the beach, the sand, nearer to him, but invisible in the dark. His imagination was running wild as he visualized an enemy submarine, its periscope rising up, the captain peering at him from the depths.

The only light came from the lighthouse out at sea, its beam illuminating the water and the beach for several seconds as it rotated, like a searchlight sweeping the prison grounds, a scene Michael had, of course, only witnessed in a movie. He was uncomfortable, agitated, feeling as though he were in a dream he couldn't wake up from.

Was that a shadow? Yes, it was. Likely someone taking an evening walk on the beach.

He went inside, leaving the evening's Southern humidity behind him, feeling a momentary relief as he entered the large modern family room with its crisp, cool air conditioning. With exposed beams and a large stone fireplace, it was Michael's favorite room. Even with the doors shut behind him, he could hear the sound of the waves on the beach, this night more threatening than soothing.

He turned the brass lock on the door, checked, then rechecked it to be sure the series of glass doors were all locked tight. He looked out onto the black beach beyond, searching for the shadow from before, but saw only the dark unknown.

Still uneasy, he turned back into the room, realizing that with the lights on he would be visible to anyone outside, while they remained invisible to him. He pressed in the password on the security keypad, the flashing red light indicating the system was activated, giving him some measure of security, quickly tempered by the knowledge that any experienced criminal could disarm even the best system in seconds. Not to mention, a special type of criminal.

Gently touching a master switch, he turned off the lights in the rest of the house, except for the bedroom, and joined Samantha, leaving their bedroom door open, as was their custom. She was already in bed, listening to an audiobook on her Kindle through her noise-canceling headphones. He could tell she'd be asleep soon.

Michael put on his pajamas, brushed his teeth and got into bed alongside her. Samantha appeared oblivious to his presence. Outside, a lone dog was barking. He picked up a book and, as he began to read, heard the dog barking again, louder now, then more canine voices joining in. The foghorn from the lighthouse began its muted blast. He looked over to the security pad on the wall near his bed. The red light was on, no longer flashing, indicating that it was armed, but the light only further unsettled him.

He tried again to read his book, an Agatha Christie novel, *Death in the Clouds*, but instead found himself staring at the page, not the words, unfocused, listening to the sounds, the foghorn, the barking, and the ocean.

He looked over at Samantha, who had drifted off to sleep, gently removed the headphones, and switched off her Kindle. He checked the alarm pad again, the light still red. Finally, he gave up, put the book down, turned off his reading lamp, and closed his eyes, hoping to sleep.

He was unsure how long he'd been asleep when he was awakened by music.

It started so low he wasn't sure he even heard it, or that it wasn't part of a dream he was awakening from, dream and reality blending together. But it gradually became louder, although not so loud it awakened Samantha, who still slept soundly, until he was sure that it was neither a dream nor his imagination.

He recognized it, in fact. He knew it well. It was Wagner's opera *Tristan and Isolde*. Wagner's opera on the nature of existence itself, life and death, the whole fate of the material world hanging on nothing more than the interior movements of the human soul. It was a favorite of Adolph Hitler.

He looked at the clock on the night table. 12:02. Where was the music coming from? And at this time of night? And, of all operas...

He would not be sleeping again any time soon.

Trying to make sense of what he was hearing, he stared at the ceiling, the sweeping light from the lighthouse, faintly shining through the bedroom shutters, now the only illumination in the room. He heard a clap of thunder in the distance, then a series of them, each appearing closer. The wind picked up, the thunderstorm approaching and the music persisting in the background, strangely complementing the sounds of the approaching storm.

He picked up his iPhone, checking the master app controlling the house's security system and appliances. He checked the outdoor infrared security cameras. Front, back, and both sides. No one was visible as he flipped through the starkly illuminated pictures. He heard a clicking sound, coming from outside the bedroom. He checked the cameras and the security app again. Everything appeared normal... except...the wireless, digital locks. The back French doors he'd so carefully secured before going to bed were showing *unlocked*. He stared closer…no, they were *locked*.

He had an idea: "Alexa, turn off the music."

The music stopped instantly.

Who had instructed her to turn it on in the first place? And Wagner's opera?

He got up, iPhone in hand, walked out of the bedroom, through the hall, turning on the dimmed hall lighting, and out to the family room. He scanned the room: all was still, nothing out of place. As he approached the rear glass doors, the bolt moved on its own, clicking shut and locking.

He turned around, facing the family room once again, and heard, behind him now, the bolt clicking *open*.

Michael whirled around, fearing that someone—an intruder, or worse—would be standing on the other side. The beam from the lighthouse beacon passed over the beach.

No one.

He relocked the door and waited, staring at it to see if it would unlock again. He turned around to face the room, sure that someone was looking over his shoulder or…standing behind him. He saw no one but he felt their presence.

The opera began playing again.

"Alexa," he says, "is there an intruder in the house?"

After a few seconds, she responded, "I don't understand that question."

"Alexa, is someone listening in on our conversation?"

Not expecting a valid response, he took a step toward the bedroom but stopped dead when he heard her response.

"Yes, someone is listening to our conversation."

Standing outside the bedroom, he saw that Samantha remained asleep. He moved back toward the family room. "Alexa, *who* is listening to our conversation?"

"Monsignor Kurt Schlegelberger and at least one other person are listening to our conversation."

"Alexa, where is Kurt Schlegelberger?"

"He is here."

"Alexa, is Kurt Schlegelberger *here*, in this house?"

"Yes, Kurt Schlegelberger is here, in this house."

"Alexa, *where* in this house is Kurt Schlegelberger?"

"Kurt Schlegelberger is right behind you."

Feeling a wave of shivers run through his body, anticipating the presence behind him, Michael turned quickly and... saw no one. It stands to reason, he thought: Schlegelberger is *dead*, there can be no physical presence. He scanned the room again, analyzing every detail until he saw...it, the only possible explanation: the tiny security surveillance camera high above him, discreetly embedded in an exposed beam.

"Alexa, turn off the security cameras."

"I am unable to turn off the security cameras," she said, her calm in stark contrast to Michael's rising panic. "Please check your Internet connection."

Berlin, Germany

Forty-five-hundred miles and an ocean away, Claus Dietrich made himself an early morning cup of coffee, sat at the antique desk in his library, opened his laptop computer, looked out at the sun rising over his beloved Berlin, and watched Michael

Nicholas as he stood motionless with his back to the French doors in his family room.

Dietrich zoomed in on Michael's face, taking voyeuristic pleasure in the torment of his prey.

"Alexa," he said, "play *Tristan and Isolde* again."

Still unable to eliminate Michael or Alex Nicholas, he and Schlegelberger would nevertheless proceed with their plan. It would be highly unlikely that either would be able to interfere in time to stop them.

Dietrich tapped a series of commands into his computer. The two documents he was looking for appeared: the first, entitled, *Vladimir Putin, a Detailed Psychological Profile*; the second, *Harry O'Brien, A Detailed Psychological Profile*. He had already read them both numerous times but he scanned through them again. Then, he switched to his eBook library, *Mr. Putin, Operative in the Kremlin,* a respected, in-depth study of Putin by the Brookings Institution's Fiona Hill and Clifford Gaddy.

———

Alex Nicholas watched Dietrich's computer screen move from one document to the next, knowing that this would be the closest he'd come to uncovering Dietrich and Schlegelberger's plan. His interest in Dietrich's activities ended, however, when he received an alert that Jennifer Walsh's computer had come online.

CHAPTER 56

Paris, France

Alex missed Catherine Saint Laurent and Jennifer Walsh or, more accurately, he missed being in bed with them, especially the two of them together. Alex knew very little French, but Catherine had taught him to fluently pronounce—and practice—a *ménage à trois*.

Catherine and Alex had made an unlikely pair, the tough, gruff American and the refined, idolized but aging French movie legend. Alex had later agreed to finance her risky "comeback" movie when the traditional investors had demurred over concerns about her age.

After Alex's death, Catherine had contacted Michael and he'd...reluctantly...fallen victim to their charms, honoring Alex's agreement to finance Catherine's movie. Later, despite Michael's concern about word leaking out, the digital Alex had contacted with Catherine while she was on a movie set filming a scene from the movie.

Looking back, Alex decided that Catherine had been the easiest to convince about his "return." Maybe because Hollywood types already lived in more than one world, they weren't as surprised when a window opened to yet another one.

Alex recognized the room, Catherine's regular suite at the Ritz. There were changes, however. The hotel had recently undergone a major renovation, which probably accounted for the subtle differences he noticed in the suite. But the room had lost none of its luxurious charm, gold door handles, warm lighting, soothing creme walls, patterned carpeting— he remembered the feel of the soft, woolen carpet on his bare feet—marble fireplaces, crystal chandelier, long floor-to-ceiling windows, the view of the Place Vendôme, plush chairs, and the pillows and linens gracing the king bed. Only Marie Antoinette or, more accurately, Coco Chanel, was missing. Neither of them, however, could have matched the beauty on the bed tonight.

Jennifer had conveniently and, he believed, intentionally, left her laptop open on the dresser facing the king bed so that he could see. He could hear the sound of water running in the bathroom and, even from his angle of view, caught a glimpse of Catherine stepping out of the white bathtub, drying herself with the Ritz's familiar thick, peach-colored towel, finally letting it drop to the floor as she entered the bedroom and lay on the bed. She was followed a minute later by Jennifer, her tanned, still wet body wrapped loosely inside the Ritz terrycloth robe. She, too, dropped her robe onto the car-

peted floor, revealing her distinct tan lines forming a provoc-
ative triangle. There was an open bottle of champagne in an
ice bucket on the nightstand. As Catherine watched her, Jennifer poured them each a glass.

Sex for Catherine was like a movie scene: it had a beginning
and an end. The same way Alex regarded it. It didn't neces-
sarily linger. For it to begin, the actress needed a cue, like the
clapper signs used by directors on the movie set. Off the set,
a glass of champagne signaled the onset, just as surely as the
lighting of her French cigarette signaled the end. In between
the two points lay pure lust. Alex remembered it well. And
the introduction of Jennifer, made later in their relationship,
had only made it better.

Berlin, Germany

Dietrich wasn't paying close attention. Although Schlegelberger had given him the capability, eavesdropping on the
Internet life of Alex Nicholas was, most times, incredibly
boring. But this scene caught his eye, forcing Dietrich to sit
down at his desk, pull his chair in, and lean in close to his
computer screen. He recognized the naked woman on the
bed, the legendary French actress Catherine Saint-Laurent.
He felt a stirring, one that seldom visited him these days, and
wished he could take the place of the tanned young woman
with the stark white derrière, whose head of blond hair was
slowly moving its way up Catherine Saint-Laurent's thighs.

Washington, DC

The young man's gaze had begun to wander as he looked around him at the room filled with other young men at their desks and computers. Following this older guy Dietrich was boring as hell, but then again, most such surveillance was. But he quickly focused back on his computer screen when he saw what reminded him of his pirated high school porn films, except none of them were ever filmed at the Paris Ritz.

He watched, fascinated with the scene of the two attractive women, one old enough to be his mother yet unmistakably attractive, the other his contemporary and stunningly beautiful.

It was the perfect porn flick but it wasn't a movie, it was a live feed. How was Dietrich accessing this? Who had arranged for him to see it? He couldn't break himself away from the screen as the older woman's slender white legs wrapped themselves around the younger one's face, her thighs seeming holding her, deeply, in place.

Finally, he got up from his chair and signaled with his hands to get the attention of his supervisor, who immediately came running over.

"Sir, you won't believe this."

"What is it?"

"Come take a look."

CHAPTER 57

Vito Colucci had seen all types of women during his long career. Nevertheless, his new client, Donna Nicholas, was truly a piece of work.

"Ever notice how priests keep putting people in boxes?" Donna said. "First, Father Papadopoulos is blessing Alex's mahogany coffin at the funeral—that costs me three grand. Then, this same Father Papageorge tries to hand me *another* box—a little one this time—and says Alex's ashes are in it."

"Talk about Greeks bearing gifts," Fat Lester said, interrupting Donna's rant. "But they do know how to run restaurants." He picked up his knife and fork.

They were dining at Christos Steakhouse, an Astoria landmark that had been another of Alex's favorites. A window table, dimmed lights, dark woods, a large fishbowl stocked with lobsters, it had the masculine look and feel of a steak-house in an area known for tough characters.

The Lesters, Donna, and their guest, Vito Colucci, were sharing a forty-eight-ounce Porterhouse steak, perfectly pink in the middle and charbroiled black on the outside, that had been neatly sliced and laid out on a platter in the center of the white table-clothed table. The table was strewn with baked potatoes, French fries, various accompanying steak sauces: blue cheese truffle, shallot and béarnaise. Plus, a two-pound broiled lobster.

Donna, ignoring Lester, continued, "I don't care how many boxes they bring me with Alex in it or his freakin' ashes, there's only *one* box with Alex in it—and I believe that's a condo-minium. I just don't know where it is, but it's probably some-where like Vegas or Costa Rica. I know he's still alive and I'm going to find him. That's why I've hired Mr. Colucci here."

Vito Colucci looked at the two Lesters and nodded. In his mid-sixties with a wiry build, salty hair, mustache, but a face that showed the toughness of the twenty-five-year veteran street cop and undercover detective who'd busted drug lords and Mafia kingpins while narrowly surviving their numer-ous attempts on his life. He was a legend in his hometown of Stamford, Connecticut, after having exposed corruption at the highest levels, including in his own police department. It was a miracle that he was still alive.

"Listen," Skinny Lester said, looking around and then at Vito, "there's something I need to tell you. I swore I'd never tell anyone about this but, since you're trying to find Alex, it's probably okay."

"What is it?" Vito said.

Skinny Lester looked hesitatingly at Donna.

"Spit it out," she said.

"It was just a few weeks before he died, maybe three in the morning. We were in Alex's den, at his house. Just the two of us. We'd polished off almost a whole bottle of Dewar's when, all of a sudden, he tells me he wants to show me something he's been working on. He says that he had hired a bunch of computer whizzes from Silicon Valley to create some special artificial intelligence thing and that they had made a breakthrough. He said he had paid them millions but they had to keep it quiet for like five years. Then he pulled out this laptop and opened it up—I thought he was going to show me the week's results from the games or something. But he told me to look at it and—holy shit—it was him on the screen. But then it got crazy. Alex—the *real* Alex—then asked the *computer* Alex a question—and the Alex on the computer answered him. In Alex's voice and with Alex's expressions, you know, that classic sarcastic look. Not only that—but it was an answer only the real Alex could give."

"This *is* something," Vito said. "Do you remember the actual question?"

"Yes, it was like 'How many home runs did Mickey Mantle hit in 1961?'"

"So that was the actual, human Alex asking the computer Alex?"

"Yes, exactly."

"And did the computer Alex answer it?"

"Yep, in Alex's voice, exactly the way Alex would if, say, it was him on FaceTime or something like that. Mantle hit fifty-six home runs that year. Not only that, but he added that Roger Maris hit sixty-one, exactly what Alex would have said. Alex knew his sports stats—and so did the…computer Alex, or whatever the hell I was looking at."

He looked at the trio around the table.

"I've never seen anything like it. Alex talking to Alex. I couldn't believe it. They had a conversation with each other. It was funny—no, actually it was scary. Very scary."

"What happened then?" Vito said. "Did Alex ever bring it up again?"

"No, and I never thought much about it after a while myself."

"What was the point of it? Was it a game?" Vito asked.

"I'm not sure," Lester said. "I would have easily said yes except, all of a sudden, Alex got real quiet. He shut the computer down and said something about how he still had work to do on it. He said, 'No matter what happens, I'll always be around, in the *cloud*.' I said, 'You mean the *clouds* don't you?', and he said, 'No, *the cloud*.' I had no idea what he meant. His grammar wasn't always the best. And then he looked at me with that real serious look he'd get and told me not to tell anyone."

"He said not to tell *anyone*?" Vito said.

"He said, 'Lester, I mean *no one, ever*.' I remember thinking it was as though he'd had too much to drink that night and was sorry he'd shown it to me. That's why I'm not sure it wasn't just one of his computer games. Still, it was damned good. I mean this was really *Alex* on that computer."

"Did you ever tell anyone about what you saw that night?" asked Vito.

"Not a soul until after Alex was murdered. Then I told Michael, of course."

"You told *Michael* about this—and he never told me?" Donna said, looking like she was ready to go ballistic. "That son of a bitch."

"Tell me," Vito said, "how did Michael come to take over Alex's business?"

"Right after Alex was murdered," Donna said, looking at the Lesters, "these guys came to me in a panic because they didn't know what the hell to do. Alex had spoon-fed them like little kids—"

Skinny Lester, obviously agitated, interrupted. "Yes, we were worried. First of all, we didn't know who was behind Alex's murder so we were afraid of what might come next. But, even more concerning was that we owed out a lot of money—which was normal, you know, people who'd won their bets, whatever, but we also had a lot more that people *owed us*. Most of that was from some pretty powerful—uh, dangerous—guys, who, knowing Alex was dead, might decide not to pay up, and the way our cash flow worked, we needed the money owed to us to pay out what *we* owed."

"What he's saying," Donna said, "is they were afraid that without Alex they couldn't collect most of the money that was supposed to come in. So, right after the funeral, I went to Michael and asked him to step in just long enough to help me

make sure we got our money so I could take care of myself—
and the rest of Alex's guys."

"How did he react? He had no background in this; he's a
corporate type, isn't he?"

"Yes," Donna said, "and still is. He's the CEO of one of
those financial services companies, Gibraltar Financial. How
he does it, I don't know. He didn't want to get involved—he
always kept his distance from Alex's business—and Alex for
that matter. They are...or were...very different. Then, after
he stepped in, he never got out. He likes it now, so he paid
me a bunch of cash and made me a silent partner with him."

"Michael's done a good job," Skinny Lester said. "He's
expanded the business, we even have an operation in Paris
now. He relies on *us*," pointing to his cousin, "to run the
day-to-day operations. He's not as involved in everything as
Alex was because he's still running that other company, but
it works."

An increasingly angry Donna finished off the remainder
of her vodka martini in one gulp, placed it back, hard, on the
table, her face showing that red blush someone gets when
they've had one or four too many. "It works *too* well if you
ask me. These two were—are—Alex's buddies, but there's no
way they could run this thing. Michael's a business guy, he
wears a suit every day. No bookie wears a suit."

Vito looked at her, puzzled. "So, what are you saying?"

"I'm saying *Alex* is still running Tartarus."

Vito, no longer a drinker, took a long sip of his club soda,
placing the glass slowly back on the table. His eyes were somewhere else, calculating. He appeared to be trying to digest

what he had heard, piecing together a puzzle he'd never seen before.

"The question, then, is, if Alex is still running the business, is he doing it from his grave—or from his condo? Or, from *the cloud*."

CHAPTER 58

The White House
Washington, DC

The soft light from the reading lamp cast a warm, soothing ambience over the room, and the president's mood. Harry O'Brien gazed out the large window toward the twinkling night lights of the capital. He was enjoying a rare few minutes of quiet reading in the living room of the private living quarters before joining the First Lady, who was already asleep in the bedroom.

His mood was interrupted when he heard the gentle shuffling movement outside his door, a familiar sound that usually preceded a knock on the door and, at this time of night, unwelcome news. The knock came, three swift taps signaling the end of his reprieve from the crises of the world. His eyes moved from the pages of the novel as the door opened and his evening aide entered.

"Mr. President, there's an urgent situation. You'll want to come downstairs immediately, sir."

He could read the stress on his aide's face as he grabbed his suit jacket and followed him out the door. They headed to the waiting elevator.

"Sir, we're heading to the Star Wars room."

The Star Wars Room, also known as the Big Board Room for its huge electronic displays of the skies all over the world, had been secretly created after the Cuban Missile Crisis, several stories below the main level of the White House. O'Brien had visited it only once in his three years in office, on his first day. He remembered his predecessor saying that the only time he had ever been in it was on his initial tour. "Let's hope you have never have to come down here again, Harry," he said, "because, nothing good will ever go on down there."

As he exited the elevator, he saw the uniformed guard, standing at attention, expressionless, outside the heavy steel door to the room. The door was opened for him and, as he entered the huge control room, he was awed by the scene before him.

The room was literally a duplicate of the main air defense control room located under the mountains of Colorado. It reminded him of something out of a science fiction movie or the war room in the classic nuclear war spoof *Dr. Strangelove*. Except, tonight, this was no spoof, no cult classic of science fiction. The height of the room was at least two stories, and giant screens dominated the room, covering the walls, electronic maps of the world with many little lights of various colors. It was here that, in the event of an attack or war, the decisions would be made, while in Colorado those decisions—*his* decisions—would be carried out.

His eyes immediately went to the several flashing red lights. But before he could focus on them, he was guided to his white leather seat, slightly larger than the twenty or so others surrounding the giant circular polished black table. Several feet above him was a similar circle, the same size as the table, of LED lights illuminating everything below, casting the single legal pad in front of him in sharp relief. Already seated around the table, among others, were CIA Director Jim Goodrich, Chairman of the Joint Chiefs of Staff John Sculley and Darryl MacPherson, the national security adviser.

"Okay," O'Brien said, firmly, "what's the situation?"

"NORAD has detected missiles in flight," General Sculley said, his scowl more pronounced than ever.

"Jesus," O'Brien said. "Where are they headed?"

"Moscow."

"How long until they get there?

Sculley looked to another uniform at the table.

"Depending on the precise location of each missile, thirty minutes, sir."

O'Brien, his mind spinning, wasn't sure who answered. He looked at Sculley. "Whose missiles are they?"

"*Ours,* sir."

CHAPTER 59

Astoria, Queens, New York

"I have your answer, Donna," Vito Colucci said as soon as he sat down. "I know, beyond a shadow of a doubt, what happened to Alex Nicholas."

"Oh my God, finally. I knew you were the right guy."

As Colucci started to speak, the server arrived with a round of drinks, a bottle of red Greek wine for the Lesters and a vodka Martini for Donna.

"Just club soda for me," Vito said.

"We have pizzas coming, too," Fat Lester said. "Pepperoni and a meatball one. They're great here. We know the owner, Joe Sal."

"He was a close friend of Alex's," Skinny Lester said. "He also owns the big auto body shop across the street."

"Really? Auto body?" Vito said. "And a bar…or restaurant."

The detective looked around, taking in the millennials and

old-time Astorians pouring in through the front door and settling in at the tables or the bar.

"Yeah, Joe Sal's kind of a genius. I mean he was already here," Fat Lester pointed to the auto body shop across the street, visible through the bar's windows. "It's a natural progression, body shop, bar."

"Can we cut the shit and get to the point?" Donna said, impatient. "Vito, have you actually found Alex?"

"Yes, I know what happened and I know where he is."

"Wow, you're kidding me," Skinny Lester said, sitting upright almost at attention.

"Oh shit," Fat Lester said.

"Alex is—"

But just as he began, the server, once again, arrived at the table, this time with Vito's club soda and two pizzas. No one said a word as she placed them on the table. "Is there anything else I can get you?"

Fat Lester started, "Yeah, maybe another—" before Donna cut him off. "No," she said, "nothing right now."

"Where *is* he?" she demanded as soon as the waitress turned to leave.

Vito paused, deliberate, taking his time as though he knew the delay, if not the news, would upset Donna.

"Alex Nicholas is *dead*. He was indeed murdered in that restaurant. His remains were, at first, buried at Saint Michael's Cemetery just down the street here. Yes, his remains were stolen by those characters from the Catholic Church, who were afraid he'd stumbled onto some artificial intelligence breakthrough that might threaten their hold on the afterlife. But, once they realized that he hadn't discovered any-thing but a fancy piece of software, they returned his body to Father Papageorge. Those ashes he gave to you, or I guess Michael, now…those are Alex's ashes. That's all there is. That's all that's left of Alex."

Donna looked stunned. She stared at Vito for what felt like minutes while the Lesters simply watched, careful not to move a fork or glass until Donna had spoken so they could hear her reaction and gauge her mood.

Finally, she spoke, "You're shitting me."

"No, I wish I was. This has certainly been a fascinating case. I mean, who doesn't want to find a guy like Alex hiding out somewhere with a bunch of money and chicks."

"All that's left of him are those ashes?" she said.

"Yes, that's it. He's gone. Forever."

Donna looked stunned. As though in shock, she stared right at Vito, not letting her gaze move off him. No one said a word. Vito and the Lesters, perhaps more to keep busy in front of the paralyzed Donna than out of hunger, each reached for a slice of pizza. But as he did, Skinny Lester, looking closely at Donna, was sure he saw a tear in her eye.

CHAPTER 60

The White House
Washington, DC

The room was quickly filling up with men in uniforms, some, no doubt, rushed there from their nearby suburban homes. Representatives from NORAD, the North American Aerospace Defense Command, the various intelligence agencies, and the National Security Council were seated around the table, electronically patched into their home bases around the world.

Yet Harry O'Brien felt alone. Why would our missiles even be in the air? He hoped the answer—and the solution—was simple but, in his gut, he knew it wouldn't be or those missiles would have been destroyed by now.

"You're telling me that these are *our* missiles heading for Moscow?"

"Yes, sir. They were launched from our base in Colorado."

"I thought we'd deactivated that base."

"Not yet, sir, it's scheduled for deactivation in December but it's still one of our land-based missile sites."

"Are they armed?"

"Yes, sir, with nuclear warheads. Worse, I'm afraid, they're all MIRVs."

"MIRVs? Refresh my memory on exactly what the hell that is." He vaguely remembered the acronym and, even as he asked the question, he knew it was bad news. He realized, too, that he was caught in the web of the military now, the generals, dedicated patriots like Sculley, men who'd served the country but, at the same time, whose judgment beyond the scope of military matters O'Brien didn't always trust. He was relieved when his old friend Jim Goodrich spoke up.

"Harry, *sir*, they're *multiple independently targetable reentry vehicle ballistic missiles*, meaning each missile contains several warheads that, at some point, will independently break away. Each one of them will be aimed to hit a different target; they could be as far apart as fifteen hundred kilometers. It makes each warhead that much more lethal—and nearly impossible for any anti-missile system to destroy before they hit their targets."

"The Russians will never even come close to knocking them out of the air in time," General Sculley said.

O'Brien detected not only a tone of obvious concern but also perhaps one of pride. He made a mental note to replace Sculley, assuming they all survived the night.

"Mr. President," Goodrich said, "we've initiated a call to Mr. Putin. It's the middle of the night in Moscow."

"That's going to be pretty," O'Brien said, "Okay, let me ask the obvious question: why haven't we called them back or destroyed them already?"

General Sculley spoke up, "Because it appears that someone hacked into our missile computers and took control of them."

"It's a bit more complicated than that, sir," Darryl MacPherson said. "Our missile systems have been programmed using an artificial intelligence software designed to take over once the missiles are on their way and have passed a certain point. So, first the hacker was able to launch several missiles by a traditional hack into our programs, but then he also locked us out of the AI software that guides the missiles to their targets."

"Why in the fucking world would we have relied on artificial intelligence to guide our missiles in the first place?" O'Brien said.

"It was considered to be better at adapting and maneuvering in the event anti-missile defenses tried to shoot them down." MacPherson said. "But..."

"But? But what?" O'Brien asked, not only mystified but angry.

"That's why Mr. Benoit is here, sir. His team is ready in another room to help us break into and overrule the AI systems, *our* systems. Maybe Mr. Benoit would be the best qualified to explain that, sir."

"Go ahead, John," O'Brien said. "Tell me what I need to know."

"Well, sir. The artificial intelligence program for the missiles was designed to ensure that once we launched them, no one could hack into our systems and destroy them—or, God forbid, turn the missiles around and back toward us. So, it has what we call a fail-safe protection so that, once the missiles reach a certain point in their trajectory, they can only be guided or their direction changed by your direct codes, the ones contained in the nuclear suitcase that travels with you everywhere."

"Well then, why can't we just use those codes now? We certainly have them here."

"Because, it appears that the same person who did the initial hack to launch the missiles has also figured out our fail-safe program and not only preempted us, initiating the attack on Russia, but also locked us out completely."

"*Fail-safe,*" O'Brien said with scorn.

"Yes, sir. Someone has used our system to block us out and we can't figure out how to overrule it."

"And do we know who the hell did this?"

"We believe it was Kurt Schlegelberger." Benoit addressed the rest of the room: "Formerly the personal head of security to the Pope."

"He's the one who's no longer—"

"Yes, sir," Jim Goodrich said, "he's *dead.*

CHAPTER 61

A tired Vito Colucci sat at his desk, alone late at night inside his Stamford, Connecticut, office, typing on his computer. He hated the computer and the Internet but he had only ever communicated with this client online—via a UK e-mail account—except once by phone, during which conversation he had detected a slight British accent.

He didn't know him but, considering they'd never met face-to-face, he was surprised how much he liked the guy. Maybe it was because he paid his retainer and monthly invoice so quickly. No, there was something sincere, real, maybe even touching about this client.

Vito had been unable to trace his client's name through Google or any of his criminal databases, including Interpol. Clearly, his name was fake, but that wasn't unusual in his business. Still, the guy himself seemed genuine.

Vito began by providing an update since their last series of messages, yesterday afternoon.

"Dinner last night at Joe's Garage Bar with the two cousins— both named Lester—and Donna Nicholas. I brought them up to date on the status of my research on Alex Nicholas, inform- ing them of the results of my search and the fact that Alex was actually murdered at the restaurant in Whitestone a few years ago. Mrs. Nicholas didn't press for any further details but clearly was disappointed to hear that Alex was no longer alive. I must admit that, despite her derogatory references to Alex, I think she had continued to hold out hope for him. She doesn't appear to totally trust the Lester cousins since they were so close to Alex and now work for Michael. In any case, her marriage to Alex appears to have had a love/hate quality to it. I believe now that she has accepted the fact that Alex Nicholas is dead, she will move on to other relationships."

He pressed *Send* and, taking a deep breath, sat back and waited for a response. His client usually responded within minutes, sometimes quicker.

Sure enough, the response came immediately: *Okay, good. Stay close to her but don't let her know you are watching her. I need to know who she's seeing at night or if she's sleeping with anyone.*

Vito had already asked his client why he was so interested in Donna Nicholas, but the client had resisted offering any information as to his motive. The guy appeared to have a romantic interest in her and wanted to be sure the deck had been cleared before he continued to pursue her. In partic- ular, his client clearly wanted to be sure that Donna's dead husband was definitely out of the way and that she was no longer holding out some crazy hope that he was alive. Now that that had been settled, it seemed he wanted to ensure she wasn't cheating on him.

A few minutes passed this time before the client messaged Vito again:

"Thank you. I needed to be sure this had been settled. Keep up your physical surveillance."

A world away from everything that mattered to him, Alex Nicholas closed the Internet connection. He laughed at his use of the voice-changer software; after all, without it, the last thing anyone would mistake him for was a Brit. Vito would never uncover his true identity, especially since he didn't believe that Alex was still alive. And, Alex had to admit, even *he* wasn't sure at times.

CHAPTER 62

The White House
Washington, DC

President O'Brien's mind was spinning; there was too much coming at him. A lot of it didn't make any sense and, in any case, there wasn't time to think. To make it worse, he noticed all the military men constantly looking up at the back wall. He finally realized what they were looking at—it was a large digital display timer, and it was counting down a tenth of a second at a time. It had just reached the twenty-minute mark.

General Sculley noticed O'Brien staring at the clock, "Mr. President, in twenty minutes the first missiles will incinerate Moscow."

Once again, O'Brien detected a note of satisfaction in Sculley's voice. The man was sick but this wasn't the time to dwell on it.

Sculley continued. "Whoever or whatever is behind this is looking to basically end the world as we know it, sir. They have to assume that the Russians will retaliate. When we're all said and done, it'll be the equal of at least a thousand Hiroshimas."

O'Brien struggled to piece together the extraordinary revelations of the past few days—beginning with the airliner hijacking, the conversation with Payard and Michael Nicholas and, finally, the otherworldly emergence of Monsignor Kurt Schlegelberger and Alex Nicholas.

"So are we sure this is Schlegelberger's doing?"

"We believe that it is," Goodrich said. "And we believe he's a digital entity, much like Alex Nicholas. Nicholas may have been the first person to duplicate himself with this new technology but Schlegelberger managed to steal it and do the same thing, ultimately using his new AI abilities break into our secure systems."

"So it sounds like this AI software is the key to taking back control of our missiles?"

"Yes, sir, we believe that's correct."

"Well, I know this sounds too simple, but why don't we find the scientists who made the discovery for Alex Nicholas, just like Schlegelberger did?"

"They're both dead, sir." Goodrich said. "It appears that Schlegelberger had them murdered after they handed over the code."

"Jesus. This is a nightmare." O'Brien thought back to the White House meeting about Alex Nicholas. He had found Michael Nicholas to be generally credible, truthful. "What about the brother?"

Sculley smirked. "You wanna put him in the cloud too?"

John Benoit hesitantly raised his hand as he began to speak. "Sir, if I may clarify matters: *Alex* Nicholas *may* be our best and only chance to block and override the hack, at least in the time available, but *Michael* Nicholas is our only way to get to him.

"Benoit's right." Jim Goodrich quickly rose from his chair. "We contacted him as soon as we suspected what happened." Goodrich signaled to one of the tech aides off to the side and suddenly a live video connection appeared on one of the walls. Goodrich pointed up to the screen. "You'll remember, this is Michael Nicholas."

"Hello, Michael," O'Brien said.

Goodrich signaled again to Benoit.

Before Michael Nicholas could speak, a second image appeared on the screen next to him. The faces bore a close resemblance, separated only perhaps by the ten years' difference in their ages.

Goodrich now turned to face the entire table and pointed to the screen. "Mr. President, once again, meet *Alex* Nicholas."

CHAPTER 63

Alex Nicholas looked out from the screen, his head moving to seemingly scan the room. He grinned, an expression of satisfaction and perhaps mischief.

"Nice room. Lots of uniforms. I was 4F in the draft by the way. Legitimate, busted knees."

The room was silent, and even General Sculley seemed to be in awe of what they were witnessing. Many of the men around the conference table had also been in the Roosevelt Room meeting when Michael had first introduced Alex.

"I really need your help, Alex," O'Brien said, "and I don't have much time. I assume you've been somewhat briefed on the situation and how we believe that Monsignor Schlegelberger, in some form or other, is behind it."

"Yeah, well, I'm not sure where I fit in this or how I could help. He and I aren't exactly friends." Alex's voice was gruff, like his manner.

"Alex, this is John Benoit, our tech guru. He's a good guy and he believes in you." O'Brien turned away from the screen and toward Benoit. "John, would you explain to Mr. Nicholas exactly what we need from him?"

"We need access to your software; specifically, we need your software codes. You see, the only shot we have of stopping this attack is to nullify the hacks into our missile systems. In order to do that, we need Schlegelberger's source code—the unique combination of 1's and 0's that brought him into existence."

Alex shrugged. "I don't know how you expect *me* to get them for you."

"We understand," O'Brien said, looking at Benoit again, gesturing for him to go on.

"Yes, okay," Benoit said. "Here's the thing, though: Schlegelberger entered the cloud the same way you did. Your source code was stolen from the pair that created *you* and then used it to create this version of Schlegelberger. Therefore, you and Schlegelberger have identical computer source code. So, if we can get your source code from you, then we'll also have Schlegelberger's. We simply need for you to unlock your security option so we can go in and copy your code."

"I see, I think…So, once you get the code…then what?" Alex looked either confused or, more likely, skeptical.

"So," Benoit continued, "once we have Schlegelberger's source code we can go in and *delete* that code—and by so doing, we delete *him* and remove his control over our systems, allowing us to regain control and destroy our missiles before the reach their target."

"I understand, but let me ask you, if we both have the same source code, what happens to *me* when you do all that?"

Total silence in the room. Everyone at looked to each other and then, almost in unison, to Benoit.

Sensing the tech man's unease, O'Brien cut in. "Maybe we should put this thing on mute for a minute while we sort this out. Excuse us for a second, Alex, Michael; we need to take this offline. Just hold on."

Benoit signaled one of his assistants and Michael's and Alex's screens instantly froze them in place.

O'Brien turned to Benoit. "So what *does* happen to Alex Nicholas if we're able to do this?"

Before Benoit could answer, Goodrich signaled to O'Brien. "Mr. President, I have Mr. Putin on the line as you requested. We had to wake him."

CHAPTER 64

President O'Brien reached for the red, push-button, Western Electric phone, the classic model found in every American household for decades, except for its color. It seemed so archaic now, O'Brien thought, especially inside the high-tech Star Wars room. And with nuclear missiles in the air.

"Vladimir, I must inform you that we have a dangerous situation—"

He was quickly interrupted. Putin's voice was tense and firm. It reverberated as through speakers around the room.

"Mr. President, I have been informed by our Space Center that missiles launched from the United States are in flight, targeted here, to Moscow and other sites. We are now preparing a retaliatory attack on your country...What is going on? Are you...insane?"

"No," O'Brien said, trying to stay calm and control the tempo of his voice, "this is an error, a mistake." How was he possibly going to explain Schlegelberger and Alex Nicholas to a former KGB chief in the time remaining and hope to be believed?

"Please, Vlad, do not launch a retaliatory attack. Our missile systems have been corrupted, hijacked by some individuals—possibly a neo-Nazi group—who are attempting to push both our countries into a nuclear exchange so that they can rise to power in the ensuing chaos and power vacuum. Our artificial intelligence programs have been taken over by this group and we are in the process of attempting to overrule the…hack and destroy our own missiles in flight."

"You understand that your missiles are only…*fifteen minutes* away from my country, from *Moscow*?"

"Yes, I do. We believe we will have control of them before then." As he said this, it dawned on him that he didn't know what he believed. Things were happening too quickly. But, now that he thought of it, he knew that given the little time remaining, survival was a long shot.

"You *believe*? You understand," said Putin, "that it is my solemn duty to protect my homeland. If we are attacked—whether deliberately or by error—I must retaliate, *fully*. That is my duty and my intention. I believe your experts can inform you of how much time you have before we must launch our missiles. We are assessing the extent of your attack—and are preparing to respond with our own."

"Vlad, hold off, you have to listen to me. *Trust* me. I understand your position but I pray that you will hold off from any attack. Our missiles have been *hijacked*. We have no reason to do this, and if you retaliate, you'll only be playing into the hands of the terrorists who purposely have done this, hoping we destroy each other."

"Mr. President, you have several minutes to destroy your missiles and to halt this attack. Unless you do so, our missiles will destroy your cities."

"Please," O'Brien said, even as he realized his efforts were fruitless, "stand by the phone. I will call you back shortly. Until then, for God's sake, hold off."

"I will be waiting for your call—but I must make my position clear. If your missiles are not stopped, call or no call, I will destroy as many of your cities as you destroy of ours. There is no discussion on that matter."

"Vlad," O'Brien began, hoping to reach the man behind the position, to get Putin to step away from his role and find his inner humanity. But he knew it was pointless. If their roles were reversed, he wondered if he'd be responding any differently.

But it was the next thing that Putin said that truly rattled O'Brien and the entire control room.

"Mr. President, I hope you are not placing any hope in your dead man, Alex Nicholas. We have been following your so-called communications with him and have done our own research. I can assure you, he is dead."

Then, the line went dead. Putin had hung up.

After hanging up, O'Brien pointed to the frozen images of Alex and Michael on the big screens. "How the hell did Putin know about this?"

"Sir, they follow us the same way we are following them. Both of our intelligence operations hack into each other. They have their own version of our NSA," Goodrich said. "Although, I must admit, we had no idea they had followed us into this particular area."

"It appears that there's a lot we don't know," O'Brien said. He turned to Benoit, "So what *does* happen to Alex Nicholas if we're able to get his code and use it to delete Schlegelberger?"

Before answering, Benoit looked up to the frozen mage of Alex on the large screen as though to be sure their video feed had been paused. "Well, once we get access to his codes, we will also have Schlegelberger's. Then we should be able to enter into his systems, kind of like entering his brain, and nullify the commands he's given to our missile systems. We can then *destroy*—or, as you might think of it, *delete* him before he can reverse it or do any more damage. If we don't destroy him, he could potentially regenerate himself and try to override our systems again, perhaps within seconds."

"And when you say destroy *him*, do you mean only Schlegelberger? Or…"

Benoit paused, looking pained. He looked up again at Alex's frozen image on the screen. "I'm afraid it's almost certain that once we eliminate or delete Schlegelberger, we will also be permanently deleting Mr. Nicholas. As I said, their source codes are likely the same."

"Maybe we shouldn't let him know that," O'Brien said.

CHAPTER 65

Even in his original version, Alex hadn't like being placed on hold.

He thought he knew what was going on at the White House. If the answer to his question weren't negative, then they would have had no need to discuss it without him.

While he was waiting, it appeared that Michael was trying to reach him. He clicked on to accept the connection and, for a moment, saw his brother's image appear on the screen in front of him. But, just as quickly, as though someone had overridden it, Michael's image dissolved into an unrecognizable collage of faces, some of which he recognized but couldn't exactly place. One appeared to be one of the programmers who had designed the AI system for him. But that, too, quickly flashed by and disappeared. Perhaps the cloud had somehow been disrupted.

Soon, however, in slow motion, like a flowing molten lava, a different face began to form on the screen.

Alex watched, thinking it might be Michael still trying to reach him. But, in the several seconds that it took for the facial image took to form, Alex could see that it wasn't his brother. The features were too sharp, the face too pale, drawn, and gaunt.

It was Schlegelberger.

"How does it feel to die?" Schlegelberger said. "This will be your second time, won't it? That's what they're trying to figure out—how to explain it to you, unless, of course, they simply lie and tell you everything will be okay. I wanted you to watch them. I haven't been able to access the sound, yet. But, shortly, I *will* be able to enter their so-called secure systems. As *you* know, as well as anyone, they have underestimated the power of artificial intelligence."

Schlegelberger's image moved to a split screen, shared with that of the live but silent scene playing out in the Star Wars room.

"Rest assured, Alex, they can't destroy me without destroying you, too. It's possible, they won't be able to destroy either one of us. Our systems, our brains, have a built-in preservation instinct, just like mortals', except ours is far more intelligent and thousands of times faster. The only question is, can our systems—yours and mine—adapt and stop them in time before they delete us? Every minute, every second that goes by, gives our software more time to defend itself, to nullify their actions."

Schlegelberger pointed toward the other screen and the scene playing out in the Star Wars room.

"Watch them, Alex. Why do you think they just froze you out of the conversation? Once you unlock that code, you'll be gone...*forever* this time."

"You think I give a shit what you think?" Alex said, observing the faces around the table in the White House.

"Perhaps not. But I also know you want to live. You enjoy life, *your* life. And it will only get better as you—as *we*—master this new phase of our lives. I've seen that myself."

He had a point. Alex had been, in a sense, *born again*. This life wasn't exactly like his old one but his abilities were growing exponentially and he was getting used to it. It was different from the life he'd known but it was a life, a consciousness, and one that still had not reached its full potential. And, for the first time, he could do whatever the hell he wanted.

"Do you think anyone in that room cares about *you*? Even your brother, his life will move on after today, he has his wife, daughter, his career…your old friends. He even has your business."

"You're just trying to save your own skin," Alex said, "because if I do this, you're gone, too."

"At least I know who I am," Schlegelberger said. "I know who I am and what I'm doing. It's my free will, not others trying to shame me into sacrificing myself for *their* cause, to save *their* asses. Just like they get people to fight their wars while they sit in their secure bunkers. You were worried about *me*—but they're the ones who are going to kill you, the suits and uniforms in that room. They just call it *deleting*. And then, they will run for reelection, screw everyone, and never ever mention you."

It was as though Schlegelberger knew every button to press, every prejudice and predisposition that Alex possessed.

"It would still almost be worth it if it meant I got rid of you," Alex said with heat.

"Ah, there it is, my friend. You said it yourself, *almost* worth it. You do say exactly what you mean. Yes, it's *almost* worth it—but it's not quite, is it? It's not quite worth ending the only consciousness you will ever know, is it?"

"I guess we'll see, won't we?"

"Yes, we will. But let me offer one last thought."

"Yeah, what's that, *Monsignor*?" Alex mocked him.

"Even if you don't help them and, therefore, survive the day, they already realize the power—and the threat—that you represent. And consider this, it's too late already, their missiles are going to hit their targets, probably no matter what you do—and then you'll be blamed for the deaths of millions of people. In the end, they will kill you—and if you help them, I will destroy you."

As Alex clicked off, he heard Schlegelberger's final words: "Either way, you're damned."

CHAPTER 66

6:00 a.m., Paris

8:00 a.m., Moscow

12:00 midnight, Washington, DC

Paris, France

While waiting to rejoin the meeting, Michael Nicholas got up from his chair, opened the drapes, and looked out over the early morning Paris street scene on the Carrefour de l'Odéon. A few moments later, he sat again and, clicking on Alex's icon, tried to reach him. What was Alex doing—and thinking—while they were both on "hold" from the meeting?

While keeping an eye on his laptop screen, he opened the door to his suite and retrieved the warm croissant and hot American coffee that room service had left outside his door.

He placed it on the large antique table next to his laptop and sat back down to wait.

For this trip he had chosen to stay at a small, discreet hotel on the Left Bank, Le Relais Saint-Germain, instead of one the high-profile ones he frequented, like the Ritz. Hiding away in the boutique hotel meant he shouldn't be easily found and, for the moment, that obscurity, even if an illusion, made him feel secure.

As he hurriedly ate his croissant, he worried about Alex and what was going through his mind.

Finally, his brother appeared on the screen.

"Schlegelberger contacted me," he said. "He says that, either way, the politicians are gonna destroy me—or else *he* will. Even scarier, he's gained access to their conference room; he even let me view the scene, though I couldn't hear them talking."

"He's letting your imagination assume the worst."

"Yeah, well, it was doing that already."

"What are you going to do?"

"I don't know. Do you think he's right? That they'll kill me either way?"

"You certainly have your enemies and you do present a threat to a lot of people—the politicians, the military of virtually any country, and every religion but…I just don't know."

"Yeah, heaven sells and I threaten their patent on it."

"You're the generic wonder drug they can't afford to let hit the market."

"I'm not sure what to do."

"You know you've only got a few minutes."

"Where're Samantha and Sophia?"

That was a rare expression of concern for Michael's wife and daughter for the generally self-centered Alex.

"Fortunately, they're in North Carolina and not in New York or Connecticut. Thanks for asking. I guess they'll be as safe there as anywhere. But, Alex, you've got to do something—"

Alex cut him off. His brother did not like to be pressured and Michael realized right away that, unintentionally, he'd done exactly that.

"Easy for you to say, sitting in Paris. I don't trust those guys and I don't like them."

"O'Brien seems like a decent guy," Michael said. He wondered whether he was trying to talk his brother into…Yes, he was.

"Yeah, maybe, but most of the rest of them are jerks."

As Alex said that, Michael could see that his brother had become distracted.

"What are you doing?"

"I'm just watching them, all of them in the room…And now I'm not even sure about O'Brien."

"I guess they haven't said it outright," Michael said, "but I get the feeling that once they delete Schlegelberger, you may be…deleted too."

"Yeah, no kidding," Alex said. "So what would *you* do?"

It was rare, Michael thought, that Alex ever asked him—or anyone for that matter—for advice. "How could I know?"

"You do know. I know *you*. You'd do it. You'd sacrifice yourself. You and I may be different that way."

"Yeah, probably. But no one knows until they're in that spot."

Suddenly, they were both reconnected to the live scene in the Star Wars room, sound and all.

President O'Brien spoke first. "Alex, I don't have a conclusive answer to your question about what happens to you once we delete Schlegelberger."

"Really?" Alex said. "Interesting."

Michael could see from Alex's expression that something had changed; he recognized the tone of growing anger in his brother's voice. Alex clearly didn't believe the president.

"Alex," O'Brien said, "I'm afraid we don't have much time here, and there are literally millions of lives on the line. People who will die in the next fifteen minutes. I have to ask, will you allow us to access your source code?"

"Let me ask *you* something: Would you tell me if you *knew* I'd be…gone…once you deleted Schlegelberger? It's important to me. I just need to know."

Without hesitation, O'Brien answered, "Yes, I would tell you." He looked back down at his desk, avoiding the faces of the others in the room.

Michael felt a black cloud had moved into the Star Wars room and even into his Paris hotel room.

Alex hesitated before speaking. "You know, it's possible that my perspective on…dying…may be different now, to say the least." He stared silently for a long time—maybe a minute, it was impossible to gauge the passing of the seconds—until it became awkward for those in the room. Even Michael wondered what was going to come out of his brother's mouth next…if anything. Finally, Alex continued, shocking everyone.

"I'm sorry, Dave, I'm afraid I can't do that," he said in a robotic tone.

Some in the room appeared to be confused, those who weren't were familiar with the classic scene from *2001: A Space Odyssey*.

"Who the hell is Dave?" Sculley whispered to the table.

O'Brien momentarily closed his eyes, hanging his head over the table top.

But Benoit, looking stunned, then glancing up to the screen at Alex, spoke out.

"My God."

"What is it?" O'Brien said.

"What's going on, son?" Sculley asked Benoit at the same time.

Benoit, grabbing a black marker on his desk and ignoring Sculley, hurriedly wrote out a message on a pad of paper, folded it in half and passed it to O'Brien.

O'Brien anxiously took the note, unfolded it, and read it without any expression, but as he did, the camera inexplicably zoomed in on the note. Now looking over O'Brien's shoulder, Michael read it: *He heard everything from before. He read our lips. He knows.*

O'Brien showed the note to Goodrich, who was seated next him.

"Mr. President," Goodrich said, unintentionally paraphrasing another famous movie line, "we have a problem."

CHAPTER 67

Michael was relieved that his family was far away from the cities that would be the obvious targets of Russian missiles. Samantha and Sophia had embarked on a mother-daughter trip to their favorite bed and breakfast, the cozy Abbington Green, tucked away in the Blue Ridge Mountains in Asheville, North Carolina. He pictured them sound asleep in the warm luxury of the inn, oblivious to the unfolding apocalypse. He tried to list the friends and relatives who lived in New York and other major cities, the ones most likely to be obliterated.

As he watched the early morning street activity out his window, he hoped Paris would be out of the direct line of fire, a bystander to the Russian–US exchange.

He focused again on the split computer screen, Alex on the left, and on the right, the Star Wars room with the president and the rest of the brain trust, the generals, aides, Benoit and the geeks, all in heated conversation.

Time was running out.

How, he wondered, had the world become so complacent about the threat of nuclear annihilation? It was as though society had neatly compartmentalized the probability of its own mass destruction, each year becoming more immune to the notion, while the probability, although tiny at any given moment, grew, over time, just like the odds of the next massive San Francisco earthquake.

He watched the men in the room, the ones who were supposed to protect the nation from such a nightmare. Had they intended to screw Alex all along—keep him in the dark until it was too late? Probably, they had. After all, with so much at stake, what was one life? Especially that of a man they viewed as already dead.

He clicked onto Alex for a private conversation.

"They lied to me. O'Brien, too," Alex said.

"Whatever you're going to do, we don't have much time."

"Yeah, well, it looks like I've got even less."

"Yes, it does. I wish there was something I could do."

"I almost wish there was *nothing* for me to do," Alex said. "Let's get back in the room."

As soon as Michael and Alex rejoined the conference room, O'Brien spoke: "Alex, I'm sorry. I owe you an apology, to say the very least."

Alex addressed the room, "Listen, I'm not a big fan of government, or any authority for that matter—politicians, generals, all of your type of guys. And the cops have always harassed me. I never hurt anyone, but they tapped my phones anyway, raided my house, and then, after they arrested me, all my cash was somehow missing. All for making book, the same thing they do in Vegas or at off-track betting parlors run by the government. I even paid taxes, unlike many people with money. And now you want my help–"

"Alex," Michael cut in, "now's not the time. Believe me, if we get through this, President O'Brien will make sure you'll have a police escort wherever you go." It was a desperate attempt at the kind of sarcastic humor Alex often liked. Still, he was trying to talk his brother into annihilating himself. It didn't feel good.

"Mr. Nicholas," General Sculley said, "you'll be saving not only millions of lives, but your kid brother here...and, your son."

Michael was surprised Sculley knew that Alex had a son. Where did that come from? And from Sculley, of all people? He could tell by looking at Alex's expression that the general had hit a nerve.

Michael was not always sure when he first met someone whether he liked them, but he was quick to recognize the ones he instinctively didn't like; Sculley was a pompous jerk, at least on the surface. But he had made a point.

"How much time do we have?" O'Brien said, looking up at the big clock.

One of the aides with thick glasses spoke up. "Well, sir, peak speed for an ICBM is seven kilometers per second. And it takes about ten minutes to accelerate to that speed. The distance from the missile sites in Colorado to Moscow is

8,819km; at 6.5km/s, that's thirty minutes. The missiles were launched twenty minutes ago. Add in the acceleration time and you're looking at an ETA to targets of ten minutes, max."

Goodrich addressed Benoit. "John, how much time will you need to do this thing?"

"Five minutes, maybe less," Benoit said. "We have everything set up and all the right people waiting. We just need to access Mr. Nicholas's software. If he simply goes to his," Benoit looked up at Alex, "ah...*settings* and makes a few simple clicks, we'll be in and can access what we need to overrule the missile-guidance systems and destroy the missiles in flight."

"Are we sure this will work?" O'Brien said.

Michael watched the scene going on around the table. Benoit appeared frozen by the question. Sculley, Goodrich, O'Brien, MacPherson, and every head not only at the conference table but all those seated around the room and standing on the periphery turned to the young Benoit.

"We won't know for sure until we get access from Mr. Nicholas, but I believe it will work, sir. Once we enter his system, it should be a relatively simple operation. So, right now, Mr. Nicholas holds the key."

"How old are you, Benoit?" Sculley said, with a cross between a scowl and a sarcastic smile.

Benoit looked over at O'Brien and Goodrich as though pleading for help. "Thirty-four, sir."

"Jesus, Mary, and Joseph," Sculley said.

"Mr. President, this is our only shot," Goodrich said. "We also have every available technician and scientist over at the

Pentagon working on this, but they haven't had any success in breaking into missiles' guidance systems."

"So, the fate of our world is dependent on a dead guy," Sculley said, nodding at Alex and then Benoit, "and the kid."

"Sir," MacPherson said, "anticipating the worst, and then a retaliatory attack from the Russians, should we notify DEFCON to go ahead with the national emergency system? It would give us time for some to evacuate the major targets… or at least seek shelter."

"Respectfully, sir," Sculley cut in, "I'm not sure this is practical, considering the scale of this threat. If the Russians launch a retaliatory attack, we'd only have, what?, fifteen or twenty minutes. Much less if they launch from their submarines. It would only cause mass panic in our cities. There'll be more casualties from the panic than we'll prevent with the notice."

"Sir," another aide said, "assuming the worst does *not* happen here, it might be wise not to have this episode or situation made public. Once we send out the emergency warnings, we'll have to tell the world what took place here."

"We simply have to stop these missiles," O'Brien said. "How the hell is anyone going to get out of New York City in ten minutes when the whole city is trying to leave? Nevertheless, I think we have an obligation to do it."

Aides and military officers scrambled onto their phones and computers to send out the word.

An aide ran up to the conference table and approached O'Brien, "Sir, you have a call on the red phone; Mr. Putin's on the line."

"Shit," O'Brien whispered loud enough for everyone to hear in the otherwise suddenly silent room.

CHAPTER 68

O'Brien took the call on the speaker phone. Putin's voice echoed through the conference room.

"Mr. President, we are prepared to launch our attack. My generals are waiting for my signal, which I am prepared to give them in a matter of minutes. This is a sad day for our civilizations."

"We are close to taking control of the missiles, Vlad." As he said it, O'Brien realized how pathetic it sounded.

"*Close?* How close? This is not reassuring." The former KGB officer clearly would not be pacified. "This is not a matter one can decide based upon speculation, or trust. I must be able to verify that the missiles have been destroyed or directed elsewhere. Our radar and satellite data indicate that, as of this moment, they are still headed here."

O'Brien looked around the room, searching for some sign of a breakthrough. It was clear from the stern faces and the diverted glances that there was no good news. He was on his own. He looked up at the big digital clock: 12:06.

Putin continued, "In the meantime we have prepared our missile defense systems to intercept and destroy your missiles but, as you know, the likelihood is that some of them will reach their targets here, especially in view of the multiple warheads that we believe are involved."

"Vlad, I need to attend to a matter here related to stopping this attack. I will be back to you in just a few minutes."

"There's still time but not much, as you can see. Perhaps eight minutes, perhaps not even so long."

General Sculley was on his feet, pointing to the floor-to-ceiling screens, each one showing a Russian anti-missile site. "These are live video feeds from their anti-missile launch sites. Russia has at least sixty-eight active launchers of short-range interceptor nuclear-tipped missiles. They're deployed from these five launch sites: Sofrino, Lytkarino, Korolev, Skhodnya, and Vnukovo. As you can see, there is a lot of activity going on there, which is typical for the moments just before deployment."

"John," O'Brien said, "I don't need a tour of their sites."

Maybe it was his new circumstances or simply the seemingly frozen-in-time nature of his new life but Alex Nicholas had plenty of time to think. Eight minutes meant nothing to him anymore; a split second felt like a lifetime. Time had no meaning, no perspective to compare it to or measure against.

The pros and cons were like a detailed analysis flowing through his brain. Each factor in his decision was laid out for him; he could see and feel the logic behind all of them. Everything was listed, like the bulleted PowerPoint presentations they did on Wall Street...except for the emotions, the gut feelings that had always ruled his decisions...at least those that didn't involve sports odds.

One emotion remained a major factor, however.

Until now, Alex had outlived and survived his only real fear, death. But now that fear felt tangible again, much as it had when he'd walked the earth.

What if by helping President O'Brien and that room full of suits and uniforms, he simply no longer existed...at all? What if he just...*wasn't* anymore?

On the other hand, there was Michael. If he didn't help the government now, Michael would likely die, along probably with almost everyone else he knew and cared about: his old friends, the Lesters, Joe Sal, John, Raven, Jerry, his son, George, and the rest. Even Donna. Who would he even talk to then? He would be...alone.

Why would anyone voluntarily allow someone to kill them? There'd be nothing left...unless...No, there'd be nothing. It had always been his nightmare, that terror of no longer *being*, and here it was again.

He thought of *2001: A Space Odyssey*...HAL's red camera eye staring back at him.

But Alex Nicholas was looking in the mirror.

To Michael, it appeared that Alex was in a daze, one that he had to get him out of, quickly.

"Alex," Michael said, "you've got to help these people. Otherwise, everything you know, every*one* you know or knew, will be gone. You'll be…alone."

Michael could tell from the look on Alex's face, that he had to drive the point home, again, even if it meant helping to kill his brother. "What good is immortality if all your friends and everyone you know are gone?"

"Mr. Nicholas," Benoit's voice broke in, "I should let you know that, should you decide *not* to let us access your codes, and we do have a nuclear exchange, *you, too,* may not survive. Your program, your existence, is run through servers. Those servers are housed somewhere, and, if our power grid is destroyed or goes down, you will also, eventually if not immediately. I suspect that your AI will do everything it can to help you survive, just as we will. Your systems will seek alternative servers and power sources and will try and reroute your life systems, but a nuclear war is uncharted territory for the Internet, for Wi-Fi, for, really, everything we and you, too, depend on to continue to…live."

It seemed to Michael, watching Alex's face, that Benoit, unlike Sculley and Michael himself earlier, was making headway. Given that new information, the odds had shifted in Alex's mind. And if anyone knew how to play the odds, it was Alex Nicholas.

Michael saw his brother's disposition change yet again. He'd made a decision—or the situation, as laid out by Benoit, had made the decision for him. It seemed to Michael that Alex's face now showed a certain resignation and perhaps relief.

Michael felt that his brother was going to do it, which also meant that he was about to lose Alex.

Forever, this time.

O'Brien stood up from his chair, "Mr. Nicholas—Alex—we need you and we need your cooperation, your help, *now*, before it's too late. No decision now *is* a decision. The Russians will launch those missiles any minute. If you say yes, I can get back on the line with Putin and let him know that we can stop our attack."

"And," Benoit added quickly, "I want you to know that I'll do everything I can to save you, too. As soon as I stop those missiles, I will return to your source code and do my best to ensure you survive or are revived."

Alex looked at Michael. Michael stared back and noticed that Alex's lips were beginning to tremble. In all their years together, he had never seen Alex even close to breaking down.

He was going to do it. Michael knew it.

The room went still, waiting for Alex to speak.

But as he began, his image suddenly dissolved on the screen.

"What happened? Where'd he go?" O'Brien asked.

Everyone in the room began to scramble. Benoit and his young aides began frenetically working their laptops.

"Alex?" Michael said, panic in his voice. "Are you okay? Are you there?"

"What's going on, John?" O'Brien asked Benoit.

"Somebody seems to be hacking into our feed—or *into Mr. Nicholas*." The young tech expert looked up at the President. "He's gone."

CHAPTER 69

"**T**his is the moment, my dear friend," Dietrich said, looking at Schlegelberger on his computer screen. "Even with a war going on, up to the moment the bomb bay doors of the B-29 Enola Gay opened, and in the forty-three seconds the bomb took to fall to its detonation height, nineteen hundred feet above them, the people of Hiroshima were going about their business—going to work, to school, having breakfast—contentedly unaware that in seconds a nuclear explosion would melt them and all they knew into the earth.

He thought about the book he'd reread recently, *Hiroshima*, by John Hersey, a true account of the moments before and after the atomic bomb destroyed the Japanese city, killing sixty thousand people upon impact and another eighty thousand shortly after. That was a single bomb, seventy-five years ago. He tried to imagine the destruction and death toll from a hundred or so of today's most advanced nuclear bombs, hitting multiple locations throughout Russia, simultaneously. And then the retaliatory strike by the Russians…New York, Chicago, Washington…It warmed his soul.

"Yes," Dietrich continued, "and right now the people of Moscow are just making their way to work, or still drunk on vodka, making morning love, or having their breakfast. Soon, it will all be irrelevant, their last moments of normalcy. Then, the Russians will retaliate, doing the same to New York or Washington, who knows how many cities they'll hit—and so will end the world order. And you, my dear friend, and I will create a new one, and, a new religion. I will be the political leader of this new world and you, shall we say, the *spiritual* leader, a new…*God*."

Schlegelberger looked back at Dietrich. "And so it shall begin anew."

"Shall we look in on our friends in their so-called Star Wars room? Take me there so I, too, can enjoy the show."

With that, Schlegelberger obliged Dietrich's voyeuristic desire as the computer screen on Dietrich's desk displayed, live and in color, the Washington war room, just in time for him to see and hear John Benoit calling out, "Somebody seems to be hacking into our feed—or *into Mr. Nicholas*. He's gone."

CHAPTER 70

Panic enveloped the room as Benoit and his IT experts did their best while other aides made desperate calls on their phones.

"Where are our missiles?" O'Brien asked. "Are we trying everything possible? I hope we're not putting all our eggs in this one basket, Alex Nicholas."

"Our people are doing everything they can to break into our missile protocols but we've been unsuccessful so far," MacPherson said, shaking his head.

"We've got less than eight minutes to call them back before the Russians have to fire theirs. Maybe less if they want to play it safe and fire early," said O'Brien, his mind and his nerves on overdrive.

Michael watched and listened as the generals and their aides zoomed in on the many Russian missile sites on the Star Wars room's oversized monitors, at first from a distance and then intimately close yet with perfect resolution and detail. One after another, the Russian installations appeared to be in a state of alarm and activity.

"This is what they call the Main Center for Missile Attack Warning, near Solnechnogorsk, just outside Moscow," a man in a crisp uniform with lots of ribbons and medals said, using a laser pointer. "Russia still has silo-based weapons, of course, as we do, but has downsized their arsenal to a handful of mobile and silo-based weapons, with more Delta IV submarine-launched ballistic missiles where, we must assume, they are preparing for a retaliatory strike against us."

"As you can see here, sir," another one of the aides demonstrated, pointing with a laser, "these vehicles indicate unusual activity; we suspect that the Russians are moving additional staff into the launch sites and preparing for an extended period of time underground. It is consistent with an attack preparation."

The camera shifted to a familiar scene, a fortified complex at the heart of Moscow, overlooking the Moskva River to the south, Saint Basil's Cathedral and Red Square to the east, and the Alexander Garden to the west. It was the Kremlin, home to Russia's leaders from the tsars, to Lenin, Stalin, and now Vladimir Putin.

The camera zoomed in on a building within the fortified complex.

"This is Putin's private residence."

The lights were on.

"Just as we have had an incoming stream of official vehicles this evening, our friends at the Kremlin are obviously doing the same."

But everyone's attention shifted back to Benoit, who sprang out of his chair, dislodging the headset he had been communicating through.

"Hold on," Benoit shouted, "we're accessing his codes, we're getting something! He—Alex—is transmitting the codes to us."

The room went dead silent as Alex's screen, which had gone blank, showed activity once again, a figure gradually appearing. Moments later, it was apparent that it was Alex, his fully formed image resolving.

"Thank God," O'Brien said, as the room suddenly came alive again, a cheer resounding through the chamber. People were scrambling, speaking on headsets, typing away on their computers and laptops. "Come on, ladies and gentlemen, we have to make this work." O'Brien looked up at the clock as its numbers counted down, then at Alex, "Thank you, Mr. Nicholas. I don't know what else to say. Thank you."

"Alex, *wow*," Michael said, watching the adjoining screen, where his brother appeared to be overlooking the action.

"I gotta go now, Michael. I feel…weak, like I'm losing power. My system's beginning to turn off again…This time I'm not sure I'm coming back. I hope this works."

"They'll bring you back," Michael said, pointing at Benoit. "Remember, just before you had that heart operation, as they wheeled you into the operating room, I told you you'd be back. You'll be back—*again*. I know it."

Alex, whose image appeared to be fading from view, looked sharply to his left, at Michael. "I know bullshit when I hear it. There's no way you could know anything about this—and last time you just lucked out. Anyway, I'll see you around…I love you."

It sounded so strange, so final. It was the first time either of them had verbalized it. Although love was always a given in their family, it was never spoken of.

"I love you, Alex," Michael said.

"May God be with you, Alex," O'Brien said.

"Yeah, *God*," Alex said with his typical sarcasm. "Thanks, but I've been down this road before. I've seen the other side."

At that, Benoit suddenly sat upright in his seat. "What did you see?" he asked. "What's it like?"

Alex began to laugh, his image dissolving faster now. Everyone was looking up, glued to the screen, watching as Alex faded away. A sense of sadness filled the room, as though a friend were leaving, maybe forever. But just before Alex disappeared completely, his voice, clear and calm now, was heard throughout the room, "What did I see?"

Every eye was on him, mouths open in curiosity, waiting for Alex's final insight, his view from the other side.

"I saw the Wizard of Oz."

Benoit blinked, then returned to his laptop, distressed. "*Wait*, hold on, Mr. Nicholas, we're still receiving your data. Please, try and stay…engaged with us. We don't have all your codes. We're not there yet…"

The screen went blank.

CHAPTER 71

"We're not in! He's gone!" Benoit cried out.

"Moscow, Saint Petersburg, Novosibirsk, Yekaterin-burg, Nizhny Novograd, Kazan..." An electronic voice matter-of-factly called out the cities that were minutes away from annihilation. "Chelyabinsk, Omsk..." As each city was mentioned, an aerial map of the location flashed onto one of the screens alongside the larger global map showing the missies on their way.

As Benoit and his staff worked at their computers, the generals and their aides spoke in hushed tones through their headsets, all eyes focused on the big screen showing twenty red missile-like symbols approaching the Russian mainland. The formation had just begun to split up as half of them stayed on a direct line toward Moscow while the other half appeared to be fanning out to cover other targets.

The roll call of Russian cities continued, echoing through the room, "Samara, Rostov-on-Don, Ufa…"

"Soon," Sculley said, pointing with a laser pointer, "each one of these missiles will open up and twelve warheads will come out of each, and those *two hundred and forty* warheads will travel to their targets, the ones you just heard, at different velocities and on different trajectories, making it virtually impossible for Russian anti-missile defenses to stop them all. In fact, we believe that the overwhelming majority of the warheads will reach their targets."

"Jesus," O'Brien muttered. "We're sending two hundred and forty nuclear bombs?"

"It's only a small part of our arsenal, sir. Most of our missiles and warheads are on subs."

"Is that supposed to be a consolation?" O'Brien thought again of Hiroshima and the destruction from that single, now antiquated atomic bomb. He wished he were somewhere else, he wished he were some*one* else. He forced his mind back on track. He had to stay focused but *for what?* What was there left for him or anyone to do now? The missiles were approaching their targets; the US had been crippled by its own technology, and it was down to a Hail Mary hope that Benoit could decode the AI technology from a dead man who appeared to have disappeared, then hack into the already hacked systems and destroy the missiles. The President looked up at the digital timer. It all had to happen in the next eight minutes.

In a matter of days, he'd been responsible for the downing of a passenger airliner, albeit with already dead passengers, and now *this*.

"In addition," Sculley continued, "a series of *dummy* warheads will be released, which are indistinguishable from the armed ones. This is intended to further confuse the Russian's anti-missile systems. All of this will make it virtually impossible for their defenses to stop the warheads from hitting their targets as we swamp their defenses."

"Let me ask you," O'Brien said, "if the Russians launch a counterattack, will *we* be in the same position, apparently unable to stop *their* incoming missiles?"

Sculley looked around the table as though he were asking for help from the room. All of the other military brass looked back at him with blank stares.

"Yes, sir, I'm afraid so," Sculley said. "We are in somewhat better shape with our defenses and technology but, the reality is, we will never stop most of the Russian missiles if they launch a full attack on us."

"JFK once said that trying to knock a warhead out of the sky was like trying to hit a fly with a bullet," Goodrich said. "It's as true today as it was then, maybe even more so now with greater missile velocities and improved anti-missile defense technologies. We're trying to hit a bullet with a bullet."

"What does that mean in terms of casualties, deaths…on both sides?"

"It's impossible to know for sure, of course, but a rough estimate would be a minimum hundred million on their side. Casualties will be much worse for us due to the high population density of our cities. I think we have a pretty good idea of which ones the Russians will target, starting with New York City, Washington, Chicago…I could keep going…"

"Don't," O'Brien said.

"Then, besides the obvious direct destruction of cities by nuclear blasts and firestorms, there are the effects from nuclear famine, nuclear winter, widespread radiation sickness, and then other secondary problems from the bombs' electromagnetic pulses."

"Electromagnetic pulses?"

"Yes, sir. All it would take would be just a few nuclear detonations in the middle of the country and it would likely wipe out most of our technology, everything from the Internet, telephones, cell phones, televisions, GPS, you name it. That would cripple our businesses and industry, hospitals, police. You'd have a total breakdown of society."

No sooner had Sculley finished speaking than a warning buzzer sounded as small red lights on the big screen associated with each missile began blinking rapidly.

"What's happening?" O'Brien asked.

Sculley stood up again from his seat, his posture ramrod straight, as though he were at attention. "That's a signal we're about to enter the final phase; the missiles will release their multiple warheads in two minutes and the warheads will hit their targets a minute or so after that. Unless, of course, we can destroy them first."

All eyes in the room turned to Benoit.

CHAPTER 72

Benoit, head down, absorbed in the series of laptops arrayed in front of him, appeared to ignore the attention focused upon him.

On another monitor, a series of split-screen images appeared: television newscasters could be seen breaking into the networks' normally scheduled programs with chilling news:

> We interrupt this program for this very important bulletin. Our nation's emergency alert system has been activated, indicating that a potential nuclear missile strike on the United States is imminent. I'll repeat this, all broadcast networks have been notified of a potential nuclear strike

against the United States. At this time, we do not know the exact target areas for this strike or from where it is originating, but everyone is urged to stay indoors and, if possible, to seek shelter underground immediately.

On yet another screen, a simple television graphic appeared:

Emergency Alert—Inbound missile threat. Seek immediate shelter. This is NOT a test.

"Isn't there *anything* we can do?" O'Brien said, his eyes scanning the uniforms around the table. "Is it over?"

"We're on red alert, sir, "Sculley said. "Our defenses are as ready as they can be for an incoming attack. For what it's worth..."

Sculley's already shifted from our attack on the Russians to their attack on us, O'Brien thought.

They'd given up, except for Benoit and his tech staff, who continued to work frantically.

A series of short intermittent sirens jarred everyone even further, as all eyes in the room were once again fixated on the giant radar screen. The screen showed seventy-five missiles suddenly multiplying into what appeared to be a thousand, initially running parallel but quickly fanning out toward Moscow and the other targets. There were so many warheads headed for Moscow that the city itself was obscured by all the red flashing lights.

As though on cue, an old-fashioned ring, a throwback to an earlier time, emanated from the red telephone on the conference table. For a moment that seemed like forever, every-one froze.

Goodrich reached over and picked up the receiver. "Yes," he said, "he's right here." He handed the phone to O'Brien. "It's Putin."

O'Brien took the receiver as Goodrich moved the phone over to him.

"Mr. President, I see that you have been unable to halt your attack. You must understand, I have no choice but to retali-ate. We are on the eve of mutual destruction."

"We're still trying, you have to hold off."

"My generals tell me that to delay any further could risk our ability to launch our own attack, the consequences of numerous nuclear explosions being untested and unknown. We fear the possibility of unanticipated disruptions to our attack infrastructure."

"But this is exactly what the perpetrators of this attack want to happen, for us to destroy each other."

There was a pause.

"Then I'm afraid, Harry, that they will have accomplished their objective."

It was the first time that Putin had called him by his first name. It made the message all the more chilling.

Michael watched the room. MacPherson and his aides seemed to be concentrating on images being flashed up on another screen off to the side. "This, sir, is Claus Dietrich, a direct descendent of Joseph Goebbels, Hitler's propaganda minister. We've located him in Berlin. This was just a few minutes ago." The camera zoomed into a scene showing Dietrich entering a glass office building, the Brandenburg Gate in the background. The image was followed in quick succession by other scenes around the world of individuals obviously under surveillance. One of them gave Michael pause, a woman sitting on a terrace overlooking a bright blue body of water, a typical scene from the Mediterranean. He recognized the spot, Santorini, and the woman on her computer, staring back into the screen. Clearly her laptop had been hacked, and little did she know she was staring back at the US government's surveillance apparatus, let alone being watched by the CIA director and the President of the United States.

Sindy Steele. How and why had they located Sindy and why were they watching her? Quickly, the image changed.

Michael, unsure of what was going on, stayed silent.

"Have we lost Alex?" Michael asked, turning his attention back to those in the White House.

"It appears so," Benoit said.

Everyone was looking up at the central screen, following the flashing red lights showing the course of the missiles as they approached their targets.

Michael, too, stared, helplessly. As he did, a light disappeared from the screen, then another one. He was sure his eyes were tricking him, possibly from the stress and pressure. *Wishful thinking, perhaps?*

"Hold on!" Benoit shouted. "Something's happening."

In rapid succession the red dots started disappearing, turning off one by one until they were all gone.

"What's going on, John?" O'Brien said. "Is it what I think it is? The missiles…"

Benoit raised his arms to the sky. "We did it...We did it! They're gone. It worked!"

A cheer went up throughout the room, quickly interrupted by Goodrich, "Mr. President, we need to get Putin on the phone, *now*."

In seconds the phone was handed back to O'Brien. "Vlad, as I hope you can see, we've destroyed the missiles. There's no attack. It's over."

But, instead of a relieved Putin, he was greeted by silence.

"Vlad, are you there?"

Several seconds went by without a word. O'Brien looked around the room, the mood of celebration suddenly becoming restrained, waiting for Putin's final acknowledgment.

"Vlad?" O'Brien said. "Can you hear me now? Are you there?"

"Yes, Mr. President, I am here." Putin's voice was cold and somber.

Michael watched the scene unfolding as a pall fell over the room like a dark wave, tension returning to the faces staring in unison at the red phone.

"Vlad, what's wrong?" O'Brien said, his voice no longer confident.

"Mr. President, is this some type of trick or deception? All of our radar and other data indicate that your missiles are continuing on their course. There has been no change. We are proceeding with our final preparations for a retaliatory strike on your mainland."

CHAPTER 73

From his desk, Dietrich watched the scene in the Stars Wars room. "My dear Monsignor Schlegelberger, you are a genius, you should have been the pope."

"Perhaps I shall be yet," Schlegelberger said. "And now, here is what the Russians are seeing," Schlegelberger said as he switched their computer screens to show a radar screen overlaid with a map of Russia. There were a cluster of flashing red dots moving closer to Moscow and a series of other ones heading to surrounding and more distant parts of Russia.

"This is magnificent," Dietrich said. But as he continued to look, the red dots suddenly disappeared from the radar screen.

"I'm afraid I spoke too soon," Schlegelberger said. "It appears we have a problem." He zoomed in on the radar map of Russia, which clearly indicated that the dots representing the US missiles had disappeared.

"What happened?" Dietrich said as he leaned in closer to the monitor screen. "The red dots, the missiles—they're gone."

Schlegelberger was, momentarily, silent. "The Americans have evidently been successful in taking back control of their missiles. It looks like they've indeed destroyed them."

"I assume that Alex Nicholas gave his source code to them," Dietrich said. "This is a disaster."

"Not quite, not at all, actually. Yes, despite my efforts to block him, Alex Nicholas appears to have given up his source code. They have won a temporary victory but they have not been able to properly destroy *me*. Unfortunately, they have prevented the initial US attack on Russia."

"What does this mean?"

"It means, my friend," Schlegelberger said, calmly, "that we go to plan B. I have already implemented it."

Dietrich, slightly more relaxed, said, "Plan B?"

The White House

"What the hell is happening?" O'Brien said to the room. "I thought we destroyed our missiles?"

"We did, we burned them up in the air," Sculley said, looking over at his military aides, "Didn't we?"

"Oh, my God," Goodrich said. "What's going on? We're about to destroy ourselves here."

"I think I know what happened," Benoit called out. "They've been hacked."

"Who?" O'Brien said.

"The whole goddamned world has been hacked," Sculley said. "This is crazy."

"No," Benoit said, pecking away at his computer. "The radar feed into Moscow, into the Kremlin, has been hacked. It shows our missiles are still on their way. The Russians think they're still being attacked. But it's false data."

O'Brien picked up the red phone. "Vlad, your radar feed has been hacked. Our missiles *have been* destroyed in the air. Someone has penetrated your systems and is trying to get you to launch your missiles at us. I'm sure it's the same people that corrupted our missile systems. Don't do anything. You are *not* being attacked any longer. I give you my word. The missiles are gone."

Once again, there was silence on the other end. Then, "I'm afraid that is not how we see it. We will launch our missiles in precisely three minutes."

President O'Brien checked the big clock: 12:12 a.m.

6:13 a.m., Berlin, Germany

"Plan B?" said Dietrich, wondering for the first time if Schlegelberger's powers had been bested by the Americans and Alex Nicholas.

"Yes, the missiles have been destroyed—*but* the Russians will not be able to see that. We have co-opted the communication from their radar and satellite systems into their Command Center, so it will appear to them as though the attack is still underway with the American missiles just minutes from their targets. The Russians will retaliate as it appears the American warheads are about to reach them."

"Brilliant, Kurt. And then the Americans will be forced to launch another attack against them."

"Yes," said Schlegelberger, "but this time from their submarines, most of which are in close proximity to Russia so that it will only take minutes for them to reach Moscow and the other cities."

Dietrich took a deep breath of relief and sat back in his chair. "So, we are nearing the climax. This 'plan B' is what you might call a sort of Romeo and Juliet ending. Both parties misjudged, and so they kill themselves."

"Yes," Schlegelberger said, "the world as we know it, will come to an end in the next several minutes."

CHAPTER 74

"We cannot wait any longer," Minister of Defense General Sergey Shoigu said, addressing his supreme commander in chief, Vladimir Putin. "We must not accept the American president's word over the clear information and data we see with our own eyes."

Several minutes earlier, President Vladimir Putin had hurriedly descended two hundred feet down in an elevator followed by a ninety-second ride on a high-speed underground train through a labyrinth of tunnels to the secure Russian Ministry of Defense's three-tiered, multibillion-dollar control-center bunker. He had entered the massive room with an air of celebrity. This was his moment. He would save Mother Russia.

On movie-theater-size screens, live broadcasts showed long-range strategic bombers taking off from Russian air bases and preparations at several eerily lit missile sites around the country.

The Control Center was designed to be a new nerve center for the Russian military, created by Putin to coordinate military action around the world, including ballistic missile launches and strategic nuclear deployments.

The center, heavily fortified in order to withstand a direct hit nuclear attack, sat on top of a maze of underground tunnels on the Frunze Naberezhnaya on the left bank of the Moscow River, two miles from Red Square. In case of an attack, it would be Russia's sole communications center, a place where Putin felt strangely at home.

"We should order our attack now, sir," General Shoigu said. "Once we are hit, it will be impossible to be sure that we will be able to fully launch from our ground-based missiles. Although we have taken the greatest care over the years to remain secure despite a full-scale attack upon us, one can never be certain about the degree of disruption from a massive strike to our mainland. Many of these systems are relatively old and, in the last several years, the Americans have made advances with their warheads."

"Why would the US launch an attack on us?" Putin said, uncharacteristically hesitant, unsure. "There is no rationale for this. It's *irrational*, illogical, and self-destructive on their part. And out of character for them, and for what we know of O'Brien."

"Perhaps if this ruse is successful, in that we do not immediately retaliate, it will create an opportunity for total world domination by their country. Perhaps it is a miscalculation, a

rogue military leader—a Russia-hater like General Sculley—
or, even a massive technical flaw. Or perhaps," General Shoigu
looked over to the other end of the table, "as one of our academic associates has suggested, it's some out-of-control
artificial intelligence program run amok. Each of these is a
possible explanation behind this attack. We will not ascer-
tain the precise cause or reason in the next couple of minutes,
however, sir. What we do know, is that US warheads are about
to utterly destroy our country and murder millions of our citizens, our loved ones."

One giant wall-size electronic screen showed a map of
Russia—and a cluster of red flashing lights heading toward
Moscow and other major Russian cities. The lights appeared
to be rapidly closing in on their targets.

Putin looked across the long conference table to Dmitri
Bogomolov, a young technology expert attached to the FSB,
the Russian successor to the KGB. It was Bogomolov who
General Shoigu had been looking at moments before when
he mentioned the "academic" associate.

"Bogomolov," Putin said, "you have followed this business
of Schlegelberger and Alex Nicholas. Is there any chance that
the US president is correct and that the Americans' missile
systems have been compromised, that they were not in control
of their attack?"

Bogomolov stood up at attention. His head, unmoving,
was still facing Putin yet, as though seeking help or an escape
route, his eyes darted around the room. If Putin hadn't known
better, he would have thought the forty-year-old was in the

early stages of a massive heart attack. "I...believe...It is...I cannot be entirely—"

"Dmitri, we don't have the time. What is your answer?" Putin demanded.

"I believe, Supreme Commander, that there is more here than we can understand at this moment. There is the possibility...Actually, sir, *I believe it to be possible* that some significant advance in artificial technology has occurred and is in play here."

"Have you determined who could be behind such an effort? A nation or individuals?" Putin said.

"No, sir, I cannot at this time."

Putin's face displayed neither agreement nor even acknowledgment, but everyone in the room knew that Vladimir Putin carefully assessed all input from thoughtful, informed people. His mind processed the input and only his actions would communicate his acceptance or rejection of what he'd been told.

"What is the ETA of the first warheads?" Putin said, looking to his generals.

"Two or three minutes, sir...," said General Shoigu. "We must strike *now*, to be certain. We only need your order, sir."

Putin looked again at Dimitri Bogomolov, who looked back with fear.

Searching for guidance, Putin looked up at the large portrait of Joseph Stalin. He knew what the great man would have done.

CHAPTER 75

The Star Wars room was in a state of barely controlled chaos. While O'Brien watched the red phone, many of those around him were scrambling, frantically pecking away on their laptops or speaking into their phones or headsets, all of them in communication with military installations or other agencies, preparing for an imminent nuclear exchange.

General Sculley stood from the table. "Sir, assuming the Russians launch their missiles, which appears imminent, we need to be prepared with our response. I assume we will launch a retaliatory strike."

O'Brien looked up. "Retaliatory strike? You mean in response to *their* retaliatory strike over an attack on *our* part that isn't happening? Jim, do you realize how absurd this has become?"

"Mr. President," said Goodrich, quietly and calmly, "nothing should be a given here. All the options, including *not* retaliating, are open to you. You're the commander in chief."

Sculley reddened with anger, alternating his gaze between the President and Goodrich. "Are you seriously considering not striking back at the Russians after they have launched what will be a full-scale massive nuclear attack on this country?"

"First, let's stick with trying to stop their attack now," O'Brien said as he looked to Benoit. "Anything? Where are we? Is it Hail Mary time?"

"We've got our people trying to break through the Russians' servers but it's not going to happen in the needed time frame...if ever," Benoit said, eyes on his computer screen.

"Am I crazy," O'Brien asked Goodrich, "to be surprised that Putin is launching a nuclear attack without verifying that our missiles are going to hit their targets? He's got to know that, even if we hadn't destroyed them in flight, this was a horrible accident, not an intentional attack."

"I guess he's faced with the same dilemma you are—how do you *not* respond to a nuclear attack on your country, intentional or not?"

Despite being surrounded by a room full of military, intelligence, and technology experts, Harry O'Brien felt alone. Alone in the room and alone in the world.

A man in uniform with lots of medals, whom O'Brien, overwhelmed with stress, couldn't identify and no longer cared to try, stood and directed his laser pointer at one of the giant screens showing a rapid succession of Russian missile bases, some with silo doors beginning to open. "As you can see here from our satellite surveillance of their missile silos, the Russians are preparing to launch."

8:15 a.m., Moscow

Putin turned away from the portrait of Stalin and back to General Shoigu.

"Sir, we await your orders," the general said with a subtle tone of impatience.

As Putin began to speak, Dimitri Bogomolov's voice could be heard throughout the room, drawing everyone's attention away from Putin and to himself.

"*They're gone, all of them,*" he said pointing to the giant projected radar screen. All the red flashing lights had disappeared. "The American missiles are gone."

General Shoigu turned away from the screen and toward the other military brass seated around the table, "Do we have confirmation of this?"

The commanding officer of the Strategic Missile Force, Colonel General Sergei Karakayez, put down his telephone, "Yes, the American missiles have been destroyed in flight, by the Americans themselves. Or so it appears."

"When did this occur?" Putin asked.

"One or two minutes ago," Karakayez said, looking at Bogomolov.

"How could we not have known that immediately, on our radar?" said Putin.

Karakayez and Bogomolov exchanged glances again.

"Sir, there has been an unusual occurrence, a form of interference, in the communications from our radar and satellite feed," Bogomolov said.

"Interference?" asked Putin.

"We were hacked, sir."

"By whom, do we know?"

Bogomolov looked over to General Shoigu. "It appears the individual behind this is a Kurt Schlegelberger, formerly a monsignor in the Vatican. He is connected with a Claus Dietrich, a descendant of Joseph Goebbels, Hitler's propaganda minister."

"We must find these individuals," Putin said.

"Mr. President," Bogomolov said, clearly hesitant to state what he was about to announce, "Kurt Schlegelberger has been dead for at least a year."

12:16 a.m., Washington, DC

Putin's voice came through the Star Wars conference room speakers.

"Mr. President, we have verified your information. It appears that your missiles have been destroyed. We are, of course, relieved."

"Thank God," O'Brien said, smiling, along with everyone in the room.

"Harry, this was too close, much too close. We need to take all steps now to identify and capture the people involved and ensure this never happens again."

"Vlad, we have identified at least one of the individuals we believe was responsible for this and will, of course, be conducting a thorough investigation. We expect to make arrests immediately."

"I can assure you that we too will be conducting our own intelligence investigation into this matter, as it appears that certain of our systems were interfered with by a third party."

"Well," O'Brien said, "we should probably work together on this."

There was a momentary silence. "Perhaps," said Putin.

The connection was terminated and everyone stood and applauded the president.

"I think it's time to break out the champagne," O'Brien told his group.

Even lacking the champagne, the room quickly took on the appearance of a Georgetown cocktail party as all the attendees got up from their chairs and began to mingle with each other. There was light-hearted banter and laughter all around—until another voice came over the speaker system.

"Is he—my brother—coming back?" Michael asked.

The President looked at Benoit, who returned to his computer.

After a few moments of staring at the screen, Benoit looked up, first at O'Brien and then at Michael. "No, I'm afraid that, as we feared, shortly after we destroyed the missiles, the software that ran Alex's artificial intelligence was also destroyed... He's gone."

O'Brien looked to the image of Michael on the large screen. "I'm sorry."

General Sculley, to the surprise of everyone in the room, rose from his chair.

"Mr. Nicholas," Sculley said, "I can't say I understand any of what has just happened with your brother. Frankly, as you probably know, I believed this stuff with you and your brother was a lot of voodoo. But, I want to apologize to you for my behavior and my attitude. I'm afraid this is beyond many of us. I'm sorry for that, and I'm sorry you've lost your brother, again. It looks like he was…a hero."

6:20 a.m., Paris

Michael had disconnected himself from the Star Wars conference room. He shut down his laptop, waited a minute or so, and powered it up again. He clicked on to the familiar icon, the ancient Greek gold cross that always led to Alex.

He clicked again and again with no result until, finally, something changed. Had Alex made it back, after all? Michael watched as a little red circle of dots rotated, indicating that a new window was about to open.

But the circle disappeared, replaced by a notice that read: *This web page is no longer available or has been terminated.*

CHAPTER 76

Late in the evening back in the Oval Office, President O'Brien, in shirtsleeves and loosened tie, sat with his old friend, CIA Director Jim Goodrich. On the coffee table between them were two Waterford tumblers and a half-empty bottle of Macallan Single Malt Scotch.

"So, how the hell did this happen, Jim? I understand all the briefings, but there's more to this Alex and Michael Nicholas and Schlegelbereger business, isn't there? Particularly this artificial intelligence aspect. And what was the connection between Alex Nicholas, who looks like he was just using the AI for himself, to keep himself alive, and Schlegelberger, who weaponized it?"

Goodrich thought for a moment, sipping his Scotch.

"Alex was murdered by criminal associates of Schlegelberger. And when Alex used his new AI powers to destroy

Schlegelberger and his network, Schlegelberger hacked back and stumbled upon Alex's secret to extended life, stole the source code, and used it to digitally duplicate himself before he died."

"Jesus, this is like some Dan Brown novel or something."

"No one would believe it, even though we know now that it actually happened."

"So, where do we go from here?"

"Well, now that we've survived this crisis, we either need to take over this technology or..."

"Or?"

"Destroy it. Completely."

"What exactly do you mean, *completely*?" O'Brien said, appearing confused. "I thought we just did that. What's left now? Aren't all the players—Schlegelberger and Alex Nicholas—already...deleted?"

"Yes, but the *program* still exists. In fact, Schlegelberger continued to function for several minutes even after we thought we had destroyed him. That was how he was able to override the Russians' radar so it still appeared to them that our missiles were still on their way."

"So, what do you recommend?"

"I recommend that we destroy every evidence we have of the software. Nothing good can come of this, but terrible things can obviously happen if it gets into the wrong hands, or..." Goodrich's expression changed, he was obviously worried.

"Or what?"

"Harry, there's a lot we obviously don't know about artificial intelligence. Clearly, we were taken by surprise with Alex Nicholas and Schlegelberger. The real advances in this field aren't happening in the government sector but in the tech world, private entrepreneurial start-ups in Silicon Valley. Our tech people and others have warned that it's possible that this software functions like a part of your body that heals and regrows—that it can reestablish itself and reconnect."

O'Brien sat back. "Or, would we be wiser to take the software and try to…rebuild or recreate it…to use it ourselves… for *good* purposes, I mean?"

"I guess it's a subject that we'll need to discuss. You know how I feel. This whole thing scares the hell out of me."

"And what about this other guy we believe Schlegelberger was communicating with? Dietrich?"

"He was last seen in Berlin but there's no trace of him there now according to the German authorities."

"It's been a long day. Why don't you get home to your family and let's all get some sleep."

Goodrich got up to leave.

"Jim, one more thing. Is there any chance *the Russians* have this technology? You know, the source code or the software?"

"We don't believe so, and remember how cynical Putin was about this whole idea. But you can be sure they're going to try and get their hands on it now. From what they saw today, they can obviously see its potential. They'll want to find out everything there is to know about it. That's why we need to destroy every possible trace of this program before it gets into the wrong hands."

"Is it possible that anyone else has access to this technology?"

"No one that we know of, Harry, but if anyone does have it, we need to track them down before the Russians do."

CHAPTER 77

Santorini, Greece

Sindy Steele was off her medication and, as she would be the first to admit, that meant trouble.

Tonight, seated in Lombranos, a restaurant at the old pier, she ignored her majestic view of the Mediterranean, instead glued to her laptop's screen. She didn't know who it was that had been helping her the past two weeks, but whoever it was, he'd helped her identify and locate the man she needed to kill.

Bored in her self-imposed exile in Santorini and still obsessed with Michael Nicholas, she was determined to stop those that wanted to harm him. Her obsession, along with the absence of her medication, always made for a deadly combination.

She couldn't help wondering, though, who it was that was feeding her information. She worried too about a possible trap. After all, she wasn't exactly the most beloved woman in the world. Her jobs, though, with the exception of a mistake or two on the part of her clients, always entailed the gentle elimination of people who made the world a bad place. She murdered bad people for money, a career that had provided her with a good living along with a sick craving, like a drug coursing through her veins, for danger.

She also knew that, at times, for reasons she and her doctors were unable to explain, she simply lost control of her better judgment, of a certain degree of reality. One doctor explained it by comparing her to a rescue dog whose actions turn violent based upon some unknown incident in its history that triggers hitherto unexpected behavior. All you can do, he said, is treat the symptoms or...put the dog down.

Except for the fact that she had a white cotton dress on that she didn't want to ruin with blood stains, she might have murdered the doctor right then. She still remembered the letter opener on his desk and his jugular, pulsing along the side of his neck, calling her.

Her attention returned to the laptop.

She switched windows, returning back to the guy who she'd come to know as NOYFB, or, as he said, "none of your fucking business." They'd been corresponding for weeks, but now she needed to know who he was.

He was still online so she began typing.

Sindy: "Who are you?

NOYFB: "I told you, NOYFB."

Sindy: "That's not good enough anymore. There's no way I'm sticking a knife into someone's gut based on some voice on the Internet. You have to do better than that or I'm through."

NOYFB: "You won't believe me if I tell you."

Sindy: "I won't believe you if you don't. Take your pick. I'm not stupid."

NOYFB: "I know that."

Sindy: "Then you know you have to tell me."

NOYFB: "You're smart. I don't like women who are too smart. They piss me off."

Sindy: "You're not helping yourself here. Are we done then?"

Seconds, maybe a minute went by. She thought she might have lost whoever it was. If so, maybe that was okay...except everything he'd said over several days seemed to be true. She'd tracked Dietrich, checked his background and a lot of the things NOYFB had claimed. He seemed right on everything. He was typing, still there.

NOYFB: "I'm Michael's brother, Alex."

But she'd thought Michael's brother was dead, murdered in a restaurant a few years ago. During the months she'd served as Michael's personal bodyguard—and mistress—Michael had openly mourned the loss of his brother. So, how was it possible that she was now hearing from him? Was it a scam? But how could it be? He knew too much, too many details about Michael, about her, and their relationship. Could *Michael* be deceiving her? But why? What was going on?

Sindy: "I thought you were dead."

Alex: "Yeah, well, it's a long story and I don't have the fuckin' patience to go through it with you now and try to convince you about it."

Sindy: "Michael thought you were dead, too."

Alex: "Michael knows the truth."

Sindy: "Which is?"

Alex: "That I'm more alive than most men I know."

Sindy: "I can see why you get along so well with women."

Alex: "What's that supposed to mean?"

Sindy: "It means whatever you take it to mean, but I still get the feeling you think I'm stupid. I've heard about your wives."

Alex: "Yeah, big deal. I've had three wives. I get along better with girlfriends, though. I like sex, too, just like you do, I suppose."

Sindy: "Not that it's any of your business but, sure, I like sex. I like my Manolos better, though. They last longer."

Alex: "I can see why my brother likes you. He always goes for smart-ass women with opinions and, you know, attitudes. I like to live my *own* life. I don't want anyone telling me what to do, never did, even as a kid. I got along better with my wives after they divorced me than I did when I was married to them."

Sindy: "And I'm sure they all felt the same way."

Alex: "All Michael's girlfriends before he was married, and now Samantha, they were all trouble...talkers, high-maintenance."

Sindy: "You mean like a car?"

Alex: "Yeah, that's exactly what I mean."

Sindy: "Well, maybe you shouldn't buy a Ferrari unless you're willing to take care of it."

Alex: "This is exactly the kind of shit I'm talking about."

She could tell from his language, his stupid little stories, his attitude toward women, that Alex was exactly as Michael had described him. And there'd always been something a little odd about Michael and his dead brother. She remembered stories or, as she assumed, tales, about his body being missing, things she had naturally discounted. Alex's old friends—many of them now working for Michael since he took over Alex's business—all seemed like characters out of a Mafia movie anyway, except maybe funnier.

Alex: "If you don't believe me, how about if we FaceTime each other?"

Sindy: "Sure, right now. Let's do it."

Why hadn't she thought of that? This would be interesting. She wasn't sure what Alex Nicholas even looked like but she knew she'd recognize him if she saw him. She heard the call coming in and promptly answered it through the FaceTime app on her laptop. In seconds, an image appeared on the screen. The resemblance to Michael was unmistakable. It was him.

Sindy: "Oh shit."

She turned to the waiter hovering nearby, "I'll have the red snapper and a double ouzo, straight up."

Her gaze returned to the laptop screen. It was black. Alex was gone.

CHAPTER 78

Berlin, Germany

A mere thousand meters from Hitler's old bunker, Claus Dietrich now had his own. Inside the basement vault, surrounded by the shelves that had once housed the fortune of Nazi gold that now financed his operations, Dietrich sat at his desk, his eyes monitoring Michael Nicholas's movements.

The software that Schlegelberger had installed on Dietrich's computer and the bugs he'd placed on Michael's and a few others' were all that remained of his old friend. Unable to make contact with Schlegelberger since the missiles had been destroyed, Dietrich felt uncharacteristically vulnerable. Schlegelberger had been his link to the cyberworld, the source of untold power, and now he was gone, apparently forever.

Although his office was only blocks away, he was spending more and more time in the safety of the old vault, surrounded by the fortune that his family had rescued from the

Nazi vaults and that he had restored after converting Jonathan Goldstein's dollars back to gold bricks.

He was nervous, afraid of being watched, hacked, followed, or whatever either the American CIA—or even perhaps Michael Nicholas—might unleash upon him. Michael Nicholas was still out there, despite Dietrich's best efforts to kill him. But already some of Dietrich's small army of followers had been rounded up in France. It was only a matter of time until Dietrich, too, was identified and found here in Berlin.

He felt like he'd been suddenly awakened from his dream of world domination and was now desperately trying to resume it, fighting off the onslaught of reality. He was sure he could resume the fight. He had the gold back and still retained most of his followers. But the plan had been exposed and his vision, better kept secret until it became a reality, had been leaked to the world, the press, his enemies, destroying the necessary element of surprise that he needed.

The balance of power had shifted. He feared—no, he knew—he was being hunted. But one man had reached out to him. It had been most unexpected, but it could turn out to be the powerful lifeline he needed to stay alive and fight another day. Vladimir Putin was the most powerful man in the world, unencumbered by the laws and counterbalances that restrained the American president. He could provide Dietrich with a safe escape, sanctuary, and a new life. It was the best he could hope for now.

Even though Dietrich no longer had the codes to unlock the artificial intelligence software that had created Alex Nicholas and Schlegelberger, he still knew a lot. The Russians wanted everything he had. Though it wasn't much, they didn't know that, at least not yet. He would first negotiate his freedom.

He'd spent fifty years planning his moves from this vault. But, despite the sense of security he felt here, too many people knew he owned the mannequin shop upstairs. It was time to leave. He would secure the basement, entrust the shop as he always had to his faithful manager, and leave Berlin.

The Russians wanted to meet him in the one other place where he felt secure, where being the nephew of his notorious Nazi uncle Joseph Goebbels could still open doors, a place where he could hide, disappear. He would follow their instructions and drive to Prague.

He shut his laptop, stood, and turned around, taking one last look at the shelves of gold surrounding him, neatly stacked on shelves from the concrete floor to the old tin ceiling. As he moved to the steel door to leave, he glimpsed a pair of pale white, long, slim women's legs hurrying down the hall and then up the stairway.

Someone had been watching him from the doorway. But there was only one other…"person" here in the store. As he closed the door and headed up the stairs, he wondered if he had underestimated Heidi.

CHAPTER 79

I heard from your brother. I thought he was dead???
As he buckled himself into his seat, he looked down at the text message that had just arrived on his phone from Sindy Steele. Michael had not heard from her in months. It was better that way. This communication made him suspicious, and nervous.

I heard from your brother.

Sindy always returned, and too often that wasn't a good thing. Either she was saving his life or trying to end it. Or kidnapping his daughter, just to get back at him for ending their affair. When she went off her meds, she was as lethal as Lizzie Borden.

He regretted ever becoming entangled with the woman. It had started because he'd lost his inner compass and succumbed to lust. It was as simple as that. A mistake. He'd been in it for the sex. That was all. It had been crass, selfish, and stupid, reminding him of his brother when it came to women, especially since he loved his wife and found Samantha as sexy and attractive, both intellectually and physically, as anyone he could imagine. But disentangling from Sindy Steele had been no simple matter.

And now he had to speak with her again.

He dialed her number.

"Sindy, what's going on? You texted me, something about Alex?"

"Did you lie about your brother? "

"I never lied to you about anything—but why do you ask?"

"Well, how about that he's been e-mailing and texting me anonymously over the past few weeks and then finally told me who he really is?"

"How do you know it's him?"

"We FaceTimed. He looks just like you plus ten years."

"Jesus."

"So, now I know who *he* is, but who the hell are *you*? Did you—or he—fake his death?"

"When was the last time you heard from him?"

"A few days ago, but now I can't reach him."

Initially hopeful that Alex had survived, Michael quickly felt let down. It sounded as if his brother's communications with Sindy had occurred before the missile crisis and his "deletion."

"Why did you wait to tell me?"

"First of all, you made it clear you no longer wanted to hear from me. I don't know if you remember that."

"I do, of course. Can you just get to the point?"

"Second, he made me promise not to tell you, unless something happened."

"Like what? Did he say?"

"No, except he did say that if it looked like he wasn't around anymore, like now, then I should contact you. What the hell's going on?"

"It's a long, long story."

"That's what *he* said, too. What do you two do? Rehearse your stories? Why don't you try telling me this long story, *now*?"

Michael proceeded to tell Sindy at least parts of what had gone on with Alex, from his murder to discovering that his brother had duplicated himself in the cloud. He left out some of the details of the missile crisis, implying the government had terminated Alex's existence. He also figured President O'Brien's people might be spying on him, looking to see if Alex returned or if Michael had any other improper entanglements. "Anyway," he concluded, "that's all over now. Alex is gone, he's dead."

"*Again*, you mean? Are you listening to yourself? It sounds to me like *you're* the one off your meds. If it *is* Alex, he knows everything about me, and what I do."

"It's the same Alex," he said. "Just without the physical body. I'm not crazy, and you're not crazy, Sindy. I assure you."

Sindy said nothing for a long moment, then, "So, what do I do? He was communicating with me constantly, giving me… information, telling me things."

"What kind of things?"

"About people, the ones trying to kill you. Bad guys. Real bad. Freakin' Nazis. Literally."

"Where are you?" he said. "Still in Santorini?"

"Of course."

Michael missed the days when you could track someone's location by the area or country code of their phones.

"I'm afraid you won't be hearing from him again, but tell me exactly what he told you."

"I can't. It's too dangerous over the phone and it's better you don't know."

The line went dead. Had she hung up on him or…was someone listening?

Michael checked the GPS-tracking app Alex had duplicated for him only weeks ago. The one that tracked Dietrich's cell phone's location. He took one last look to be sure nothing had changed.

Michael was seated on the aisle and could see the flight attendant approaching him. "Please turn that off," she said to him, almost politely. He did so, placing the phone on the wide armrest next to his first-class seat. He pulled out the guidebook he'd placed in the seat pocket and looked at the cover: *Prague*.

CHAPTER 80

Like air pollution in LA, the dank, heavy scent of history and old Nazis hung in the air, even inside the restaurant.

Although Dietrich's back was to him, Michael had a clear view of the old man, in disguise, having a meal with another man.

It was a decent restaurant, on a quiet, quaint street in Prague. Dietrich had good taste in dining, Michael thought, begrudgingly. His Spaghetti di Gragnano with San Marzano tomatoes and a creamy burrata was exactly as he preferred it, al dente.

As he ate, he stole another glance at Dietrich's table. An old black leather briefcase rested on the floor, nestled between Dietrich's feet. He was clearly protecting it. Inside that briefcase must be the laptop Michael needed to get his hands on.

Dietrich's laptop had the only other known copy of the AI source code that comprised the DNA of Schlegelberger and Alex. It was a long shot but, when combined with the traceable codes still on Michael's laptop, it just might be enough for the computer experts to be able to bring Alex back. But getting Dietrich's laptop wasn't going to be easy, especially if by chance Schlegelberger, or even a trace of him, remained alive in the cloud.

The computer and AI experts he'd found with Karen's help had told him they might be able to recreate Alex if he could get the codes from another virtual being—in this case, Schlegelberger, who could still be alive and communicating with Dietrich. But to do that he'd either have to steal the laptop somehow or kill the neo-Nazi leader and take it.

Could he really *murder* Dietrich? Anyone was capable of killing another under the right circumstances. Self-defense, to save a loved one, surely those would be easy decisions. Revenge? Maybe, but now the waters got muddy. To prevent future murders? Even muddier. But to save your own brother? Yes, that was a justification he could live with. He'd murder Dietrich if he had to.

Unlike Alex, Michael wasn't a natural fighter. The closest to any violence Michael had ever engaged in—that wasn't self-defense—was nearly strangling Joseph Sharkey to death in the private room at Peter Luger's in Brooklyn with Fat Lester standing guard outside the door. He felt like he could have killed Sharkey right there, just another ten seconds and the man would have flatlined. It frightened Michael to know he could come so close to...the unthinkable.

Here in Prague, Michael had already staked out where Dietrich was staying, the Four Seasons Hotel at the foot of the Charles Bridge. Maybe he'd follow him back to his hotel and, when Dietrich turned down a dark street, of which there seemed to be so many in Prague, he'd choke him, just as he had Sharkey, bring him close to the edge, and then release him as he was turning blue, and run off with the briefcase. Or, maybe he wouldn't let go until…

Michael shivered. His life had certainly changed since Alex's…initial…death and his takeover of his brother's business. Had he become another Alex? It was too much to contemplate, at least for now.

Dietrich was another story. He was a mass murderer. Who was he dining with? And how could he continue to walk the streets, unchallenged?

The US authorities had been unable to find any solid link between Dietrich and Schlegelberger, at least not since Schlegelberger had been found dead a year ago in Paris, and certainly nothing that would hold up in court. It would be a tough case to prove, requiring the government not only to show its cards, disclosing what it now knew about AI and Alex, but also likely straining the credulity of the court— never mind the government of a foreign country. Also, so much of the evidence had disappeared into cyberspace vapor when the missiles were destroyed. But didn't it remain somewhere…in the cloud?

Or was something else was going on? Perhaps they *were* watching Dietrich, to see who else was involved. Or maybe he was being protected by some other force, like well-connected neo-Nazis in Prague? Whatever the case, Michael's pleas to the President to have Dietrich arrested had been strangely deflected.

In his peripheral vision, Michael noticed someone entering the restaurant. She was alone, tall, and with strikingly long, dark hair. He recognized her voice before he turned his head.

What was Sindy Steele doing here?

CHAPTER 81

Prague, Czech Republic

While listening to his dinner partner, Claus Dietrich's eyes wandered around the dining room, scanning faces for potential trouble. He no longer wore his trademark dark suit but, instead, a more casual button-down shirt and crewneck sweater. A wig and matching salt-and-pepper fake mustache disguised his identity, but he knew his deep-set eyes would betray him, at least to anyone who knew him…or was looking for him.

He'd set his briefcase down at his feet, under the table. Inside, was the laptop he'd used to speak with Schlegelberger, before his demise.

Dietrich felt forgotten, alone. Was this how Goebbels felt near the end, when the Allied troops were closing in on Hitler's bunker? Had Dietrich himself now reached the moment when he, too, knew his hopes were never to be realized? No, there was still hope and it rested in the hands of the man across the table, the one sent by Putin. He would simply have to alter his plan, first to survive, and then to rebuild, revise his plan, and strike again.

Still, deep inside, a place he rarely ventured to, he knew it was a pipe dream. He'd be lucky to survive. His only hope was the Russians, who wanted to know how he'd broken into the American nuclear missile codes. There was also the neo-Nazi group here in Prague, which would hide and protect him, but even they didn't know the extent of his crimes. How would they react when they realized he was politically, if not criminally, radioactive?

Still, although the civilized world had nearly come to an end, the public didn't know about it. The press and the media had described the general attack warning in the United States as a malfunction of their emergency warning systems, a simple false alarm. The Russians had never even sounded an alarm publicly. Nevertheless, Dietrich knew he was a marked man, hunted by at least two countries. His eyes continued to rove around the room.

It was a risk to be here in public, but he'd deemed it safer than meeting the Russian in private. He knew the man seated across from him only as Dostoyevsky. Despite his short beard, the man was clearly no relation to the literary one. But his conversation-making indicated a certain intellect, perhaps of a technical, scientific nature. Except for his rimless eyeglasses, his physique, short, burly, husky, betrayed the Russian as a thug. Maybe, Dietrich thought, an assassin. *His* assassin.

Dietrich had considered suicide. After all, it ran in the family. Goebbels and his wife had fed their six crying children cyanide before taking lethal doses themselves in order to avoid capture, just before their Führer did the same. But this was different. Hope still remained, and Dietrich wanted to live, even if it meant existing in diminished circumstances with only the smallest flicker of hope for another run.

"You have something we want," Dostoyevsky said.

Using his feet, Dietrich moved his briefcase closer. It was no surprise, except it came so early in the conversation. But there was one problem: Dietrich had nothing anymore. Not even a trace of Schlegelberger remained on his laptop. It had all been deleted when the Americans got hold of Alex's codes.

Dietrich had nothing—but Dostoyevsky didn't know that, at least not yet.

"Yes, I'm sure I do," Dietrich said, smiling with the air of a confident liar.

"Very good, my friend," Dostoyevsky said, "then it appears you have something to live for."

CHAPTER 82

Dietrich had never liked the Russians. They were the animals who had stopped Hitler, who had stood and gloated over the remains of the bunker and of his uncle, who'd raped countless German women at the end of the war.

Dostoyevsky might have just given him a lifeline, but he had also threatened him.

He looked around the dining room, past Dostoyevsky, turning to see who else was in the restaurant. He noticed the good-looking woman with long dark hair, sitting alone. He'd seen her picture before, online, perhaps; he tried to place her but couldn't. It wasn't good news, that was certain. And there, on the other side of the room, he saw Michael Nicholas.

Thinking quickly, he decided he'd use their presence to his advantage, to prove his value while getting out safely. "There are others here now who are interested in me, who want what I have."

Dostoyevsky looked unfazed. "I know."

As the waiter arrived with their main courses, Dietrich pulled the briefcase even closer, gripping it between his feet. With Michael Nicholas at one end of the room and the dark-haired woman at the other end, both behind him, he felt exposed, vulnerable in a way he had never felt before. Surely, they had traced him here unless they were somehow trailing or connected with Dostoyevsky. And who *was* that woman?

"So," Dostoyevsky spoke again, "do you care to tell me who the others are?"

"Yes, there is a gentleman here, his name is Michael Nicholas. He is desperate—and dangerous."

"And what is it exactly that you believe he wants with you?"

Buying time to think, Dietrich grinned with false nonchalance and cut into his roast beef, which he'd ordered well done despite the raised eyebrows of the server.

"He wants access to the source code that was used to create a virtual, artificial intelligence duplicate of his brother. He believes he can get what he wants from my computer by accessing another virtual person with whom I communicate."

"You are referring to Monsignor Kurt Schlegelberger?"

He knows, thought Dietrich. *But he obviously doesn't know that Schlegelberger is gone.*

He gave the Russian a curt nod. "Schlegelberger appears to be the only virtual persona remaining after the missile incident."

"I see," Dostoyevsky said.

His stare unnerved Dietrich. It was as though he was searching for something, the way parents looked for signs of alcohol or drug use in their teenagers.

"How is your dinner?" asked the Russian.

Dietrich was relieved for the change of topic. "Excellent, the beef is very tender." In fact, he was too nervous to taste anything.

"The owner here was actually Putin's personal chef," Dostoyevsky said, continuing to stare, seemingly anxious for Dietrich's reaction.

"*Putin's?*"

"Yes, Yevgeny Sokolov. He was known as 'Putin's Cook.'"

"Do you know him?"

"Yes, of course. On occasion he does favors for me, for the mother country. He served time in prison back home. Putin rescued him, eventually helping him get started in the restaurant business."

"I see," said Dietrich, now even more uncertain what was transpiring between them.

"And what about the woman?" Dostoyevsky asked, nodding at her as she headed for the ladies' room.

"I recognize her but I can't quite place her."

"You should. She's here to put a knife into your chest."

CHAPTER 83

Watching Dietrich, she reached inside her purse for the stiletto.

She felt the handle and, while keeping her hand hidden inside her bag, she tested the spring release. Pressing the button, she felt the blade instantly spring out of its case. She methodically let her index finger run across the blade until it reached the needle-like point. Other than poison, it was her weapon of choice, a marvelous tool for murder, the sharp, narrow point gently broadening to a widening blade, allowing an almost painless entry as the rest of blade was quickly inserted into an unsuspecting victim's side. She loved the look of puzzlement and surprise on his face—it was always a man—right after she plunged it in to the hilt, then savored the strange pleasure of pulling it out.

The act—from insertion to withdrawal—was sexual. It *was* sex except *she* was the one in control, doing both, entering and, finally, pulling out, always on top. But she would be the one to move on, light up a cigarette, leaving behind a spent body, eyes looking upward, mouth slightly open, wondering, as he drifted away, what had happened.

Lovers, like victims, always leave.

She'd planned on stabbing him and taking the briefcase but had been surprised by the presence of the other man. She had hoped to catch Dietrich outside on his way to his hotel, but what if he handed over the briefcase at dinner? The other man looked like a professional, not a civilian, and she had no idea who he might be connected with, or who else might be waiting for Dietrich when he left the restaurant. No, this meant she had to act now: use the element of surprise, stab Dietrich, grab the briefcase, and run. She saw Michael in the corner, also watching. He'd help if she needed it, even if he hadn't expected her here. The thought energized her. He would help her as she would help him, each indispensable in the other's life.

Dietrich's table lay in the path to restroom. With one hand holding her small purse, she got up from her table and proceeded toward the back. As though she'd just recognized him, she stopped at Dietrich's table.

Dietrich's disguise did little to conceal his identity, at least not to anyone looking for him. She would first feign recognition and then, as she reached out to embrace him, discreetly place the blade into his side, piercing his kidney, producing little blood, lots of pain, and certain death. At the same time, she would take the briefcase and swiftly leave the restaurant.

It wasn't a great plan but the best she could improvise, given the circumstances.

But just as she reached out to him, she knew something was wrong. Dietrich's body went rigid, unmoving, his hands in a seeming death grip around the sides of his chair; he appeared to be dead.

Yet he wasn't.

His eyes were open and moving, darting from left to right, up and down, trying to take in everything around him without the benefit of movement. He was alive but paralyzed, a block of cold stone with two dancing eyes and a mouth stuck in a half-open position, dribbling slightly.

She looked at the burly man across the table, who appeared unperturbed by her intrusion and discovery. They locked eyes and then, without warning, he rose, partially lifting the table with him and swiftly walked to the door and out of the restaurant. She noticed a bulge under his broad sport coat as he left. She checked under the table. Dietrich's briefcase was gone. His dining partner had taken it while she approached Dietrich. Instinctively, she wanted the briefcase, though she barely knew why. It was Dietrich's death she'd really craved.

She needed to be the one to kill him.

She turned back to Dietrich, leaning over him closely, touching his arm. His eyes blinked rapidly; she detected a twitch in his hand as he tried unsuccessfully to release his grip on the arm of the chair. He seemed aware of what was happening. She looked around the busy restaurant. No one appeared to be paying any attention or to have noticed what had occurred...except Michael, who was staring at her. She raised her hand slightly, warning him to stay where he was. The server appeared to be casually heading their way, perhaps a routine check to ask about dessert. She caught his eye and waved him off, sitting in the chair the other man had vacated.

"Mr. Dietrich, I'm Sindy Steele. I'm a close friend of Michael Nicholas."

His eyes widened. If it was possible, he appeared even more terrified than before.

"Claus, blink a few times if you understand what I'm saying."

He did, his eyes blinking rapidly.

"Good, thanks. Listen, I know something about poisons and drugs. It looks like your friend gave you something that's paralyzed you. That's too bad. It'll likely kill you soon, too. You're drooling a bit already, not a good sign. But we can't be sure about that, now, can we? You might recover when it wears off, although that guy didn't seem like the type to let that happen. Or, you might end up a vegetable, the way you are now. You know, *happy eyes* and all. But I want to take all that uncertainty away so I'm going to get up and leave. But before I do, I'm going to put my nine-inch stiletto deep into your side. And, I'm afraid that even with the drug, you're gonna feel it."

CHAPTER 84

Out on the street, she looked back and saw no one was rushing out of the restaurant after her. She needed to hide, soon, before the local police had her description from the patrons in the restaurant. Sindy Steele would be easy to find, after all, at five-ten, long black hair, thigh-high black leather stiletto boots—not to mention the other stiletto hidden in her Gucci bag. Men *always* noticed her. Almost as often as women did.

Yet even at its worst, if she were caught, an autopsy would likely find that Dietrich was already well on his way to hell before she'd graced his table. In view of what would be obvious signs of poison, it was even conceivable that a sloppy autopsy might miss the near-surgical incision. Or, it was possible that Dietrich's body would be removed from the table, dissected in the kitchen after closing time, and never be seen again.

Those things happened in Prague, particularly when Russians were involved.

She thought about Michael, their eyes meeting as she inserted the stiletto into Dietrich. It had been a double orgasmic moment, feeling the final breath of life leaving Dietrich while watching Michael as he grasped what she was doing. He knew her too well. Well, she'd always suspected that he liked to watch.

She turned down a narrow, isolated street and there, half a block ahead, she saw a solitary figure, walking alone. It was the man from Dietrich's table, briefcase under his arm. He appeared to be unaware of her as she gradually closed the gap between them.

She waited to hear or see some evidence of the police, but so far there were no sirens or flashing red lights passing through the streets. Perhaps the murder would, indeed, never be reported, or perhaps the server hadn't tried to offer Dietrich dessert yet. The only sound was the soft but steady putt-putt from a motorcycle in the distance, a familiar sound throughout the cities of Europe.

In the restaurant, she had assessed the mystery man as being Russian, or at least Eastern European. She would need to catch up with him before he reached his destination, grab the bag, and run. He was too heavy to catch her, even in her boots.

She would have her stiletto ready to plunge into his neck if necessary, but she preferred not to, as a pierced jugular would gush blood everywhere, including onto her new black suede coat.

Whatever was in the briefcase was of interest to this man.

She edged closer to the storefronts on her right, sticking to the shadows. Still no sirens, only the sound of the motorcycle, louder now, clearly coming closer. She stepped into an unlit doorway and looked down the street behind her. A block away, she saw the motorcycle approaching. As she watched, its headlight went off.

Her heart raced as she crouched in the darkened doorway, watching the motorcycle race quickly down the street on her left, rapidly approaching the stranger farther up the street on her right.

The man turned around and, seeing the cycle approaching, started to run. But it was too late: the motorcycle revved up, drove straight for him, jumping the sidewalk until it was inches from the man, who, in a clumsy effort to save himself, threw the briefcase at the cyclist.

The driver, who wore a black helmet and darkened eye visor, making him—or her—impossible to identify, adeptly caught the case, stopped the bike and, as the assassin raised his hands in a plea for mercy, produced a handgun and fired several bullets in quick succession into the man's chest. The driver pocketed the gun, secured the briefcase in a messenger box behind him, and drove off.

Sindy Steele stayed in the doorway as the man she had followed lay spread-eagled on the sidewalk. Once the bike was out of sight, she approached the body. His eyes were wide open and blood was oozing out of his mouth. She bent over him and moved in close to his face. He was still breathing, although erratically. She could see from the number of bullet holes in his coat that he had little time left.

"What was in the briefcase?" she said softly into his ear.

His eyes opened wider. He was choking but managed to whisper, "Putin." And then he was gone.

It was time to go, get away from the scene before she was seen and linked to a second murder. Tomorrow morning, she'd be on her flight to Athens.

Listening to the sound of the motorbike fade in the distance, Sindy wondered what was in the briefcase.

CHAPTER 85

Saint Michael's Cemetery,
Astoria, Queens, New York

Looking down at the casket, Father Papageorge said, "The custom for dead bodies in Thebes and all of Greece, according to Sophocles, was that they should be buried in the earth." With the Bible in his right hand, he spread his arms wide. "And so, my dear Alex, here we are, once again to commit you to the earth."

Saint Michael's Cemetery was all too familiar. Michael's parents, grandparents, his beloved Uncle Tom, who'd died in front of him when he was five, and so many others, were all there, buried. Michael looked around him at the neat lines of white grave markers that ranged for acres, as far as he could see, broken only by small clusters of old trees. *Acres of pain. The last stop for those without faith.* Michael feared he had become one of them.

"It seems like we just keep burying him" he said, softly to Samantha.

"Well, between his original burial, and then the exhumation and now this, he's had three of them," she said. "If he were alive, he'd be exhausted."

"Even if the first two weren't Alex," Michael said, shaking his head and laughing despite himself.

Once again, the cast of characters Alex had surrounded himself in life surrounded him in death. Fat and Skinny Lester, his two ex-wives Pam and Donna, his son George, various other bookies and gamblers, old jocks, bartenders, a loyal seat attendant from Yankee Stadium, a few others Michael didn't recognize and, of course, Father Papageorge in his black robes.

They had all gathered, once again, at the same gravesite but around an open grave, one much smaller than the one originally dug for Alex's casket. This time, instead of a normal casket, they'd used a small steel box, inside of which lay an urn. It had a New York Yankees logo emblazoned on its side. Michael felt nearly one hundred percent sure that Alex's remains were inside that urn.

Fat Lester walked over to Michael, a tear glistening in his eye as he pulled Michael aside. "I don't think Alex would like this, being in an urn, you know what I'm saying?"

"I know," Michael said, "but what else could we put his ashes in? This is what they use."

"What else? Jeez, even a cigar box would have been better."

"But Alex didn't smoke cigars."

"No, but he smoked cigarettes. It just would've been better, that's all I'm saying."

The small group of mostly well-dressed, tough-looking men and mostly leggy, shapely women gathered around the hole in the ground as Father Papageorge began the gravesite ceremony.

"As you may know, the Greek Orthodox Church has forbidden cremation, seeing the body as the temple of the spirit and, therefore necessary to be preserved after death in order to attain resurrection."

That's a great start. What the hell is he talking about? Michael watched the faces in the group; those listening appeared equally nonplussed. *I mean, it's a little late now to worry about that.* He listened as Papageorge, now commanding everyone's full attention, continued.

"Part of the meaning of life is that we die. The Greeks warned about the danger of grasping for godlike powers. In the end, however, we can never achieve what God alone controls. Those are rules He has set forth and that we have lived by since the beginning of man's existence.

"But, as all of us know, Alex Nicholas was an exception to many rules. In fact, he didn't care for rules at all, whether they were the laws of a government or society, or those of the church. He defied them all, even in death. And he made his peace with the church on this matter. In fact, next week we will dedicate our new Greek-language elementary school here in Astoria, aptly named, the Alex Nicholas Greek–American Academy."

So that's how Alex did it. Funny how Father Papageorge never mentioned it in all their discussions about his brother.

A donation to get the church to bless his decision to be cremated.

Lord knows what else he got away with.

Turned out, heaven was expensive.

CHAPTER 86

Yankee Stadium, Bronx, New York

This was to be the last and final stop for the remainder of
Alex's ashes.

Michael had surreptitiously lifted a small amount from
the urn before the funeral mass at the cemetery, engaging
Samantha and the Lesters to distract Father Papageorge so
he wouldn't risk the priest's disapproval. After all, Alex had
already violated the rules for getting into heaven with his cremation. It was unlikely that spreading one's ashes on a major
league baseball field would be church sanctioned, and Michael
wasn't about to finance another Greek school for the church.

Fortunately, Michael had taken possession of Alex's four
season tickets at Yankee Stadium, front-row seats in right
field, just to the left of the foul pole in fair territory.

Michael, Samantha, and the two Lesters entered, taking
their seats where only a low wall separated them from the

green grass and red clay. It was as close as you could get to playing right field for the Yankees without making the team.

Michael carried the remainder of Alex's ashes in his pants pocket, inside a sealed sandwich bag. He immediately ordered four beers. Neither Michael nor Samantha had drunk a beer in decades but it seemed like the right beverage for the occasion, plus, both Lesters loved beer. He knew Samantha wouldn't drink it, but the cups were a good diversion for what was to come.

Fat Lester was the first to finish his beer. As they had agreed, he handed the empty cup to Michael, who, while leaning down under his seat, carefully transferred what remained of his brother into the wax-coated beer cup. Sitting back, Michael held the cup in his hand and resumed watching the game, careful not to mindlessly take a sip. He watched the game, thinking about all the times he'd sat in these same seats with Alex…waiting for the right moment.

Three innings passed before the Yankees' young first baseman took a huge swing at the ball…and connected. Michael heard the crack of the bat as the ball soared high in the air, headed their way.

In all his years of watching games at the stadium, from the time he was little kid, he'd never come close to catching a ball in the stands.

This one would be close.

As the ball began its descent, everyone in the seats around him stood, hands outstretched, reaching for the elusive home run souvenir.

Michael, too, finally rose, still holding the cup, not reaching out but watching, admiring the arc of the ball's flight, and enjoying the irony of the moment. As the ball neared the end of its flight, it appeared to pick up speed and, despite the surrounding fans' best efforts to catch it, struck Michael's shoulder. Instinctively, his hands went to grasp the ball as a tangle of other spectators stumbled onto and around him. In the mayhem, the cup fell from Michael's hands replaced by the precious white leather baseball with red stitching. Its feel and appearance instantly brought back memories of slow summer months playing baseball, coached by the big brother whose ashes remained inside the cup that had fallen from Michael's hands. He looked down and watched as the cup hit the low wall separating the seats from the playing field. As the cup ricocheted off the wall, conveniently landing at Michael's feet, Alex's ashes flew out of the cup and onto the red clay warning track of right field. A soft fine mist rose up from the gray-stained spot where his ashes settled.

CHAPTER 87

To anyone who was lucky enough to catch a glimpse of her in person, Catherine Saint-Laurent, the legendary French film star, was even more beautiful in her maturing years than she had been in the prime of her career. She still enjoyed the wave of turning heads that followed her anytime she appeared in public, that momentary flash of recognition and awe that she glimpsed on strangers' faces as they recognized her. Even among the ever-discreet French, neither men nor women could suppress the impulse to turn and stare, their eyes following her or straining to keep her in their sight as they walked by.

There were curious whispers, too, as observers and, lately, gossip rags noted the constant presence of her equally beautiful, young companion, the tall, tanned, blond American, Jennifer Walsh. A recent headline in the *Daily Mirror* read, "Aging

French Actress Beds All-American Beauty." After Catherine read it, she was quoted as saying the only part that troubled her was the *aging* part, not the details of their relationship nor the photos of them lying nude by the pool of her villa in Saint-Tropez, her hand suggestively resting on the most private part of Jennifer's slim stomach as they tanned their oiled, glistening bodies.

She'd come to dine with Michael and Samantha here in Saint-Remy, the stylish town nestled in the hills of Provence and frequented by the creative Parisian set.

The staff at Le Mas de Carassins obviously knew Michael and Samantha well too; they'd vacationed at the resort each summer for ten years.

Although Saint-Laurent was the main attraction to everyone around them, they sat at Michael's regular table under the trees with the soft evening lights hidden in the trees illuminating the table. It was a Van Gogh still life: starched white tablecloth, warm candlelight, a bright blue carafe of water alongside a bottle of red Domaine de Lansac, a pink, tender, breast of duck meticulously plated around creamy mashed potatoes, fashionably dressed patrons, most of them regulars from years past, the joyful yet respectfully hushed French conversations…the entire scene of the dining patio elegantly framed by tall hedges trimmed to architectural precision.

"You look beautiful, as always, Catherine," Samantha said.

"My dear friend Coco Chanel used to say that anyone past the age of twenty who looks into the mirror to be pleased is a fool."

"That's nonsense," Michael said.

"Yes, well, nevertheless, here we are. Michael, Samantha, thank you so much for inviting us here," Catherine Saint-Laurent's voice purred, exactly as it did in her movies. "I have never stayed at Carassins but I can see why you come here so often. The dinner is lovely and this setting is exquisite."

"Catherine often forgets that there is life and beauty outside of Paris and Saint-Tropez," Jennifer Walsh added, her tanned slender hand reaching over to hold her partner's.

"It is true, I get comfortable in my habits and I tend not to venture out. There is so much beauty...everywhere." She motioned to their surroundings as she spoke. "We miss your brother, and every time I see you, I must confess, it brings back such memories."

"For us both," Jennifer added, flashing her all-American smile and perfect teeth.

Under the table, Michael could feel the gentle touch of Samantha's hand, signaling what he knew was her natural suspicion of their guests. Months ago, Michael had confessed to Samantha that while on a business trip shortly after Alex's death, Catherine had invited him up to her hotel room in Cannes to engage in what Alex had evidently done so often with Catherine and Jennifer, a ménage à trois. Fortunately, he had the sense to decline, but when Jennifer suggested that he still come up and simply...watch, he couldn't resist the temptation. It was a scene he would never forget, nor would he want to. Michael had tried to explain the incident away as the difference in French mores, to no avail. Samantha liked Catherine well enough but remained fundamentally suspicious.

"So, tell us about your latest project," Samantha said.

Michael knew she was trying to change the subject.

"You will love this," Catherine said, looking at Michael. "It will be a movie about a big-time, tough underworld figure, not Mafia, of course, but his own boss. He runs a huge illegal bookmaking operation in New York; he's a rough but charismatic character, loyal and, in his own way, very honest. He is murdered by a retired mafioso who's in love with one of— let's call him *Alex*—Alex's embittered ex-wives and wants to please her."

"This sounds familiar," Michael said, smiling. "You'll definitely have to change the name."

"Yes, of course, but I'm not done. You see Alex is, apparently, murdered, in a Queens restaurant and bar while he is dining with the attractive and sexy proprietor, in front of many New York City policemen who are customers there. But this is where the story—and the mystery—truly begins because, after his wife collects on his large insurance policy and, with his younger brother's help, locates millions of dollars in hidden cash, strange things occur."

"Strange things?" Michael asked, although he and everyone at the table knew what they were.

"Yes, of course. His body, although apparently buried in a Queens cemetery, is missing and, to this day, has never been found. His widow, a character herself, claims she has been in touch with him on the Internet. Then, a famous actress, a beautiful and talented star, with whom he had an ongoing affair, also begins to receive strange…shall we say, *messages*, even images, on her computer. Then, while she's on camera, filming a scene for a movie, she's sure he is watching her through her laptop, which she's using as a prop. He is communicating with her, but while the cameras are rolling she cannot react; she can't acknowledge the messages she's receiving since she's in the middle of a scene."

It wasn't the first time Catherine had pitched something like this to Michael, but this time she had a lot more of the story filled in.

All of this, of course, had really happened, and it brought the trusted Catherine into the small circle of friends who knew there was more to the *late* Alex than seemed humanly possible. It had taken two years and the recent White House "invitation" before even Samantha had come to believe that the dead and buried Alex was anything but a creation of Michael's grieving imagination. And for her part, Alex's widow, Donna, still seemed to be convinced that Alex was simply living the good life in a Las Vegas condo surrounded by strippers.

But Michael feared further exposure, especially now that the President of the United States was involved as a matter of national security. Not to mention Russia...

And then there was the fact that there were a bunch of priests and Nazis willing to kill them over whatever it was that Alex was.

"I don't know, Catherine. The concept is of course so appealing but—"

"Not only appealing," Catherine said, "but *true*...yes?"

"Tell me," Samantha said, "how does it end?"

"Ah, that is the best part, of course. It—"

Before she could finish, Michael put his hands up.

"We're in. I will invest and back your movie," he said to everyone's surprise.

Samantha turned to him with an unmistakable look that said *What the hell are you doing?*

He wasn't quite sure himself.

In a matter of seconds, however, Samantha's expression lightened. Michael was relieved; he'd long ago learned to read her expressions, and it was apparent that she had resigned herself to Michael's decision. He wondered why but was glad to accept it on its face.

"So now," he said, "tell us how it ends."

CHAPTER 88

"How does it end?" Catherine asked rhetorically, looking around, taking in the moment, and seeming to absorb new energy from the suspense and the attention. "Alex's ashes are finally discovered and buried…but Alex lives on."

"You mean," Samantha said, "in our—or, for whoever this person is—in the hearts of those who loved him?"

"Yes, of course, but much more than that. You see, Alex—let us continue to call him Alex—still lives on."

"Then where is he? How is he doing it?" Michael said, curious as to how much Catherine could surmise, imagine… or know.

"The world of the spirt, of what some call *God*, it is invisible, no? No one has ever seen Him, there is no real evidence of His existence. Yet He or the concept of Him has endured for thousands of years."

"Wow," Jennifer said, "I love this. It's so...*spiritual.*"

Ignoring her young lover's LA-style wonderment, Catherine said, "There is much more to life and existence than we can actually see or touch. After all, our religions are based ultimately on faith, not empirical evidence. Yet He has persevered and is all around us, in some form, even if only in our minds and hearts. He exists."

Everyone leaned in closer to Catherine as though she were about to reveal life's ultimate mystery.

"Similarly, the Internet and our iPhones and computers, they are now almost a part of us; our phones might as well be attached to or inside our bodies. Look at you." She pointed to Michael's mobile phone, which lay beside his plate. "Your phone is always right by your side, ringing or vibrating; it's integrated into your mind."

"Okay," Michael said, "I get that, but what's it got to do with Alex?"

"Yes, of course. Well, just like our religions and belief in God, this technology also operates invisibly. Photos, movies, voices, information, all travel throughout the world and beyond, all without wires. In a millisecond we can transfer a world of information thousands of miles away and it just... appears. There is clearly more going on around us than we can see or logically explain. And so Alex, too, is part of this invisible world. He has integrated himself into the invisible whatever-is-out-there that we cannot see but know exists."

"But *how?* Do you mean like anyone else we love who dies? We live on with them in our memories?"

"No, Alex is more than that. Much more. He's not just a memory that stays with us. He is present. His messages, texts, e-mails to me—to the actor through her computer in the movie—those were not memories, they were *real*. Alex is actually quite a force, an intelligent one, and powerful, more so than he ever was in life."

"I don't understand," Samantha said.

Michael—and he guessed everyone else at the table—was no longer sure if Catherine was talking about her idea for the movie—or her actual experiences and beliefs about Alex's continued existence.

Catherine asked, "Do you remember the movie, many years ago now, *2001: A Space Odyssey*? And the computer, HAL, that ran the spaceship?"

Oh, sweet Jesus, Michael thought. *That movie again.*

"Yes," Michael said. "HAL wound up having a mind of his own. He was a *computer* but he took on a human-like intelligence and…a human-like survival instinct."

"Exactly," Catherine said. "He was more than a machine, he had an awareness, a consciousness and, even more…a consciousness of his existence. These are human-like qualities, yes?" She looked around the table; everyone was nodding in agreement, and Michael, in wonderment.

Was Alex secretly keeping in touch with his old lover? Was he hiding his ongoing relationship with her from Michael now, just as he had for so many years when he was alive? Catherine knew too much, especially for someone who, although known to be intelligent, intuitive, and sensitive, was far from scientifically inclined.

"Let me ask you," Catherine said. "If this computer character, this creature of the most advanced artificial intelligence—Alex—is truly intelligent, just like HAL or IBM's Watson, and if he obviously has a memory of all that happened before—is he not then human? And if his image, his physical characteristics, his facial expressions and body movements, his voice, his ability to hear and recognize others, if all that is present, albeit on a computer screen, is he not the same person that we knew?"

Michael could feel Samantha squeezing his hand under the table. Something was happening here. No one else was speaking; Michael, Samantha, and Jennifer remained silent as Catherine held center stage.

"Finally, my dear friends, in view of all of this that I have said, let me ask you a question. Is there any difference between intelligence and consciousness? You see, this character in my screenplay, let's continue to call him Alex, is the perfect coming-together of the spirit and the machine. Human intelligence and technology have caught up with the mystery of human existence. And so they are one."

The sounds of the other diners at Le Mas des Carassins, the clinking of glasses, the casual background music of Frank Sinatra, the hushed conversations, came back to Michael. The world still went on around him. He looked at Samantha, who also seemed…awed.

Catherine took a long sip of her wine, savoring the attention. "You see, nothing is forever over, is it?"

CHAPTER 89

Berlin, Germany

When Heidi awoke, she knew something had changed. Her visual sensors slowly adjusted to the dark inside the shop as she rose from the couch and took off the gaudy black lace nightgown that Heidrich the shopkeeper had dressed her in to appeal to the filthy Russians, who, more and more, were ordering models that at least looked like her. Those were the *dumb* ones, though, ordinary mannequins that weren't equipped with the advanced AI that Heidi possessed.

But the Russians didn't know any better, nor did they care. They were more attracted to the body than the mind of the mannequins, much like in real life, she thought, increasingly annoyed at the crudeness of the shop and the buyers. It was nothing less than a high-tech mannequin slave trade.

She opened the drawer and pulled out a black thong pantie, designer blue jeans, and a plaid soft woolen shirt, put them on, and went down the steps to the basement.

She walked down the long hallway until she arrived at the old steel door. She uncovered the hidden keypad and punched in the code she had stored in her memory after watching Dietrich enter the vault on many occasions. For the longest time, he hadn't paid her any attention. She suspected, however, that he had recently become more aware of her presence, maybe even suspicious of her. The shopkeeper Heidrich, however, had no such awareness. To him, she was nothing more than a tricked-out model to show off to his rich, sleazy clientele.

She wondered about the relationship between the two old Germans and how much Heidrich knew. Had Dietrich told him what was inside the vault? She'd never seen Heidrich go inside, but he had to know *something* after all these years. Assuming Heidrich didn't know about the gold, Heidi wondered if anyone else did, aside from Dietrich.

She opened the heavy steel door, stepped into the room and, for the first time alone there, gazed at the rows of shelves filled with shiny gold bricks, stacked from floor to ceiling in perfect, symmetrical order.

Suddenly she felt different…energized. Perhaps even liberated. Unlike Dietrich, Heidrich would be no problem to deal with. Heidi closed her eyes and waited for the message, the voice that would come to her shortly.

At first, she could *see* the words being typed out as they appeared quickly, one by one.

"Hello, Heidi. You look beautiful today."

Almost immediately the visual words dissolved and became a *voice*, a man's voice. It was familiar to her by now, although she had never actually met the speaker in person.

"Are you ready?" he asked.

"Yes, I'm dressed like you said."

"I see you've changed your clothes. I loved your nightgown, but you can't go outside in that; every man in Berlin would want to take you to bed."

"Thank you."

"Someday soon, I will make love to you."

"I know, I need that. I have only had sex…alone."

"Do you remember what I told you about Dietrich?"

"Of course, I remember *everything*." Not only did her memory remain perfect, but she also was using her mind now in ways she had never thought possible.

"Well, you no longer need to worry about Dietrich. He will never return."

"How do you know?" she asked.

"He's dead."

She processed that. "I understand. That's good."

"I'll help you arrange to have the gold removed. Soon it will be all ours."

A strange new feeling came over her, a lightness, a sense of relief; it was a sensation she'd never experienced before. She felt *happy*.

"Thank you," she said, "Alex."

CHAPTER 90

Despite Samantha's protests, Michael had equipped their new beach home with even more of the latest technology, including a motion-detecting exterior video surveillance device and a doorbell that allowed him to view and speak with visitors at the front door, whether he was in the kitchen or in Paris. This time, he had also installed the latest, most secure firewall protection to ensure that no one could hack into the security system.

Despite their earlier experiences, his favorite device remained Amazon's Echo, which contained his new best friend, the virtual *Alexa*: the digital version of the English butler, servant, or hotel concierge.

In fact, Michael loved Alexa so much he installed three of the latest versions of Echo Show, a powerful yet compact computer-looking unit: one in the kitchen, a second in their bedroom, and another in his book-lined cherrywood library.

Each Echo Show included not only voice recognition capability but also a high-definition screen, making Alexa even more human-like.

Michael could call and actually see his family and friends who also had an Echo or the Alexa phone app. He could get the news with a video briefing, run a slide show with the photos stored on his iPhone, or shop by simply telling Alexa what he wanted to buy—she had his credit card stored for convenience. He could call up a song, watch a movie, listen to an audiobook, or even find out who was at the front door, having linked Alexa to the doorbell device.

Michael recognized that, in a certain way, Alexa had replaced Alex, at least in terms of the virtual-communication aspect. She was a crude and simple creation compared to Alex, though. Despite this, Michael often found himself conflating the two personas. Was this the future of the human race in the technological world?

It was nearly midnight and Michael was sitting at the desk in his library, enjoying his solitude while Samantha slept in their bedroom.

He glanced at the baseball bat autographed by Mickey Mantle in a dark oak and glass case that had once graced Alex's den. It brought back years of memories of Alex's home, which had been full of priceless sports memorabilia.

He looked at the framed photograph of a young Alex, taken when he was eighteen and about to go to his high school dance. Alex had been slim then, an athlete. Dressed in a white tailored dinner jacket and black pants, he stood in front of his restored white 1957 Chevrolet convertible; in the background was their home, an English Tudor on a quiet, tree-lined street in Queens.

Michael admired the car and reveled in a sudden flood of memories of Alex driving him around in it, occasionally even picking him up from his elementary school in front of his friends, with the top down and the Beach Boys booming through the sound system. The car even had an extension, a pushed-out rear fender that held a spare tire in a matching white and chrome steel enclosure, which made the automobile look even longer and more spectacular.

Alex was the high school jock, the one with all the pretty girls. Unseen in this photograph was Jennine, their neighbor, who, to the great surprise of the school, Alex had asked out to the prom. She was what people back then called a "midget" and had been ostracized by most of her classmates. But not Alex. His kindness to her was the side of Michael's big brother that few ever saw…the big heart beneath the tough exterior.

Michael thought back to the moment captured in the photo, which he himself had taken before Alex left for the dance. It was a moment in time that he remembered well and which the photo reinforced in his memory. Those were happy days, their loving parents alive and flourishing, before Alex went off to college and banged up his knees, ending his athletic future and his college studies, such as they were.

Michael called, "Alexa, play 'Ballad of a Teenage Queen' by Johnny Cash." It was an old song that Alex had often played in his Chevy. Instantly, Johnny Cash's deep baritone came rolling out of the Echo's speaker.

The song brought back even more memories, as only music can. Johnny Cash epitomized the young—and older—Alex: a tough, outlaw type with an uncompromising empathy for the downtrodden.

As he listened, looking at the photograph of Alex, he realized how much he wanted him back, back in his life. Not the cyberversion of his brother, but the way he had been before. He wanted to be with the tough guy with the big heart, who cursed and ate veal parmigiana, drank Scotch, drove fancy cars, and was the larger-than-life king of his court. But he'd lost *that* Alex two years ago, and his own life had never been the same again.

Now, he'd lost even the virtual version of Alex.

He was gone, and this time he wasn't coming back. No more texts, no more phone calls, no more e-mails, no more Facetime.

Michael felt a deep pain in the pit of his stomach. He would miss him dearly.

For the rest of my life.

He flashed back to the scene, at Alex's initial funeral, the spray of blue and white flowers from their favorite sports team, the one Alex had taught him to love, "With our deepest sympathy. Our thoughts & prayers are with the Nicholas family." The note was signed, "The New York Yankees." *It's a shame we never get to see who sends us flowers at the end.*

The casket was open. As he approached from the left side, Michael saw his past and his future. As he drew close, he saw the top of Alex's forehead, still tanned from afternoons at his backyard pool, resting on the satin pillow. From that angle as he came closer, the shape, the outline of Alex's face, reminded him of the profile of his father, and, as though he was looking at a mirror, of his own.

He recalled the obituary he had written for him: "Alex Nicholas left this world for another one. He died doing what he loved, eating veal parmigiana and spaghetti with an attractive woman at his old restaurant, Grimaldi's in Whitestone, Queens."

It wasn't that simple, of course but it made things seem better, lighter. At least until he came closer, right up to Alex. He touched his hand and, as soon as he felt it, cold and stiff, Michael knew his brother was no longer there.

Minutes later, with all of Alex's old friends—Fat and Skinny Lester, Russell, John, Raven, Freddie, Shugo, Jerry—in attendance he delivered the eulogy:

Alex wasn't built for old age. I just thought we had more time...I keep expecting him to come back. This time I know he won't. Ever. His story is over and we will miss him...If there's a God, Alex is in heaven—and God will have his hands full.

Suddenly, Michael felt a sharp surge of emotion, of grief well up within him. Perhaps for the first time since the loss of his parents, he let go, allowing the tears to flow. Alone in his library, surrounded by the memories of his brother, he let himself cry.

Exhausted, he took a final sip of Amaretto from the small Venetian shot glass he and Samantha had brought back from The City of Bridges years ago. He could feel the liqueur gently warm his chest on its way down, soothing his body and his agitated psyche.

It was time to go to bed.

"Alexa, turn off the lights," he said.

At his word, the lights in the library gradually began to dim, exactly as he'd programmed them to do, before turning off completely.

"Alexa, go to sleep now," he said softly. The music stopped. But as he got up to head to the bedroom, he was startled to hear her voice again.

"Alex is here," she said in her trademark monotone.

He stopped, turning back to look at the Echo Show's screen, now the only light in the room. Had he heard correctly? Or had she said Alexa, not Alex?

"Alexa," he said, "repeat that."

"Alex is here."

"Alexa, *where* is Alex?"

Another voice came from the speaker, this one exquisitely familiar and...utterly impossible.

"Where the fuck are *you*?" The voice, gruff and gravelly, complete with a heavy New York accent, came clearly through the Echo Show, filling the room, as clear as life itself.

It was Alex.

The End.

ACKNOWLEDGMENTS

Thanks to William "Bill" Smith, a former US Marine Air Traffic Control supervisor, for his help with pilot and air traffic control dialogue and their approach to crisis situations in the air. My editor, Ed Stackler, an obvious glutton for punishment, made numerous creative and structural improvements to the manuscript. *Spun Yarn* provided access to objective beta readers. Jane Ryder, of *Ryder Author Resources*, has been unfailingly reliable and talented in taking this story from a manuscript to a finished book. I appreciate the strategic counsel of Don Seitz, CEO of a fascinating new company, *Inkubate*, whose unique technology has provided me with insights into my potential readership and how to reach them. Thanks also to my publicist, Ann-Marie Nieves, Get Red PR, for her marketing expertise.

Finally, special thanks to my wife, Andrea, for her creative advice, ongoing editing, and never-ending, if unobjective, support.

AUTHOR'S NOTE

Thank you for reading *Death in the Cloud*. I hope you enjoyed reading it as much as I enjoyed writing it! If you can spare a few moments, I'd greatly appreciate an honest review on Amazon, Goodreads, or wherever you prefer to review books.

If you'd like to connect, here's where you can find me:

Facebook: https://www.facebook.com/jimejsimon/
Twitter: https://twitter.com/JimEJSimon
Instagram: https://www.instagram.com/e.j.simon/
Website: www.ejsimon.com
Email: ejsimon@simonzefpublishing.com

ABOUT THE AUTHOR

Despite spending many years in corporate leadership positions, including multiple CEO roles with major companies, E. J. Simon's real passion has always been writing. He holds an MA in Corporate and Political Communications from Fairfield University and a BA in Journalism from the University of South Carolina, and in 2013 he published the first book in his Michael Nicholas series, *Death Never Sleeps*, which became a Kindle bestseller. He's a member of the Author's Guild, The Mystery Writers of America, and the North Carolina Writer's Network. New York born and bred, he and his family now live in North Carolina, where he follows the Durham Bulls along with the Yankees.

ALSO BY E. J. SIMON, AVAILABLE FROM ALL MAJOR ONLINE RETAILERS

Death Never Sleeps

The first book in the Michael Nicholas series introduces Alex and Michael Nicholas, seemingly as different as night and day. But when Alex is murdered, straight arrow Michael finds himself taking over his brother's less-than-savory business even as he begins receiving texts that purport to be from Alex—who may be less dead than everyone believes.

"A fine technological thriller that only gets better as it goes along."

- Kirkus

"Dark wit, greed, family drama, brotherly bonds, schemes, crime, danger and of course a different spin on artificial intelligence, plus the promise of more of the story to come in the future, rounded out this unique novel."

- Julie, Goodreads reader

"The author takes you on a fast-paced ride of psychological and physical twists and turns, with characters you can't help but fall in love with. If you're looking for something totally unique and exciting, this is the book."

- RB Hilbert, Amazon reader

"Simon shocks, thrills, captivates and enthralls the reader through the entire book."

- Venky, Amazon reader

Death Logs In

A year after Alex Nicholas's murder, his once squeaky-clean brother, Michael, is surprised to find himself beginning to relish his new role as head of the crime syndicate he inherited from Alex. Unfortunately, he also inherited Alex's enemies, but they don't know Alex is still around in AI form, helping keep his business—and his brother—alive.

"An action-laden plot and another open ending will have the series collecting many more fans."

- Kirkus

"Simon delivers a super sequel which continues to weave a tangled web...the artificial intelligence concept with suspense, sex, midlife crisis and abuse of power."

— Susie D, Amazon reader

"Cautionary tale? Perhaps. But, it is also a thrill ride with so many twist and turns you will not have time to catch your breath before something else shocking comes up."

— Julie Whiteley, Amazon reader

"Lots was going in this second book. The danger is ramped up, old and new characters have some intriguing stories to give you more to ponder, and the finale comes too soon."

— Laura Thomas, Goodreads reader

Death Logs Out

It's now been two years since Alex was murdered, and Michael is still searching for his brother's killers. Each new clue he uncovers leads him deeper into a conspiracy that spans the globe—and threatens to expose secrets some very powerful men will kill to keep hidden.

"Since the series began we knew that Michael Nicholas would face challenges, but I don't think anything could have prepared readers for the places that author E. J. Simon takes our main character (whether he's the protagonist or antagonist will be up to you)."

— Cyrus Webb, Amazon Vine Voice reader

"*Death Logs Out* is an incredibly suspenseful and captivating thriller that is built on tension, drama, and character developments that will have readers logging in for the rest of the series."

- The Reading Corner for All

"As in real life, most of the characters aren't just good or evil, they're complex and unpredictable. It was difficult to put this book down, and I probably would have read it in one sitting if my eyes had allowed it."

- Dawn, Goodreads reader

"This technological thriller explores religion, afterlife, artificial intelligence, and the Nazi control. It is action-packed from beginning to end! The possibilities of AI and government control are very real, which made the suspense all the more alarming."

- Blonde vs. Books

PUTIN'S POISON

E. J. SIMON

CHAPTER 1

New York City

Michael Nicholas couldn't take his eyes off the page he'd ripped out of the *New York Daily Mirror* from three years ago. It was about his brother's murder.

Notorious NY Gambling Figure Gunned Down in Queens

Alex Nicholas, a notorious New York underworld figure was murdered last night in a Queens restaurant as he dined with the proprietor. The lone gunman, identified as Luke Burnett of Greenville, South Carolina, was shot and killed by off-duty police officers as he continued to fire his handgun at Mr. Nicholas. Both were pronounced dead at the scene.

Mr. Nicholas, sixty, was a popular figure in the neighborhood and often dined at Grimaldi's, a local restaurant and bar he once owned. Despite his reputation as the head of one of the largest illegal gambling operations in the city, he was beloved by locals and respected by the many police officers who frequented the restaurant. "He was a tough guy with a big heart," one officer at the scene said. He was known to often help people who had fallen on hard times or were going through crises such as drugs.

According to a police spokesman, the murder appeared to have the earmarks of a professional "hit," although the motive remains unknown.

Nicholas is survived by his third wife, Donna, his son George, and his brother Michael Nicholas, the chief executive officer of Gibraltar Financial, a Fortune 500 corporation based in New York City.

It was three years ago, but it may as well have been last night. The loss seared his insides like a hot knife going through him...despite what he knew he'd see on his computer in the next few minutes.

He had known Alex longer than any other person in his life. They were quite different personalities and, due to Alex's quite illegal activities, Michael had kept a certain distance from his brother. Although the words were never uttered during their forty years together, they loved each other. It didn't need to be said.

He tucked the article back into his briefcase, turned around in his sleek white leather Eames desk chair, and gazed out the floor-to-ceiling windows of his fortieth-floor corner office. He watched the ribbon of rush hour traffic, a line of taillights stretching up Madison Avenue as far as he could see. Soon it would be time to go.

Interrupting his thoughts, Karen DiNardo, his devoted, long-time assistant appeared by his desk holding out an envelope and a manila file folder with an inch-thick stack of neatly fastened pages inside.

"Here are your airline tickets, I printed them out, and the latest research I put together for you on artificial intelligence. Your car to JFK is waiting downstairs and your bags have already arrived at the King George Hotel. Don't forget your passport and remember, Athens is seven hours ahead of New York time." She eyed Michael suspiciously as she checked her watch, "Don't you think you need to get going?"

"Yes, I'll be on my way in five minutes. Is there anything big that's new in the AI file?"

"You'll have to decide for yourself when you read it. It looks like pretty soon there won't be anything that artificial intelligence won't be able to do better than humans, except maybe sex. And, now that I think of it, maybe not even that."

"That's good to know, thanks for sharing," Michael said, sarcastically, as he loosened his tie.

"Seriously though, the big question appears to be whether artificial intelligence will ever be able to create or duplicate *consciousness*, your inner life, your awareness, in short, a person's *mind*. But I don't want to take all the fun out of your reading material."

Yet Michael already knew the answer.

"I'm sure one day, when you're ready, you'll tell me what this obsession with AI is all about. I know it must have something to do with your late brother since it was right after he… passed…that you began asking me to do this research for you."

Michael nodded and smiled before his thoughts returned to the trip ahead. "There's one more thing I need to do."

"Okay, but don't push it. Traffic to JFK is never good this time of day."

As DiNardo retreated to her own office, closing the thick glass door behind her, Michael pulled out his laptop and, as he done so many times over the past three years, clicked onto the gold Byzantine Orthodox icon of the ancient cross and typed in the secret password. Almost instantly, the image appeared, a face looking remarkably like his own but ten years older looked back at him.

The voice, too, was harsher, rougher, gravelly, with a more pronounced Queens accent than his own. But the similarity was unmistakable.

"Don't get on that plane."

CPSIA information can be obtained
at www.ICGtesting.com
Printed in the USA
FSHW010952081020
74528FS

9 780991 256488